S0-AGF-154

# PRAISE FOR
# FASTBACKWARD

"*Fast Backward* is not only a page-turning, heart-stopping glimpse into an alternate outcome to WWII, it is a thought-provoking take on choices being made in contemporary times. Cocoa is an unforgettable character, fighting hard against the current of history."

> —**KIRBY LARSON**, award-winning children's author, including *Audacity Jones to the Rescue*, *Audacity Jones Steals the Show* (2018 Edgar Award Nominee), *Dash* (Scott O'Dell Historical Fiction Award), *Duke*, *Hattie Ever After*, and *Hattie Big Sky* (Newbery Honor)

"One July morning in 1945, 15-year-old paperboy Bobby Hastings witnesses an atomic bomb explosion and rescues a naked 16-year-girl beside the road. And that's just for openers. The girl claims to be from the future. Says we didn't win World War II after all. Predicts utter doom and destruction if the United States government doesn't take action immediately. *Fast Backward* is a high-stakes, tense tale about two gritty young people from different centuries who take on the impossible challenge of saving the world. David Patneaude's fast moving story involves a striking cast of characters, events, and surprises that keep the pages turning. Don't start *Fast Backward* until you have plenty of time. You won't want to put it down."

> —**DAVID HARRISON**, award-winning author; Poet Laureate, Drury University (Missouri)

"*Fast Backward* is a high-stakes thrill ride! I've long thought that we need more World War 2 stories and alternate history in young adult fiction, and this is both. Fans of *The Man in the High Castle* or Michael Grant's *Front Lines* series will love *Fast Backward*!"

> —**MIKE MULLIN**, award-winning author of the *Ashfall* series

"Imaginative, thought-provoking, and compelling, *Fast Backward* draws you in to a fascinating what-if: What might have happened if the Nazis got the bomb in time to win the war? And what if a traveler from the future gave us the chance to avert that disaster? Hurtling head-first into this challenge are lively, likeable Bobby and Cocoa, the intriguing girl who materializes out of thin desert air. But why should anyone believe two teenagers?"

—**DORI JONES YANG**, journalist and author of *Daughter of Xanadu* and *The Forbidden Temptation of Baseball*

"David Patneaude's frightening 'What if?' alternative history will have young readers turning pages to find out what happens next and also turning to history books to educate themselves about the horrors of World War II. What an accomplishment!"

—**CARL DEUKER**, award-winning author of *Heart of a Champion, Swagger,* and *Gutless*

"Past, present, and future collide in David Patneaude's soaring new novel of courage set at the dawn of the Atomic Age. One early morning in rural New Mexico, a pedaling paperboy named Bobby encounters a lost girl named Cocoa, and his fate—and the world's—are changed forever. Patneaude peels back the layers of history to glimpse the future—but is it bright or dark? A superb, enduring book, with lots of timely reverb."

—**CONRAD WESSELHOEFT**, former *New York Times* writer and author of the acclaimed novels *Adios Nirvana* and *Dirt Bikes, Drones, and Other Ways to Fly*

"Riveting! One of the best time travel stories I've read in a long time."

—**DORI HILLESTAD BUTLER**, Edgar Award-winning and Seuss Award-honored author of the *King and Kayla, Buddy Files,* and *Haunted Library* series

*Fast Backward*

by David Patneaude

© Copyright 2018 David Patneaude

ISBN 978-1-63393-616-4

All rights reserved. No part of this publication may be reproduced, stored in a retrieval system, or transmitted in any form or by any means—electronic, mechanical, photocopy, recording, or any other—except for brief quotations in printed reviews, without the prior written permission of the author.

This is a work of fiction All the characters in this book are fictitious, and any resemblance to actual persons, living or dead, is purely coincidental. The names, incidents, dialogue, and opinions expressed are products of the author's imagination and are not to be construed as real.

Published by

 köehlerbooks™

210 60th Street
Virginia Beach, VA 23451
800-435-4811
www.koehlerbooks.com

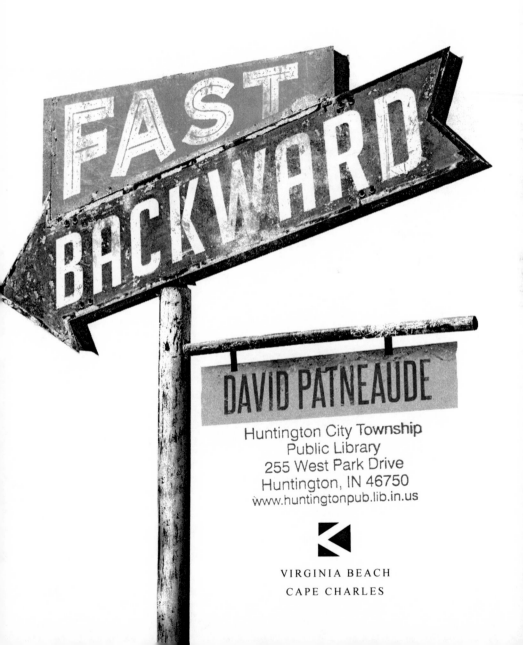

FAST BACKWARD

DAVID PATNEAUDE

Huntington City Township
Public Library
255 West Park Drive
Huntington, IN 46750
www.huntingtonpub.lib.in.us

VIRGINIA BEACH
CAPE CHARLES

# DEDICATION

Once more, to Judy, who long ago saw this writing thing smoldering in me and chose to give it oxygen. This is only the latest in a long parade of books, and the characters and conflicts and choices and voices within their covers, that wouldn't have existed without her encouragement.

# ONE

Monday, July 16, 1945

I don't often beat Leo to the newspaper shack, even though he has to *endure* an eighty-minute drive from Albuquerque. But this morning is an exception; I'm early. Above the vast desert, the sky is black and moonless, but stars flower everywhere. I can practically smell them.

I prop my bike against the lean-to and stretch out on its bench. After a sleepless night followed by seven miles of pedaling, I'm happy to rest. On the next leg of my journey I'll be shouldering sixty-seven newspapers stuffed in my *Albuquerque Journal* bag.

I've complained to Leo that he could've placed the shack closer to the base camp so I wouldn't have as far to haul the papers. But he claims the government won't allow civilian structures—even our slap-dash shelter—within the invisible outer perimeter of a hush-hush Army outpost. Even if the government were to make an exception, Leo says he'd have a longer drive, which means he'd use more gas. His bosses would have to ask for leniency on the gas rationing rules, which have already been relaxed so we can get the *Journal* to the base's hotshot workers every day.

Anyway, Leo says there's a limit to how much time he can spend on the road. He has other carriers. He has another *real job*. It doesn't matter how important the men at the base camp think they are or how vital it is to keep them happy while they work on their cloak-and-dagger project.

I'm supposed to get along with my boss. Dad, who hasn't gotten along with *any* of his bosses, tells me that regularly. But if my family didn't need the money, I'd tell Leo to keep his newspapers. And his excuses.

Breakfast is a contorted Hershey's bar I find in my bag. I take a bite, hoping it will settle my stomach. It's been an uneasy few days—a night-before-the-first-day-of-school knot of anticipation and dread.

The cause is a puzzle, but I believe it's something I've contracted during my visits to the base camp. For the past week or more, I've been exposed to increased nervous energy radiating from the men there. But whether it's borrowed anxiety or something else, the affliction kept me up until after midnight and prodded me awake before three thirty. Mom and Dad snored on. Even Lolly barely stirred when I stepped over him and out the door.

The Hershey's bar fails to calm my nerves. I breathe deep, which doesn't help either. I inhale the smells of the desert—mesquite, sagebrush, yucca, dust, a trace of overnight dew—then close my eyes and wait for the rattle and roar of Leo's road-weary '39 Ford.

I doze, but a familiar racket soon grabs my attention. Wiping drool from my chin, I stand and face the bounce and swerve of Leo's headlights. The car stops, spewing exhaust and shedding dust. To save gas, Leo turns off the engine before he gets out to open the back door.

"Bright and early this morning, huh, Bobby?" He grips the door handle and simultaneously pulls and lifts and jiggles. *The touch*, he calls it.

"Couldn't sleep." The door creaks open to reveal the nine labeled stacks of papers on the seat and floorboard. Mine isn't the tallest, but I've got farther to go than the rest of Leo's crew. And although the fresh layer of asphalt on most of the local roads has made travel easier, I won't be pedaling over city streets. Near the base, I have to get past the watchful eyes of sometimes-grumpy MPs who recently have been getting grumpier. *What city boy has to do that?*

A lot of these engineer types aren't exactly generous with the tips. When I show up at the end of each month to collect, they practically shed tears over their bill. A tip? Forget it. Other geniuses hand me cash and expect me to figure out what they owe. They can't be bothered to look at the tab. I could tell them double and they wouldn't squawk.

I don't do that, of course. They're doing their part for the war effort, people say, and I'll do my part by being honest.

I often wonder what it is they *are* doing. Outside the maze of buildings, though, no one knows—it's all guesses and rumor—and inside, nobody says anything, at least not so I can understand it. I've overheard fragments of conversations, but the soldiers, even the one who happens to be my uncle, stay mum. To my ears, the engineers could be speaking Egyptian, or Martian. Regular fellows they're not. Their bodies are here, but their minds are elsewhere.

There are ordinary but also tight-lipped worker bees at the camp, too. Somebody has to provide nourishment for the brains, clean up after them, drive them around, treat their ills. It's a small town they've built out here. Three hundred civilians, uprooted from faraway places. I've heard strange accents: East Coast, and much farther; Europe, probably, Germany, possibly.

When I stick my nose inside Leo's car, I'm overwhelmed by the fragrances of fresh newsprint and worn mohair. As usual, my brain makes its own connection—shoe polish; wet dog.

I plop my pile of papers on the bench. "They're not as heavy this morning, Leo." The darkness hasn't let up much, and the stars are now blanketed by clouds.

"Hitler and his crew are backpedaling. Not much to report from Europe anymore. But the Japs aren't about to give up, so there's still plenty of news from the Pacific. Still plenty of dying to come." He slams the door shut. I feel his eyes on me. "But you don't need to worry about that, right?"

"I'm only fifteen, remember?"

"Not talking about you, sprout."

I know who he's talking about. "My cousin," I protest, although Leo's heard this one before. "He's still in the Pacific . . . somewhere. The *Yorktown*. Torpedoes and kamikazes and shit."

"Your cousin," Leo says dismissively.

Leo lost three fingers in the Big War and two nephews in this one. A cousin on an aircraft carrier doesn't impress him. What would impress him is if my dad weren't a conscientious objector, a CO, a shirker, a slacker, a coward, a *conchie*. Leo hasn't used any of the derogatory words around me, but I haven't been able to avoid them elsewhere. If Dad were a soldier or sailor, Leo would give me more than forced friendliness and my allotment of the *Journal*.

"And what about my uncle?"

"He's *here*," Leo says. "What the hell could happen *here*?"

"He fought in Italy and France. He's still carrying around German lead in his leg." A strong argument, but Leo's a *what-have-you-done-for-me-lately* guy. Never mind that his last action was more than twenty-five years ago in the "War to End All Wars."

My uncle Pete—Mom's brother—has a Purple Heart and a Silver Star and a job on Lieutenant Bush's base security team. He's a sergeant, military police. The Army sent him home, or the closest thing to home, and that's how I got my job. Once the powers in charge decided to allow newspapers at the base camp, they wanted someone they could trust to deliver them. Uncle Pete recommended me. So far, I haven't given away any secrets, mostly because I don't know any secrets.

"Happy trails, Bobby," Leo says, shrugging. He gets back in the Ford. By the time he cranks it to life, does a U-turn, and rumbles away, I'm already rolling papers and filling my bag.

A hundred yards down the road his brake lights flash. Soon he's reversing and I'm wondering what he forgot. *Papers? Advice? Customer complaints? Did I bounce a paper off someone's door over the weekend? Did I miss the mess hall or one of the ranch houses or short-change a barracks?*

Leo stops and rolls down his window. Dust rises. "You didn't ask, Bobby."

I realize why he's returned. "I never do."

"Thirty-two," he says.

"Can you blame her?"

"I thought you were on *my* side," he complains.

"I don't take sides. But I do feel sorry for you, if that's any consolation."

"Pity's better than nothing, but I was mostly just reporting. That's what we newspaper folks do, right? Report?"

I can't tell for sure, but he may be getting in another dig at my dad, who once was a reporter for the *Journal,* and then, until six months ago, the *Socorro Chieftain.* At both places, his CO status—or more accurately his outspokenness about the peace movement—eventually got him canned. Officially, he's *1-A-O Remanded*, so he wouldn't have gotten drafted anyway. But he couldn't just cruise along, unwanted, like most forty-something nearsighted guys. He felt—and still feels—obligated to tell people his philosophy on war, especially when they don't want to hear it.

Now he does odd jobs and sends an occasional article or opinion piece to *The Nation* and crosses his fingers that someday he can get something printed in a *real* publication. The editors there have given him encouragement, but nothing more. Without Mom's night bookkeeping job at the bank we'd be eating jackrabbit and cactus.

Leo seems to be waiting for an answer to a question he didn't really ask. A *rhetorical* question. "Right," I say. "Report the news."

Because I need to keep my job, I don't mention that the position of circulation supervisor isn't even in the same ballpark as being a reporter. And now that he's "reported" to me that thirty-two days have passed since his wife last allowed him into her sacred underpants, I'm more than ready for him to move on.

"Thirty-two," he repeats, as if he can't believe it, and drives off.

Except for an occasional bird call, the morning returns to silence. I roll and tuck and stuff, thinking about the last time I got into a girl's underpants—*never*—and realizing that I feel sorrier for myself than I do for Leo.

Thirty-two days isn't a lifetime. I've barely kissed a girl, and that was Patsy Kendall, who'd practiced on half the other ninth-grade boys—rumor has it a couple of girls, too—before she kissed me. She didn't grade me, but I could tell that I was nothing special, that I wouldn't be getting any further with her. Which was probably good, because I wouldn't have known how.

By the time I finish rolling my papers, the eastern sky is a shade lighter. I get on my bike and head off, the bag balanced on my shoulders. I hardly notice it, but what I do notice is the lack of traffic. There's never much at this hour, but it's rare not to exchange waves with someone heading away from the base. And the past few mornings have been busier than usual with vehicles heading toward it.

The solitude fuels my apprehension, like a storm is coming and this is the calm. Like I'm the last boy on earth and the surviving girls are as choosy as ever, and they'll never choose me.

So, I should be eager to get to the base, but a small part of me enjoys being alone and feeling unsettled and sensing the *Let's Pretend* mood of the morning.

I brake to a stop and gaze into the dimness, straddling my bike. The air crackles with lightning. I can't see the camp, but I know it's less than a mile away. Sentinel Jeeps, maybe even a horse or two, soldiers, guns, grim faces.

Occasionally—guaranteed when Uncle Pete's on duty—I'll get a smile and maybe some conversation, but I can tell the men don't want to be out in the middle of the New Mexico desert. There are no Nazis or Japs here; the guns are for show, or the slim possibility of trouble—some bad guy trying to get at whatever the smart fellows are concocting behind the plywood walls.

I resume pedaling, but sleeplessness has my legs feeling earthbound. I have to concentrate to keep up a decent pace. My eyes have adjusted to the dark, but it's mostly instinct that keeps me on the narrow road.

Although I'm focused on the pavement, something makes me raise my eyes, slow, and glide to a stop. I feel a need to wait. *For what?* I'm surrounded by emptiness. Early morning murk. Behind me, sunrise is a thousand miles away.

But it's *not*.

With no warning, the sun erupts on the horizon. But not behind me, in *front* of me.

*Southwest.*

*Impossible.*

But it's not the sun. It's a giant dome of blinding light. For an instant, it silhouettes the structures in the camp and then the silhouettes fade as the dome turns into a ball that becomes a column that grows into a mushroom.

My heart booms. *Ride,* it says. *Turn your bike around. Ride.* But I don't. I let it drop. I stare at the vision in front of me. My eyes burn, but I can't close them. I might miss something. The heavens are dancing, electric, purple.

*Is it the engineers' doing? Their dream? Their nightmare? Or has something blown up accidentally? Has someone—genius or everyday Joe—made a horrible mistake?*

I feel faint. The newspapers are heavy on my shoulders. Gulping cool air, I drop to my bare knees, only half believing what I'm seeing. The fiery column continues to swell and rise, and I continue to watch. Light and shadow. Color and void. Thickening and thinning. Fear and curiosity.

And then a base-drum roll of thunder surrounds me. A hot wind smacks me in the face and presses my carrier bag and clothes to my body and bends me back like a playing card caught in a fast shuffle. The air tastes like dirt and something foreign—a stew of burnt vegetables and smoking tires and manure.

In an instant, the wind diminishes and debris settles to the desert floor. Quiet returns.

Brushing grit from my knees, I wobble to my feet. The silhouettes have vanished, but I'm confident the structures haven't. The explosion, or whatever it was, seemed close only because of its colossal size.

The sight—rising, swelling chaos—goes on and on. A genie from a bottle. I should go home, but I'm rooted to this spot like an old cactus.

Finally, the roiling clouds begin to dissolve and move away as purple fades to ordinary pre-dawn charcoal. I begin to feel my heartbeat, the morning cool on my skin. Suddenly I'm hungry, thirsty, exhausted.

I get back on my bike. Guided by the dimming light of the artificial dawn, I move cautiously ahead. My legs are rubber, my eyes dazzled and swimming. I've just seen something I can't explain. *Will someone at the base—Uncle Pete, maybe—explain it? Or will they all be as ignorant as I am? Or simply unwilling to talk about the most amazing thing I've ever seen?*

# TWO

Throughout the camp, excitement charges the air. People are up, staring at the horizon past the windmill and flagpole and over the tops of the tents and huts and horse stables and ranch houses and barracks buildings and mess hall and mystery structures. I toss paper after paper toward their open doors, but they ignore them.

They contain yesterday's news.

Today, there's something bigger, something ominous, at least to me. And it must mean something extra significant to the camp residents, too, because their voices rise above the usual murmurs and whispers as they stand in small clusters, half-dressed or still in their pajamas. Someone greets someone else with "Congratulations!"

Two engineers I recognize stand outside one of the McDonald ranch houses, which were converted to working spaces when the base camp was established. The men are fully dressed. One wears a fedora, tipped back. They're talking with their hands.

I usually rapid-fire three newspapers in the direction of the ranch-house door, but today I decide on something more personalized. Maybe these two guys, up early and dressed for a party, knew what was going to happen; maybe they'll tell me.

When I get closer, I notice their wallets are out. *Have they seen me approaching? Are they going to give me a tip for persevering?*

No. The hatless one hands the other one money and gets a satisfied grin in return. The wallets go back in their pockets.

I give each of them a newspaper and toss the other one at the door.

"Thank you, son," Fedora says. He has an accent and smiles. He's got reasons. Folding ones. The other guy doesn't look as happy.

"Bobby," I say.

"Yes," he says. "Bobby."

I don't beat around the bush. "Do you fellows know what happened this morning?" I glance in the direction of the shredded clouds and faded light. I can still smell something. Broiled yucca. Scorched sand. Death.

Their answer is a couple of blank looks.

"You couldn't have missed it," I say. "Monster cloud. Colors. Noise like thunder."

The blank looks become puzzled stares.

"Blinding light. My eyes still sting."

Fedora shakes his head.

"You didn't see it?"

"Not a thunderstorm?" No-Hat says.

"One blast, then nothing," I say.

Fedora lights a cigarette.

"The whole sky was boiling." I don't know why I'm trying so hard. I know they saw it.

"We must've been inside," No-Hat says.

"Thank you for the newspapers . . . Bobby," Fedora says. "Perhaps tomorrow the *Journal* will have a story on your . . . storm."

Although night hangs on, I can read their bullshit expressions. This was no *storm*. But I'm not surprised at their tight lips. I'm not supposed to know anything.

Not about this place.

Not about what goes on here.

"Right," I say. "I'm sure it'll be in the *Journal*."

I move on, rolling over the compacted desert dirt, tossing papers, snaking between buildings and groups of gawkers and talkers. I swerve close to a few of them, but like radio talk from a distant station, their spirited conversations drop in volume every time I get near.

The enthusiasm is obvious, but I sense uneasiness, too. And the foreign taste is still in my mouth: sweet, but with the promise of something bitter, giving me a too-familiar feeling of being in a place that underneath its surface is hostile and toxic. It's like the whole base camp is situated on top of a giant underground pool of sulfurous lava and at any moment the earth will open up and swallow us in one gulp.

I recognize where I've felt this before. Albuquerque. The government building. Dad's CO hearing.

I squelch the memory. It's old and unpleasant, and right here there's more exciting stuff happening.

Outside the mess hall, two cooks are taking a break. Officially, these two might not know as much as the engineers, but maybe they've heard something, and maybe they'll be more willing to tell me what it all means.

I stop next to them and pull the mess hall's unrolled allotment of newspapers—six—from my bag. "Here you go, fellows," I say, trying to hand over the thin stack.

They barely give me a glance. *I'm interrupting.*

I hold the papers out to them until I begin to feel foolish. The shorter one, who looks like he eats too much of his own cooking, finally speaks. "Just put 'em by the door, kid."

I tuck them under my arm. "Did you see the sky light up a while ago?" The sky did more than *light up,* but I want them to acknowledge that *something* happened.

The taller one glances in the direction of the blast and quickly back to me, as if he's afraid he'll give away a secret. But he already has. He *saw* it. "We were on our way to work," he says. "Helluva thing. I about shit my pants."

"I think you *did* shit your pants, Eddie," the short guy says.

"That's your cooking you smell, lard-ass," Eddie says.

"Do you know what caused it?" I ask.

"We don't *know* anything," Eddie says. "The eggheads don't talk to us. But stuff sifts down."

I think about Uncle Pete. *How much has sifted down to him?*

"Don't let anyone tell you it was an accident, kid," Lard-Ass says. "We've heard the word *accident* being thrown around this morning. But the longhairs are here for a reason. Most of 'em are celebrating over it."

"And the rest of them are paying off gambling debts," Eddie says.

"Gambling debts?" I say.

He glances around nervously. "Someone bets something is going to happen, someone else bets it won't, someone bets it'll be big, someone else bets it'll be small. That's a guess, but it's an educated one. When these guys come here to eat, they barely see us."

"And when they do," Lard-Ass says, "we're just pieces of furniture."

"Wow," I say. *But how reliable are a couple of Army cooks' guesses, educated or not? What would Dad, the ex-reporter, think of these fellows' inside scoop?*

"Shit-your-pants scary, kiddo," Eddie says. "These assholes would be happy to blow up half the world and make bets on how many of us will survive."

On that comforting note I drop the newspapers at the mess hall door and continue with my route. Maybe I'll see Uncle Pete; he'll have some real information.

But I don't find him, and finally I'm on my way out of the base camp, cruising past the last sentry. The bag over my shoulders is nearly weightless, but in my head and gut the questions are heavy and churning. *What mysterious force is powerful enough to bring dawn to the western sky?* If the engineers really cooked something up, it must have been quite some recipe.

The sun is still hiding behind the distant hills, but light starts to expose the terrain around me. With every turn of my pedals, I can see farther. And something—edginess, maybe—makes me extra alert.

Out of all the flatness and sameness, a dot of substance and possible movement emerges. It's far ahead, near the shoulder, about where the road bends to the left. The dot, which slowly takes on the shape of a shrub, then something more angular, maybe a yucca, feels out of place.

After so many back-and-forths on this barren strip of pavement, nothing should feel out of place.

I'm spooked, but also curious, so I slow down as the dot-shrub-something becomes a human being. The person, lost maybe, gazes out of the gloom. *Looking at what? Have my bike's squeaks and rattles attracted this stranger's attention?*

I don't know much about girls, but when I'm a hundred feet away it becomes obvious that I'm looking at one, and she's wearing something clingy enough that her slender girl-shape is silhouetted sharply by the daybreak glow behind her.

Timidly I move closer. My heart thumps. Then it thumps louder.

I know nothing about naked girls other than what I've managed to sneak a look at in Leo's glove-box collection of French playing cards, but soon I realize that this girl's shape isn't revealing itself because of clinging clothes. With the speed and force of lightning, I realize that this girl is naked.

*Holy shit!*

I want to stop; I want to keep pedaling. I want to look away; I want to stare.

I settle on compromise; go slow, keep my eyes on her face.

Ten feet away I stop and get my feet on the ground before I get too distracted and tip over. *Her face,* I tell myself, but my eyes have their own ideas.

"You're not wearing any clothes," I say.

*Brilliant.*

"English?" she says, trying to cover up. But her skinny arms and hands aren't much good for that, even when she angles her body sideways.

"American."

She shakes her head. Her hair is short and sparse. It looks unhealthy, like the hair of women and girls I've seen in photographs taken at liberated Nazi death camps. I order my eyes to stay above her neck. There's some spillover.

"No," she says. "You *speak* English."

Of course. I speak English. She also speaks English, but with an accent, foreign but not completely so. I've caught snatches of something similar at the base camp, where *German* is usually what pops into my head. And I've seen war movies with fake Nazi bad guys. This girl could be one of their daughters. Or a Nazi spy, dropped in by parachute.

*But would a spy parachute in naked? The opposite of inconspicuous?*

"Yes," I say. "I speak English."

"*Verboten*, once," she says, confirming my suspicions. Her arms are crossed against her chest, but there's no help for the rest of her. "But we say fuck it. The laws are archaic, and there is no one to enforce them, and we have nothing to lose."

Speaking of nothing to lose, she's lost me. *Verboten? Laws against speaking English?* I don't know what she's talking about, and I've never heard a girl say *fuck*. The morning continues to brighten.

"Where is this?" she asks.

"You're not wearing any clothes," I repeat.

"They disappeared," she says. "Sucked away. Small loss."

I toss my carrier bag to her. In it is one copy of the *Journal,* my daily bonus from Leo. She slips the bag over her head. It covers most of her top half, but still there's the bottom. I drop my bike and take off my shorts and hand them to her.

While I stand there in my sweaty T-shirt and a pair of the Navy-issue boxers my cousin Carl sent me for my birthday, she steps into the shorts and zips them up. She doesn't smile, but there's a light in her eyes as she drops a small object in the bag. *What would a naked girl carry with her?*

At last I let my eyes wander. The shorts hang on her hips. She's more than skinny. She's undernourished. I have no food to offer her. The Hershey's bar is heavy in my stomach.

"*Danke*," she says. "Thank you."

"You're in New Mexico," I say, finally overcoming the static in my head to get back to her question.

"New—" She glances around. "It looks unspoiled."

"What would spoil it?" I say, but a vision of the blinding flash and the otherworldly ball and the towering column rushes past my mind's eye, and my question, echoing in my head, sounds naïve, even to a kid who knows next to nothing.

She smiles, her teeth showing big in her gaunt face. "What year is this?" The *what* sounds like *vhat*.

*What year?* "Where are you from?" I say. "How did you get here?"

"You first, American. What year?" She takes a step closer, gazing into my eyes until I have to look away. I busy myself picking up my bike.

"It's 1945." I resist saying *of course* or *dummy* or *Have you been in a coma or impersonating Rip Van Winkle or something?*

"1945."

"July," I say, humoring her.

"Where are you going?" There are tears on her cheeks. I want to know why. I don't want her to be sad. I want to know what she's doing here.

"Now?"

"Yes."

"Home."

"I do not have a home. Here. There. Now. Then."

I feel disconnected from reality. Fire in the sky, and now this, whatever *this* is. I could be dreaming, but the pieces of this scene—what I'm sensing, thinking, saying—feel genuine. Unreal but real. Far beyond my day-to-day, but not far beyond *someone's*. "You can come with me," I say. "My mother has clothes you can wear. We have food."

Mom will know what to do.

From behind me comes the sound of a vehicle. The girl's eyes follow it as it approaches and whips past, not slowing at the sight of a kid straddling a bike and a half-naked girl. Its occupants are in a hurry.

"I have seen that kind of car," she says. "Old photographs. Middle of the last century. The Devil's War."

Cars in the middle of the last century. The Devil's War. Nothing she says makes sense, and even as the day begins to warm, I feel a chill. I tell myself it's the lack of clothes. *But is it?* Although I feel unmoored, I try to make conversation. If this isn't a dream, maybe I'm inside the pages of a comic book. "It's 1945," I repeat, imagining the words taking shape in a dialogue bubble. "That was a '41 Chevy. Last century was horse and buggy."

She shudders. *How long did she stand naked in the cool of the desert before I found her? Or is she like me, chilled by a feeling?*

"I can go home with you, American?"

"It's Bobby."

"Bobby," she says. "Robert." Coming from her lips, both names sound different, yet familiar. And nice.

"Only when my parents are mad at me."

She doesn't smile at my weak joke.

"You really can come with me," I add. "My mom and dad like taking in strays. They took me in, once."

I move closer and gesture at the sturdy rack behind my seat. I know it will hold this bony girl. "Get on."

She sits, sidesaddle at first, but she has difficulty extending her legs. She switches to cowboy style and lets them dangle. She has a different kind of smell—sweet and stale at the same time. A vanilla Coke in a locker room.

I've always liked vanilla Coke. And locker rooms.

Her hands grasp my middle as we take off. "Your parents," she says into the wind, "they did not make you?"

There are no sounds but ours; I have no trouble hearing her words. But they don't register. "*Make* me?"

"Make you, Robert. Sex. Pregnancy. Childbirth."

"Oh," I say over my shoulder. "No. The daughter of anonymous friends of friends from their church had me. She was unwed. She gave me up and took off with her parents for places unknown right after my mom and dad adopted me. I was just a few weeks old."

"Your biological father?"

"Biological? Oh. Another mystery. Some kid. Probably a famous scientist or something now."

I sense a shiver. "What day is it?" she says. "What number in July?"

For a moment, I have to think. The day already seems three days long. "The sixteenth."

"Did something happen this morning? Here, in this New Mexico place?"

"You saw it?"

"Tell me," she says.

"What's your name?"

"Tell me."

I tell her. The blinding flash, the mushroom cloud, the wind and thunder, the awestruck conversations at the base. Her ropy arms practically stop my breathing.

"Why?" I say finally.

"I have to think. Pinch myself. Wake to a familiar nightmare. Or live this one."

"Nightmare?"

The bike tires roll and hiss, the fenders rattle. The day brightens.

"I pinched myself," she says.

"And?"

"The nightmare. It begins here."

Everything about her—words, accent, nakedness, concentration-camp body—unsettles me. *What will my parents think?* "How did you get here?" I ask.

"I cannot explain it."

"Can you explain where you came from? Why you were naked?" The naked part won't be ignored. "Did your family abandon you or something?"

*Like my flesh-and-blood mother and my ghost of a father?*

"I have no family. I can explain nothing."

Because she can explain nothing and I also feel a need to pinch myself—several times—we ride along in silence. She doesn't loosen her grip, but I'm okay with that. It makes me feel anchored. Maybe it works that way for her, too.

"Cocoa," she says finally.

"What?"

"My name is Cocoa."

"That's a new one on me."

"Not so new," she says.

"Where *you* come from."

"I come from here," she says. "And there."

"Huh?"

"Never mind."

More silence. But it won't last. The sun peeks over the mountains, revealing in the distance a couple of familiar outbuildings and a familiar house. In a few minutes, when I bring this strange girl to the door of that house, we won't be greeted with silence.

# THREE

When I open the front door, I smell coffee and hear the grumble of the kitchen radio. Lolly, our yellow lab, pads down the hall and sticks his big muzzle in my crotch. I flinch. My boxer shorts don't offer much protection against dog greetings. He and Cocoa size each other up.

"Mom?" I call. I don't want to walk in on her unannounced. She's warmhearted and open-minded, but there's a limit.

"Your father's still asleep, Bobby." The words flow from the kitchen. We shuffle closer. Cocoa's eyes are wide.

"We have a visitor."

A chair scrapes. Slippers scuff across the linoleum. Cocoa shadows me as I step through the doorway. When Mom sees us, she freezes, dressed in a nightgown that's longer than her faded housecoat. Her eyes are on Cocoa, her gaze unwavering.

"This is my mom," I say. "Dottie Hastings."

"Where did you come from, dearest?" Mom says.

Cocoa doesn't answer, but there's a hint of a smile to match Mom's.

"She can't explain it," I say. "I found her out in the scrubland, standing by the side of the road." I glance at Cocoa. "She wasn't wearing any clothes."

Mom shifts her gaze to me, to my Navy-issue boxers. "You could've given her your shirt, Bobby."

"I wasn't thinking clearly. My head was spinning."

Mom's smile broadens. "I can understand that."

"I'm Cocoa," Cocoa says. I realize that my nervousness has short-circuited my manners.

"What a lovely name," Mom says. She crosses the space between us and gives Cocoa a hug. She winces when she feels Cocoa's bones through the canvas of my bag. Her fingers graze Cocoa's wispy hair.

"My mother found it."

"*Found* it?" I say.

"On a box. In a dumpster."

"A dumpster?" Mom says. She leans back but maintains a grip on Cocoa's spindly hands.

"For garbage," Cocoa says. "A garbage receptacle. Big enough to live in." Cocoa's accent leaks through, and Mom seems to notice. Her head tilts; her mouth opens.

"She has no family," I say.

Mom stares at Cocoa's blank expression. I've seen pictures of soldiers suffering from shellshock, from mistreatment in POW camps. Hers isn't the same as theirs—there's a stubborn light in her eyes—but it's close.

"How did you get here, honey? Who left you at the side of the road?"

Cocoa and I have gone over some of this, but how could Mom *not* ask? Lolly plops down nearby.

Cocoa shrugs an *I don't know*. She's discovered the newspaper in the carry bag, and hands it to me.

"There was something else," I say. "Something huge. Scary. Just before I got to the base."

"What was it, Bobby?" Mom asks. Both sets of eyes are on me.

"A giant explosion. Lit up the whole sky and made its own weather—clouds and wind and heat and thunder."

Mom nods. "The sound woke me. I thought it was thunder."

"Did you see it, Cocoa?" I say.

"I saw . . . something."

"The base is okay?" Mom asks me. "The men?" Her question carries extra urgency. Her kid brother is stationed there.

"I didn't see Uncle Pete, but everything's normal. Except the whole camp was up. Excited. They witnessed something. Expected it. But it was far enough away that nobody got hurt."

"An extraordinary morning." Mom shifts her gaze back to Cocoa. "But we can continue talking about it later. Right now, you could use a bath, sweetheart, and some real clothes. I have—"

Mom glances at Cocoa's body and then her own large chest and wide hips. "I might have something that won't look like a tent on you. And I'll dig through the things Bobby's outgrown. Not glamorous, but they'll do for now."

"Thank you," Cocoa says.

"Bobby, why don't you get down that box of your clothes from the extra bedroom closet and put it on the bed. Then boil a dozen eggs. Cocoa and I are going to be occupied for a while."

She takes Cocoa's arm and steers her toward the bedrooms and bathroom. Before I lose sight of them, Cocoa gives me a look of gratitude that's clouded with emotion—uncertainty, wariness, bewilderment, loneliness, fear.

They disappear, and I drop the *Journal* on the table and go to the extra bedroom, where I move the box of clothes to the bed, imagining Cocoa slipping into them. Then I go to my room to put on some jeans before heading out to the chicken coop with Lolly, always hopeful that I'll toss him an egg.

He was born hungry. When he was so new to our house that he was still nameless, he got into a bag of lollypops and ate every one, sticks and all, pretty much naming himself. Since then, we've mostly kept him away from candy, and eggs have become his favorite food.

The hens have been busy. I gather up a baker's dozen in no time and loft the thirteenth to Lolly, who wolfs it down. He licks his lips to clean up the last of the shiny yellow yolk and shows off his lover-boy pose—long grin, sweeping tail, brown liquid eyes. A familiar comfort on an otherwise unworldly morning.

When I return to the kitchen I hear voices down the hall and the sound of running bathwater. I get the eggs on the stove and sit at the table to read the newspaper, which Dad calls *his* paper, even though he gets it free from me every day. But it's hard to concentrate. The news—national, state, local, war, even sports—seems insignificant. Something happened this morning. Something is happening now, here, in my house.

Dad wanders silently into the kitchen, startling me. Lolly gets up from under the table, gives him the nose-in-the-crotch greeting, and gets a head-scratching in return. Dad is still wearing his pajama bottoms—striped in faded black and white, like a prisoner's—and an old white undershirt, tight across his chest. His forearms are like melons. He grew up on a farm, plowing fields and bucking hay and chopping wood and wrestling livestock, and he can still walk around our barnyard carrying a half-grown hog under each arm. Put a rifle in his hands and he'd put the fear of oblivion in any Nazi. But that won't happen, thank God.

His graying hair sticks out in three or four directions. His glasses ride low on his nose.

"Who's in the bathroom, Bobby?" He pats his abdomen in the general location of his bladder, signaling his need to pee. "I heard two voices. Your mother and—"

I'm not sure how to answer. I haven't yet explained it—*her*—to myself.

"Go outside, Dad. The pigs won't care." And neither will our neighbors. The closest ones—the Unsers—are a half-mile away and old and mostly keep to themselves and probably couldn't tell Dad's weenie from a prickly cactus.

"Thanks for the suggestion, but I can hold it. Who's in there, though?"

"A girl. Her name's Cocoa. She was lost. Confused. I brought her home."

"*Lost?*"

I tell him almost everything. I don't tell him she was naked. The image might offend his Quaker sensibilities and make him worry about how much I saw, which was everything, although my own sensibilities aren't offended.

If he finds out, it will have to be from Mom.

"Quite a morning, huh, Bobby?" Dad says when I'm done telling the story of the non-naked girl. He gets some coffee and sits. The cup looks like a plaything in his big hand.

"That's only half of it." I go on to tell him about the explosion, the reaction on the base, how good it felt to get away from there.

"The girl," Dad says.

"Cocoa."

"Yes, Cocoa. Do you think she was too close to the blast? That it disoriented her?"

"Could be. But it was far beyond the base camp. And she wasn't in that direction. I was homeward bound when I spotted her."

I imagine her near the explosion, being tossed in the air like a rag doll and flying over the base shedding clothes and landing unharmed—mostly—where I found her. But that's ridiculous. This is real life, not a cartoon.

"Maybe she'll remember more after she has a bath and some rest," Dad says.

"She has to eat." I remember the eggs. They're boiling away, almost high and dry. I wonder how rubbery they'll be. I fill the pan with cool water. "She's got roadrunner legs," I add, trying to prepare him. "She almost looks like one of those concentration camp people."

Dad shakes his head, glances at the front page of the *Journal*. "The world has turned ugly, Bobby. Madmen and sheep. Madmen and sheep. Where are the good shepherds?"

# FOUR

y the time Mom and Cocoa return to the kitchen, Dad has put on khakis and a blue work shirt and is pretending to study the sports pages. Lolly is outside, looking for shade. I'm at the stove, stirring a saucepan full of Cream of Wheat. It will take more than boiled eggs to put some meat on this mystery girl.

She looks better. Not normal, but better. Her hair is clean and mostly dry, no longer matted. Still short, of course, but it doesn't look as sparse. She's wearing a seventh-grade school shirt of mine, short-sleeved so her spaghetti arms show, and an old pair of my jeans, hiding her concentration-camp legs. I imagine what she's wearing underneath.

On her feet are some of Mom's white bobby socks, no shoes.

When Dad sees her, he lurches to his feet. He tries to keep his expression under control as Mom introduces them, but he's got an expressive face and right now it's concerned and sympathetic and curious and most of all stunned—even with the background I gave him.

"Good to meet you, Cocoa," he says, doing his best to sound breezy. "Dottie get you all fixed up?"

She nods. "I left a ring of grime in your . . . bathtub, I am afraid." She hesitates on *bathtub,* and I wonder if it's the word or the object. *Who doesn't know what a bathtub is?*

"Gone in a jiffy while you were dressing, honey," Mom says. "Anyway, with Bobby around here, we're used to grime."

"Honest dirt from honest work," I say, borrowing the expression Dad uses when he brings the filth and stink of the barnyard into the house and Mom banishes him to the bathroom.

Dad gestures to a chair and Cocoa sits. "Should we call the sheriff?" he asks. "See if he can help locate Cocoa's family?"

Cocoa shakes her head.

"She has no family," Mom and I chorus. She and I carry dishes and utensils and eggs and Cream of Wheat and milk and sugar to the table.

"No family," Dad echoes, studying Cocoa's face. *"None?"* He gets no help from her—a raised eyebrow, an apologetic half grin. He glances at me. I was once, briefly, in the no-family club. I see the questions in his eyes, but he's considerate and patient and willing—if not happy—to wait for Cocoa's story. "No need for the sheriff, then."

"This sheriff," Cocoa says. "Is he influential in the government?"

"The government?" Dad says.

"Is he someone who can talk to your president?" she says. "The others? The Congress?"

Dad stifles a laugh. "Sheriff Wally's just a county cop, Cocoa. I doubt he's ever been out of New Mexico."

"Do you know anyone else in the government?"

"Why, honey?" Mom says.

"I must talk to someone with influence; someone with connections."

"This family isn't exactly in the good graces of the government," Dad says. "And by family, I mean me."

Cocoa goes silent. We sit, and three sets of eyes watch as she raises a glass and drinks deeply, the milk trickling around the rim of the glass and down her chin in a way that makes me recall Leo's French playing cards.

I send that thought packing. She puts down her glass and

wipes her mouth with the back of her hand.

Mom hands her a napkin. "You must be hungry, Cocoa. Please start."

Still she hesitates. Her foreignness, her stick-figure body, whisper to me that she might not know how to eat, at least not this food with these utensils at this table with these people.

I ladle a glop of Cream of Wheat into my bowl and add milk and sugar and raise a spoonful to my mouth and make contented sounds like I'm trying to encourage a baby to eat something disgusting from a jar. Dad catches on. He cracks a hardboiled egg on his plate and picks away the shell and takes a bite. It looks rubbery. Mom butters a piece of toast and munches away.

Cocoa decides to follow my lead. A glop of Cream of Wheat. Milk and sugar. A tentative bite. A swallow. A smile. Then she gets serious, rapidly emptying her bowl. Her smell—shampoo and bath soap and laundry soap and mothballed air trapped in my outgrown clothes—sweetens the breakfast smells.

She starts on the eggs. Unlike Lolly, she peels hers before wolfing them down. She grabs a piece of toast while Dad and I try not to gawk. Mom puts more bread in the toaster.

"Mom's brother Pete is in the government," I tell Cocoa. "He's in the Army. He works with some big shots. He could talk to them, maybe. If he had a reason."

"Pete doesn't exactly work with them, Bobby," Dad says. "He protects them. And whatever it is they're doing."

"He knows them, though," I say. "I've seen him talking to Dr. Bainbridge, and he runs the whole place." I recall the morning sky coming alive with light and color. My eyes still sting.

Mom returns with more toast. "Why do you need the government's help, honey?" She's as inquisitive as Dad but lacks his patience. "Does it have something to do with where you're from? Did someone bring you here illegally? Against your will?"

Cocoa shakes her head. "I am from here." She sighs. "And not."

Mom and Dad exchange glances and then look at me, like I'd have a solution to the puzzle.

"What?" Dad says to her.

Cocoa taps her head. "Foggy."

We wait.

"I think some*thing*—not some*one*—brought me here," she says. "But my idea for how it happened is crazy. So maybe my brain has been injured." Tears return, and Mom lays her hand over Cocoa's. Instead of being appreciative, I decide it should be *my* hand there.

"You don't have to tell us now," I say.

"When you're feeling up to it—" Dad begins.

But Mom jumps in. "You might feel better if you talk about it, dear. We won't judge or share your story with anyone unless you want us to."

Cocoa nibbles at a piece of toast. Then she puts it down and fingers her stomach like she's overwhelmed it with something it's not used to—food. "You could decide to return me to the desert, if you think I am mad."

"Never," Mom says, squeezing Cocoa's hand.

"We kept Bobby," Dad says.

Cocoa almost giggles, and then shakes her head. "When my thoughts are less tangled, we will talk."

"We're not in a hurry," I say. Dad and Mom hold their tongues.

Cocoa studies Dad's weathered face. "How many years do you have, Mr. Hastings?"

"It's Chuck," Dad says. "And what do you mean, Cocoa? How many more years I'm going to be around?"

Cocoa smiles. "I know you do not have a crystal ball."

I decide to interpret. "She wants to know how many years you've *been* around."

"Much easier," Dad says. "I'm forty-five."

Cocoa whistles. "I have never known anyone with forty-five years," she says. Again, Mom and Dad exchange looks and eye me.

"But you are still handsome . . . Chuck," Cocoa says. Dad's already ruddy complexion gets a shade redder. "For someone with forty-five years, you look good."

Mom's enjoying Dad's embarrassment. She's six years younger and fond of reminding him of the difference. "And you, Cocoa?" she says. "How many years do you have?"

"According to my mother, I had seven years at the time she died. So now I have . . . now I have sixteen."

"Sorry," Mom and Dad say.

"I have almost sixteen," I say.

"We're sorry about your mother," Mom clarifies, ignoring me.

Dad glances at the wall calendar—July, with a picture of a beach scene. Surf and sand and people and umbrellas. "Nine more months, Bobby," Dad says.

"She has no family," I remind my parents, hoping to move past the topic of my age.

Cocoa's gaze settles on Mom's face. "You also look good, Dottie," she says, and then glances down at her own body and limbs, all narrowness and angles under the baggy clothes. "And then there is me."

What I want to say is, *What about me? My parents look good—for their years, anyway—and you don't look so good— except in my eyes. But what do you think of me, Cocoa?*

# FIVE

olly bangs his nose against the screen door and whimpers, signaling the end of breakfast. But Mom has one more thing to say to Cocoa as Dad and I start carrying dishes to the sink.

"I'm going to ask the doctor to come here, sweetheart. I won't be revealing any secrets when I tell you that you're as skinny as a fencepost and not very strong and your color isn't so good. Before he arrives, you should take a nap. Sleep cures many an ill, my mother used to say."

"Grandma?" I let Lolly in. "Grandma *never* slept."

"Up late every night," Dad says. "Reading her mysteries, smoking her Chesterfields, drinking her Jim Beam."

"Not until after my dad died," Mom says. "Besides, all that's got nothing to do with Cocoa. Look at the darkness under her eyes. If my mother had followed her own advice, she'd still be around." Mom gets teary, so Dad and I back off.

"A *doctor*," Cocoa says, pronouncing the word slowly, as if it's foreign, and it probably is, to her. But she said she's from *here.* And *not?* The day continues to make no sense. "I am okay with seeing a doctor."

"Good," Mom says.

"I need to stay healthy," Cocoa says. "But I don't need sleep." She glances at the counter. "Robert, is that the newspaper I carried here?"

"The *Albuquerque Journal.* I bring one home every day. And I go by Bobby."

"It has news of the war?" she says.

"It's hard to escape news of the war," Dad says, scowling. He brings her the *Journal.*

I pull up a chair close to Cocoa. Leo was wrong about a shortage of stories on the war with Germany. Headlines trumpet battle reports from both Europe and the Pacific. Cocoa reads quickly, working her way through the rest of the paper.

"The Nazis have not yet given up," she says.

"A matter of time," I say.

"Hitler is still alive," she says.

Dad nods. "A few weeks ago, there were rumors that he'd committed suicide. Since then he's appeared at a rally in Berlin, looking healthy and unexpectedly confident. The speech was filmed, and witnessed by neutral observers. He's still alive, continuing to cast doubt on the existence of a loving God."

"The devil," Cocoa says. "His war."

"He started it," I say. "We'll finish it."

Cocoa gives me a look, like I'd just begun a serious conversation about Santa Claus.

"The base camp," I say. "Where I deliver the papers. There's a bunch of smart fellows working on something for the Army out there." A big, scary something, I think, although, like the cooks, I don't *know.* "Some kind of surprise that Hitler and Hirohito won't like, is my guess. It's just a guess, of course," I add, mindful of the posters I've seen at the camp and elsewhere: *Loose lips sink ships! He's watching you! Careless words! The enemy is listening! Someone talked! Shhh!*

"Hitler has his own smart fellows," Cocoa says.

"Some of the brains at the base camp sound kind of like you," I say.

"Yes, Robert," she says, no sign of surprise in her words or on her face. But she seems agitated. "Your uncle—"

"Pete," I say.

"Pete," she repeats. "Peter. Could he give the important people a message?"

"What do you have to tell my kid brother, honey?" Mom says. Lolly is back at the door, wanting out. Mom frees him.

"My mind is plagued by mist and shadows," Cocoa says. "But things are beginning to emerge. Events. History. I know something horrible is going to happen. I know it. And when I have more detailed information, I need someone to give it to. Someone who can take action."

She's not giving up on this. My parents aren't looking at Cocoa. They're looking at each other, and then me again. Mom frowns. Dad's eyebrows rise. *Holy shit!* I think.

Cocoa ignores our reactions to her oddball but chilling comments. "When the time comes," she says to Mom, "will you ask your kid brother to listen to me?"

"Of course, dear. But what is it you're so worried about?"

"The world," Cocoa says. "Humanity."

More frowning and raised eyebrows. More *holy shit*.

"I would tell you more if I knew more," she adds.

I yawn. "Want to say hi to some animals, Cocoa?" I ask. Dad usually feeds our barnyard friends in the mornings, but he hasn't made a move in that direction, and I need air.

"What time will the doctor come?" Cocoa asks.

"I'll call him now," Mom says. "But it won't be for a while. Go meet the animals. But stay out of the sun."

# SIX

**W**e head for the barn, which is far enough away that the house isn't exposed to the smell of cow and pig shit (unless the wind is blowing from the east). On the way, Cocoa asks me about my parents—what they do that allows us to have a house and car and animals and food and clothing. She makes it sound like we're rich or something.

"Nothing special," I say. "My dad's a former newspaper reporter who's trying to be a freelance writer but mostly does odd jobs, and my mom works evenings in a bank. The farm makes us a little money and keeps us in as much milk, butter, and eggs as we want."

We pass the chicken coop and pen, where about half of our two dozen hens are out scratching and pecking at the dust, searching for bugs and creating shit of their own and avoiding the urges of Franklin, our rooster, who must be in the coop harassing the rest of his harem.

Lolly trots out of the barn, shaking hay and dust from his yellow coat, raising a cloud. I think of another cloud, rising above the desert floor. And maybe the sight prompts a memory in

Huntington City Township
Public Library
255 West Park Drive
Huntington, IN 46750
www.huntingtonpub.lib.in.us

Cocoa, too. She shuffles to a stop and presses her palms against her temples. Lolly circles us, perhaps trying to herd us out of the sun. Like me, he's never seen a girl as skinny and sickly as Cocoa.

*What is it that makes me want to get past all the surface weirdness—the nakedness and scrawniness and aloneness and foreign accent and mysterious statements—and get to know her?*

There's no explanation.

But I don't care.

"What's the matter?"

No answer. I take her pointy elbow and get her walking again. But she stops once more. She squints into the sun, well above the hills now. "It is so blue."

She's right. The rainstorm has cleared away everything but the deep turquoise. The sky is cloudless. Nothing God-made or manmade to blemish it. "It's New Mexico."

She locks me in a stare. "For now, Robert."

"If you don't want people to think you're crazy, you have to quit saying shit like that."

"It is okay if you think I am crazy."

"Because I don't matter?"

"Because you *do.* Because I feel comfortable talking to you. Because I do not want you to become comfortable with . . ." Her eyes take in our surroundings—house, outbuildings, car, fences, hills, mountains, sky—before returning to me. ". . . all of this."

"You keep talking in riddles."

"They are all I have for now."

I decide to take her at her word. "You're not ever going to call me Bobby, are you?"

"It is a little boy's name. You are no longer a little boy. You have seen me naked." I have. And I can't forget it. "Besides, I prefer Robert."

I glance back up at her turquoise sky, deciding that Robert isn't so bad. "What does the sky look like where you come from?"

"Until today, I have never seen blue sky. I have seen murky clouds dangling cobwebs of poisonous vapor. The glare of overheated sunlight. Dying birds dropping to the earth. Your heart would break, Robert."

"Sorry I asked." *Where on earth could such a place be? Has she really come here from Germany, where by now bombs must have turned the sky inside out?* "You must be glad to be here."

"Yes. And no."

Another riddle. But I keep my mouth shut, afraid to feed her wild imagination.

We reach the cool barn. She breathes in the thick and maybe—to her—strange stew of smells. She stares at the barrel-shaped body of our sow and the uneven row of frantic piglets tugging at her teats. Their enclosure is clean, there's fresh hay and slop. Dad—or Mom—has already been here. Farther along, the heads of the Andrews sisters, our three Jersey cows, overhang their stall doors. They stare at us uncomplainingly. Someone has already milked them.

"This is all like déjà vu, Robert," she says. "Pieces of life coming to me that seem familiar. But not just as they happen. Before they happen."

"What do you mean?"

"Nobody can explain déjà vu," she says. "But with this kind of déjà vu, there is an explanation."

She sits on a bale of hay and I join her, close enough that her smell holds its own with the sharp odors of huge animals and hay. Lolly plops on the dirt between us.

"Which is?" She's already dropped hints, but they only made me question her sanity.

"I am not crazy," she says.

"I didn't say you were." But I thought it. I *thought* it.

"Your face gives you away." She grins, making her look normal and almost healthy. "Your innocent baby face."

My baby face heats up. She tells me I'm not a little boy, then she makes me feel like one. "Mom says I'll be happy to have this face when I'm older."

"There was . . ." She pauses, and I can see the cogwheels spinning in her head. ". . . *is* a writer called H. G. Wells."

She pronounces the name *Vells,* but I know him. "*The War of the Worlds* is on my nightstand. I've read it three times."

"Always war."

"You sound like my dad. But *The War of the Worlds* was different."

"Was it?"

"We were attacked by monsters from Mars."

"Always monsters." I fill in the blanks, picturing newsreels of Hitler ranting in front of thousands of his robotic fools. I think of his extermination squads and death camps and boys my age dying for his bullshit causes. "I was thinking of another H. G. Wells book."

"*The World Set Free*?" I say. "The one about a war fought with atomic bombs?" I have war, and bombs, on the brain.

She shakes her head. "Do you know *The Time Machine*?"

"I can accept the possibility of creatures from outer space and atomic bombs," I say. "But going back and forth in time? I think H. G. Wells was drunk when he wrote that one."

She smiles. "I used to think so, too."

"What's that mean?"

"It means I no longer believe the idea of time travel is farfetched."

"Then *you* must be drunk."

"I tried drinking once. I thought it would be good for the pain."

"Pain?"

"Where do you think I came from?" she says. "Before you discovered me on the side of the road?" As if they're holding their breath for the answer, the Andrews sisters stop chewing and tail-swishing and scratching their hides against the walls.

"I'm waiting for you to tell me."

"I am waiting also."

"For what?" I ask.

"Previously, for my mind to clear. Now, for yours to open."

"It's open."

"I wish it were," she says. "If I do not have the courage to talk to you, when will I feel brave enough to talk to the people who matter?"

"I thought you said *I* matter."

"Of course, you do. I have seen the way your parents look at you." Her expression grows wistful, her eyes watery. I want to hug her, but there's no way I would. "But I must talk to people who are influential in your government, who have the capability to listen and believe and act. Then perhaps I will have my chance to matter, also."

"You can practice on me."

She stares at the dirt. "I am tired, Robert. Your mother suggested I sleep, and I am going to try. When I awake, maybe I will tell you my story."

# SEVEN

**M**om escorts Cocoa to the bedroom. Dad sits at the kitchen table, typing. He thinks and pecks, thinks and pecks. His fingers are too wide for the keys.

I pour three glasses of iced tea and sit. I wonder if Dad even knows I'm here. But when Mom returns, he notices her right away. They've been married forever, but they often create little scenes I'm more used to seeing on a school dance floor or at the drugstore fountain—a couple not much older than me sharing a soda and a look and a history and plans.

Mom sits, gives Dad, then me, a smile. The smiles are similar, but different. Cocoa says I matter to my parents, but I wonder how that compares to what they mean to each other. I was the stray, after all.

"Thanks for the tea, Bobby," Mom says. "The heat is already catching up to me."

Dad resumes typing with his sausage fingers but stops suddenly when I throw out a question meant for both of them. "What do you think about time travel?"

An awkward pause precedes Dad's answer. "I don't believe

I've thought of it at all."

"You've read *The Time Machine*."

"When I was your age, Bobby. I had a richer imagination then."

"Einstein believes in it," Mom says.

"True," Dad says. "But there's no way to prove his theory."

"Why time travel, Bobby?" Mom asks. "Do you wish you were somewhere else?" She takes a long drink of tea, preparing herself, maybe, for the possibility that I don't want to be here.

"Cocoa," I say. "She brought up H. G. Wells and *The Time Machine*. She said she used to not believe in time travel, but now she does."

"Her imagination is still intact," Dad says.

"We'll hope that's all it is," Mom says.

"Why would she change her mind?" I say. "With her next breath, she asked me where I think she came from. Is she telling me she's from another time?"

"She's obviously disoriented," Mom says after a delay. "I think we should leave it to Doctor Kersey to look into her wellbeing. She might open up to him." Mom grins. Doctor Kersey isn't some old country doctor. He's only three years out of Harvard medical school. "When he smiles, he looks like Tyrone Power," she adds.

"I don't think Cocoa is in any condition to be impressed by Doctor Kersey's looks," Dad says. "But I hope she notices. It could mean she's not as bad off as she appears."

I let Dad's words sink in, realizing I'm torn between wanting her to look at Doctor Kersey the way she'd look at an old country doctor, and wanting her to react like a regular girl meeting a Tyrone Power lookalike. I settle on hoping for mild interest—as if my hopes could have any effect on how she'll feel.

"I'll also ask Doctor Kersey if he thinks we should notify the sheriff about Cocoa's appearance here," Mom says. "She could have loved ones frantically searching for her."

"She says she doesn't," I say.

"She's said a lot of things," Dad says.

"If she had loved ones, she wouldn't look like a scarecrow," I tell him.

"If she's a runaway, she might," Mom says. "It won't hurt to ask the doctor."

"When's he coming?" I ask.

"Early afternoon," Mom says. "Before I have to leave for work."

"I hope he's looking his matinee-idol best," Dad says.

"Me, too," I lie.

I hoped Cocoa would wake up before Doctor Kersey arrived, because she said she might tell me her story. But I still haven't heard her stir when the sounds of a car approaching ride the hot air through the open windows. There's no mistaking the tenor voice of the doctor's '36 MG.

I go to the door and watch him park a safe distance from our old DeSoto. The MG seems even more exotic sitting in our yard than when parked in front of his office or whipping around town. The only one I've ever seen, it's dark green with a black convertible top that's down right now, revealing its wrong-side steering wheel.

The sun glints off the sparkling chrome of the spoked wheels and the rich polished paint of the driver's side door as the doctor opens it, unfolds his long, thin frame, and stands. He has to know his wind-tossed hair is standing on end, but he doesn't seem to care. He waves to me, grabs his black leather satchel, and heads for the house.

I think I'm in love, and I don't mean with the doctor. How glorious it would be to take Cocoa for a drive in this car.

I hear voices behind me, and when I turn, there's Cocoa, looking sleepy but rested. She's bookended by Mom and Dad. I expected Cocoa to be nervous, but she seems excited.

"Hello, Bobby," the doctor says, halfway up the steps. We shake hands. "How's your throat doing?"

"Like new, Doctor Kersey." I had tonsillitis in the spring, and everyone except the doc was talking surgery. But he gave me a shot and a jug full of some homemade, foul-tasting concoction to gargle twice a day and at the end of a week I was back to normal.

"Everybody's inside. Come on in."

Studying his face, I shadow him through the door. He shows no shock, only friendliness, as he greets my parents and they introduce him to Cocoa. Maybe Mom prepared him. He says hello and shakes Cocoa's hand. She gives him a smile, and he returns it. *If she thought Dad was handsome, what does she think of the matinee idol?*

"Is there somewhere Cocoa and I—and you, Dottie, if you'd like—can discuss her history and do a quick exam?" the doctor says.

"Cocoa asked me if she could talk to you alone," Mom says. "At least to start with. You're welcome to any room in the house. But can I speak to you first?"

They step out to the porch, but I can imagine their conversation—Mom filling him in on whatever she hasn't told him already. How I found her, her nakedness, her foreign accent, her lack of memory leading to puzzling references to where she's from and weird comments about wanting to talk to people in the government, and, last but not least, time travel. The doctor will have his hands—and brain—full.

Looking more apprehensive, Cocoa waits silently at Dad's side. We smile at her, but her focus is on the door. Doctor Kersey comes back in, and Mom signals Dad and me to remove ourselves from the house.

"Let's stretch our legs," she says when we get outside, and despite the fact that I've already gotten in more than my share of exercise, I'm glad to fall in next to her with Dad taking up a spot off her other shoulder.

Lolly catches up and slows to a trot at my side. We walk to the road and turn left, toward town. There's no traffic in sight, which isn't unusual. Few people live anywhere close to us, and gas is rationed, and there's nowhere to go. So, aside from the crunch of our shoes on the gravel road, and Lolly panting against the heat, and the soft distinctive whoops of a nearby ground dove taking cover, quiet surrounds us.

But soon my curiosity, directed at Mom, bubbles to the surface. "What did you say to the doc?"

"He'll recognize how unhealthy she is, so I stuck to her amnesia, the strange things she's said, how lost she seems, how her accent means she's not local even though she claims to be. I told him that even if we don't know what she's been through, it must have been big, so she's got a reason to be off-kilter. I told him about the explosion, that maybe she was too close to it. I told him she seems to have nobody. I asked him if we're obligated to notify the authorities."

"What did he say?" Dad asks.

"He seemed concerned but not worried. He said we'd deal with the legal questions at the proper time, but first we have to figure out her health issues and get them resolved."

"Did he say anything about how she looked?" I ask.

"He did."

I wait for the rest of her response, but it doesn't come. Instead, she swipes at her cheek and walks faster. But if she's trying to shake us, it's not working.

Finally, Dad asks the obvious question. "Which was?"

Her eyes are glassy as she turns to face us. "He said when he was still in training on the East Coast he cared for German and Polish refugees—people who had been liberated from death camps. People who had been abused and starved by the Nazis. He said Cocoa doesn't look quite as undernourished, and her spirit seems better, but she wouldn't seem out of place in the company of those unfortunates."

Mom is upset at the comparison, but I'm not shocked. It's not the first time I've thought about how I'd seen Cocoa's skeletal body and haunted eyes in newsreels, in photos in *Life* magazine.

Dad puts his big arm around Mom's waist. We resume walking. Lolly spots a roadrunner and halfheartedly chases it into the brush. By the time he rejoins us, we're another quarter-mile down the road and his tongue is hanging out like a wet sock. I imagine what's going on back at the house.

We turn around and head back. Mom wants to be around when Doctor Kersey finishes, and she needs to get ready for work. When we arrive, the MG still sits driverless in the yard and there's no sign of the doctor or Cocoa. We find shade on the porch and sit. Lolly stands at the door expecting to continue on in, but we ignore him.

Eventually we hear voices, Doctor Kersey's and Cocoa's. It sounds like a normal conversation. On the surface, at least, the findings and explanations and revelations—whatever they are—haven't caused any huge waves of emotion.

The screen door opens. "You're all here," the doctor says, looking genuinely happy—or relieved—to see us. "All finished for today. Come in." He grins. "Which sounds a bit strange, since this is your house."

I find Cocoa standing at the kitchen sink, sipping a glass of ice water. She drinks a lot of ice water.

"Did you find any other naked girls out there, Robert?" she murmurs. "Anybody like me?"

"Not this time." I'm tempted to say "There is nobody else like you." *But would she take that as a compliment?* "How did it go with Doctor Kersey?"

"No surprises. He took his time listening to my lungs, but I could have told him they are not worth a shit. He checked my heart and abdomen and reflexes. If he found anything terrible, he did not let on. He used the word 'compromised,' which does not sound so bad, does it? He did not raise an eyebrow during his examination. He is sure of himself, handsome, hot. He made me feel uncomfortable but then comfortable."

I could've skipped hearing about *handsome. And what does* hot *mean? It's New Mexico. It's July. Aren't we* all *hot?*

Voices carry to us—a question from Mom, a response from the doctor. But the words come in murky drips, and soon the conversation moves away.

"When he asked me to tell him my story, or at least my memory of it, I had only one condition."

"That he's someone who matters?"

"That he will help—or at least not hinder—me when I tell it to someone who *does* matter. That he will tell the important people that I am not crazy."

"He agreed to do that?"

"'I can see already you're not crazy, Cocoa,' he said. 'Tell me about yourself, and if I have a chance to speak to anyone in authority on your behalf, I'll do it.'"

"You told him?"

"Yes. And the more I told him, the more I remembered. Like roots exposed along the path of a landslide."

"What did you say?"

She goes to the living room doorway, and I follow her. The

voices of my parents and Doctor Kersey carry from the front yard. "Let's go visit the animals, Robert. I do not know how much your parents will share with you."

In the barn, the animals mostly ignore us. Lolly is probably with my parents. Cocoa sits on a bale of hay, but I stand, resisting the urge to pace.

"What I told him," she says, "is something fantastical. I did not know if he would believe me, but I had no choice. I will tell my story to anyone who has the power and willingness to do something about it."

I'm holding my breath. My legs are rubbery. I sit next to her, silent, afraid to push her off course with more questions.

When she finally speaks, her words come in a torrent. "I told you I believe in time travel. Time *slippage*, really, because time *travel* implies that I had a hand in it. I believe in time slippage because I come from a different time. Do not ask me how, but I think the atomic bomb blast—this morning's event was an atomic bomb test, Robert, the first one ever in the United States, as far as I can recall—was the impetus.

"When I woke up, I was clueless. Except for some fading light simmering on the horizon and a giant purplish cloud high above everything, it was dark. I was naked on the ground in a desolate desert landscape. I thought I was dead. I thought I was in heaven, or hell, but I never believed in those places.

"I got to my feet and began walking. I saw what I knew must be stars because I had seen them in photos and videos in the abandoned library that I call home. I read about them shining white and yellow and creating constellations.

"I wondered how it could be possible to have cool air around me and be able to see stars and my first thought was that I had been transported to another planet but that seemed even less likely than my next thought, which was that I had traveled through time, but that seemed ridiculous, too, so I tried not to think. I just kept walking."

She takes a deep breath. I sense images forming behind her eyes.

"Daylight crept into the darkness," she says. "I saw a distant mountain peak and headed for it so I would not walk around in circles, and I came to the road and tried to decide if I should go left or right. Then you came along and made up my mind for me."

"*Videos*?" The word is the least important piece of her puzzling story. I should be asking about atomic bombs and slipping through time and how she got naked. But *videos* might have a reasonable explanation.

"Movies. Moving pictures. Talking pictures."

"I get it." I try not to look skeptical—even though I'm beyond skeptical—because I know she's worried I'll think she's lost her mind and, if she thinks that, she won't tell me more. "I'm glad I came along," I add.

She keeps studying me, and I figure she's looking for a reason to go on, or not. "Where do you come from, Cocoa?" I say. "The past? The future? A faraway country?"

She leans closer. A small array of freckles dots her sunken cheeks. I don't remember seeing them before now. I want to touch them, but I don't, because she's wondering if I'm humoring her, and I don't want to be anything but serious, and I'm afraid of how she'd react to my fingertips on her skin.

"I told you I am from here," she says at last. "But it is a different here. Nearly a hundred years from now. Not New Mexico, but New Dresden. Not the United States of America but the Subservient States of the Fatherland. Not blue skies and clean air and order and hope, but ashy skies and toxic air and chaos and hopelessness."

*She's gone all the way off the rails*, I say to myself. But a small part of me doesn't believe that. A small part of me believes *her*. "What happens?"

"The Devil's War. *This* war." She pauses. "Hitler wins it."

She's disturbed. Fantasizing. Brainwashed. "He's on his last legs. The Nazi army's in retreat, backed up nearly to Berlin from both sides—the Russians and us. *He's* not winning. *We're* winning."

"He has people fooled. He has aces up his sleeve, ready to be played. That is why I must talk to someone."

"What aces?"

"Your generals believe they have won the race to build the first atomic bomb. This morning they successfully tested it. But, in fact, Germany won the race. The delays in the Allied invasion of France gave German scientists breathing room. Now Hitler has bombs of his own and the capacity to use them. He has a plan to move ahead. Soon."

"He *wins*?"

"And loses. Civilization goes into a tailspin. You would not believe the outcome, Robert. But look at me."

I do as I'm told. The freckles provide a random layer of normalcy and even cuteness. But there are also the sunken cheeks and the bluish veins visible under the papery skin and the pained eyes and the dark shadows under them and the wispy hair framing it all. My gaze falls to her neck and shoulders and arms and the rest of her wasted body under the baggy clothes.

"I am the face of Hitler's legacy," she says. "Your world is heaven; mine is hell. But unless I can get someone to listen to me, they will surely become one."

Her words frighten me, but I tell myself they shouldn't. I tell myself they're fiction—that they should be no more frightening than the words of H. G. Wells or H. P. Lovecraft or Edgar Allan Poe. I try to convince myself that Cocoa has been through some frightening event that's left her irrational, and she can't be from the future. I try to convince myself that Dr. Kersey has seen the nonsense in her story and he's telling my parents she needs time to recover and if the recovery doesn't take place she'll need help from a different kind of doctor.

But I study her face and I'm not convinced of anything. "I have a million questions."

"A million more?"

"At least."

"I will answer any that I can, Robert, but not now. I do not know if this passage through time will allow me to alter history, but I have to try. I have to hurry. I must reach someone in power. Maybe that will be through Doctor Kersey, or your uncle Peter, or even your father the writer. But I must start."

*Not now*, she says.

*When, then?* I ache to be convinced, one way or another.

I follow her to the front yard, where Doctor Kersey sits behind the steering wheel of his MG, still talking to Mom and

Dad. He sees us coming and waves, which I suspect is a signal to my parents that we're getting within earshot.

The MG's engine crackles to life, and then the little car heads down the driveway, trailing a cloud of exhaust and dust. Again, I'm reminded of another cloud. *Was it really just this morning that my life turned inside out and upside down and sideways?*

"Are you feeling okay, dear?" Mom asks Cocoa when we arrive.

"What did the doctor say about how I feel?" Cocoa says.

"He didn't tell us how you feel," Dad says.

"He told us you're doing fine," Mom says. "But he wants to check out some things more thoroughly. He expects to see you in his office tomorrow."

"He was impressed," Dad says. "He says you're a smart girl with an unusual amount of knowledge."

They're leaving out part of the whole truth. The part that matters.

The *time slippage* part.

"An unusual amount," Mom echoes.

"What else?" I say. "Anything about where Cocoa comes from and why she needs to talk to someone?"

"I think he told us everything Cocoa told him, Bobby," Dad says.

"Did he believe what I told him?" Cocoa says.

"Here's what he said," Dad replies. "He said, 'There's no rational reason for me to believe her story. But I'm certain she believes it.'"

"That's it?" I say. "He's not going to do anything?"

"Wait and see," Mom says. "As we told you, he wants her in his office tomorrow."

"We do not have time for *wait and see*," Cocoa says.

"Can we talk to Uncle Pete?" I say.

"Peter's a realist," Mom says.

"He's been to war," I say. "This war. He's fought. He's got scars. Do you think he wouldn't listen to a story about Hitler winning?" This is the part of Cocoa's story I can't let go of. Which means I almost have to believe the rest of it. *Will anyone else?*

"He's not exactly open-minded," Dad says.

"About pacifism," I say. "This isn't pacifism."

"I'm running late," Mom says. "I could take you and your bike to the newspaper shack, but you'd have to pedal the rest of the way and back home."

"Cocoa needs to tell him the story herself," I say. She has me half-believing her, so maybe she can half-convince Uncle Pete.

"I will ride behind you again, Robert," Cocoa says.

"Are you feeling up to it, honey?" Mom says.

"No problem," Cocoa says.

I look at her and imagine plenty of problems, but she has a determined look. I picture her arms around me.

"Put your bike in the back seat, Bobby," Mom says. "Both of you drink some water. I'll be five minutes."

"You might not be able to talk to Pete," Dad says as Mom hurries away. "With all the excitement out there, he could be unreachable."

"We'll wait," I say, and Cocoa and I head off to load my bike.

When Mom gets to the car we're already sitting in the front and kind of close, but as she slides behind the wheel she nudges Cocoa a little nearer and I get a whiff of shampoo. It's Breck, what Mom uses, but on Cocoa it smells different—stronger and sweeter but with a hint of bitter, too, like an apple picked too early.

I like green apples.

While Mom lead-foots it toward the shack, Cocoa catches me staring at her fingers, white-knuckled, digging into the seat. "I have never ridden in a car," she says.

Mom winces and slows.

She drops us off. Now it's pedal power. In two minutes I'm sweating, but Cocoa holds tight, humming something, and that's about all I get out of her for the rest of the trip. When we near the base camp and pass the two sentries in their Jeep, I wave, and one waves back. They don't seem concerned or impressed that the paperboy is bringing along a stranger. *She's a girl; she's skinny; she looks ill. Couldn't the kid do better for himself?*

No. I couldn't.

# EIGHT

Outside the enlisted men's barracks we find Uncle Pete's buddy, Joe Waller. He sits on an empty oil barrel he tipped on its side and rolled to the shade of the barebones building. He's cleaning his rifle, which he uses for hunting game, not bad guys. I introduce him to Cocoa. He tries not to stare.

"On patrol," he says when I ask him about Uncle Pete. "Took off on horseback an hour ago."

"Horseback?" Cocoa says.

"We don't use 'em often except for broom polo," Joe says. "Too much territory to cover. But today our vehicles are doing taxi duty."

"Can we see the horses?" Cocoa says.

"Sorry, honey. All checked out."

She looks disappointed, but at least her mind is sidetracked for a moment. "When will Peter return?" she asks.

Joe doesn't answer right away. Maybe it's her accent. He was in France kicking the Germans' asses before a piece of shrapnel cut him down.

"Not soon," he says finally. "Horses don't like heat. I'm guessing after midnight."

"Midnight?" Cocoa says. She turns to me. "Is there someone else?"

I shake my head. Uncle Pete will listen, at least until the story turns ridiculous. Nobody else—especially someone who *matters*, like Lieutenant Bush or Dr. Bainbridge—will give this strange girl with the stranger story the time of day.

"Can I leave Uncle Pete a note?" I say. "It's important."

"Sure."

I bum paper and pencil and scribble a note in which I ask my uncle to call me right away because I have something big to tell him. Then Cocoa and I get back on the bike and head home. Again, she doesn't say much, but three times—whether to me or to herself I can't tell—she murmurs, "We must talk to someone."

She's dragging by the time we walk through the door, and Dad tells her to go to bed. She doesn't argue. When I hear the bedroom door close, I sit at the kitchen table and fidget until Dad looks up from his typewriter. He's trying to be patient, but whatever he's working on is important.

"What did Dr. Kersey really say?"

He squirms. He rarely lies, so the bullshit he and Mom were spreading earlier must have been a struggle for him. The quiet is overridden by a news bulletin about a huge blast at the Army base caused by an *accidental explosion* of a stockpile of munitions.

Speaking of bullshit . . . the light, the thunder, the wind, the cloud. That was no *accidental* explosion. Cocoa may not have all her marbles, but the bomb part of her story makes sense.

"He wasn't quite as positive as we let on," Dad says.

I wait for him to continue.

"The doctor believes she's been traumatized by some mystery event that's affected her mentally," Dad says. "But more concerning to him is her physical health. She's malnourished, and her body systems are showing the effects of starvation combined with environmental factors akin to working in a mine. Has she said anything about that kind of history?"

"A *mine*?"

"Nonsensical, huh?"

"He's got nothing better?"

"He says she has a murmur and arrhythmia, liver enlargement, lymph node enlargement, and lungs that function at half her predicted capacity. He's puzzled, but tomorrow he'll do a more thorough exam, including lab work."

"He thinks it's okay to keep all that from her?"

"He's told her some of it. He'll tell her more tomorrow."

"Can he make her better?"

"He's going to try," Dad says. "And we can help with the nutrition part."

"Doesn't sound like he's going to go to bat for her."

"And you weren't able to talk to Pete."

"I left him a note," I say. "I asked him to call."

"He will. If he's not too busy being a soldier."

"You make it sound like a bad thing."

"We've had this discussion before, Bobby."

"Today you started it."

"Yes. And I'm sorry. But I'm not sorry I chose to conscientiously object to the war, just as Pete isn't sorry he chose to serve."

"It wasn't exactly a choice," I say. "He would've been drafted."

"He had a choice. Before he made it, I let him know his options."

"He's keeping us safe."

"And I'm not," he says. "I'm aware of that."

We *have* had this discussion before. It always ends the same—stalemate. "Do you believe Cocoa's story?"

"*Time* travel? Hitler gets off the ropes and *conquers America*? A helluva tale, Bobby, but I wouldn't bet a nickel on it being true."

"A penny?"

"If the penny were yours."

"Maybe Uncle Pete will believe it," I say.

"He's believed other things."

"You don't like him."

"I like him fine," Dad says. "But the war drove a wedge between us, and we can't seem to dislodge it."

"I hope he calls."

"Me, too, Bobby. For Cocoa's sake. But don't bring up anything outlandish over the phone. The only way Pete won't shut down at the first mention of time travel is if he hears about it from Cocoa, face-to-face. I wasn't lying that the doctor was impressed with her. We're all impressed. Maybe Pete will be, too."

I glance at the paper in his typewriter. "You could write a story about her. Submit it to the *Chieftain*, or even the *Journal*."

He laughs. "I'd never get another story published. Besides, I don't write fiction."

"You don't have to mention the time . . . uh . . . *slippage* part. Say she appeared the morning the bomb exploded. Write about her appearance, her accent, her lack of family. Isn't this what they call human interest?"

"Bomb?" Dad says. "Didn't you just hear the newsman? You believe her bomb story?"

"Maybe Uncle Pete can answer that question."

"Maybe."

"It wasn't munitions," I say. "People at the base camp don't think it was." I don't tell him the *people* are a couple of Army cooks.

"God save us, if someone's developed a super bomb." He goes back to his writing. I get up to let Lolly in, wondering what Dad has to lose by writing about Cocoa. Because of him, I've become the least popular kid at school—except for human plague Bo Crandall. He's fond of dropping pubic hairs on his classmates' desks and will start his junior year as an eighteen-year-old, if he starts at all.

People can't stand disgusting pricks like Bo Crandall, but the son of a *conchie* is a close second on almost everyone's shit list. *So why does the* conchie *himself think he has a future in newspaper writing? Why does he think a story on Cocoa would jeopardize his fictitious future?*

Mom has a pot of chicken soup simmering on the stove. I give it a stir, cut a slice of the bread she baked earlier, and wander to the living room, where Dad's old copy of *The Time Machine* resides on a low bookshelf. I take it to my room, away from the click-clack of Dad's typewriter keys knocking out a story that nobody wants to publish.

I stretch out on my bed and begin reading. Maybe the second time around, old man Wells' thought-provoking but bizarre idea about traveling through time will be just as thought-provoking but not so bizarre.

I read and doze. When I finally get up, the sun is low, the house is quiet. Through the kitchen window I see Dad outside, heading for the barn. I go to Cocoa's room; it *feels* like her room, even though she's been with us barely a day. I tap on her door. No answer. I crack it open. She's on top of the covers, eyes closed. I study her chest for a sign that she's breathing, and finally it comes—a slight rise and fall. Feeling like a peeping Tom, I shut the door and leave.

On a cutting board by the kitchen sink Dad has left me a pile of rhubarb and a note. *Bobby: One-inch chunks. I'll start the pie when I'm done milking the Andrews sisters. Thanks!*

My mouth waters. But as I rinse and cut I wonder if Cocoa will like rhubarb pie. *Do they even have rhubarb in wherever (or whenever) she's from?*

I stare at the phone, willing it to ring. It doesn't, and still there's no sound from Cocoa's room. Finished with the rhubarb, I sit to listen to the radio. Maybe the next newsman will dig deeper into the Army's cover-up story.

But when the news comes on, it's the same tall tale.

Cocoa finds me in the living room. I tell her the blast is being downplayed. I tell her I've heard nothing from Uncle Pete, and that the doctor is taking a wait-and-see approach to her story.

She's agitated. "Everyone sucks," she says.

And she's right.

We spend the rest of the evening waiting for the phone to ring, waiting for something more truthful from the radio. We hear Dad put the finishing touches on the rhubarb pie and close the oven and tap away on his typewriter. When the smells of baking rhubarb and sugar and crust reach us, Cocoa finally smiles.

We have supper—chicken soup and bread and butter and sliced tomatoes from the garden and warm pie—and Cocoa loves everything. But the news is still a lie. And Cocoa has to go see Dr. Kersey in the morning for prodding and needling and questioning. And when we finally head off to bed, Uncle Pete still hasn't called.

# NINE

I t's still dark, and Leo beat me to the shack, as usual. He left the faint stink of exhaust in the air and my stack of newspapers on the bench. I roll only half, remembering the crowd of people leaving the base camp yesterday.

I wonder how many won't return, which gets me to wondering again about Cocoa's bomb story. If the explosion *was* a test, at least some of the engineers and the people who support them would have no reason to stick around.

Maybe it's the early hour and lack of sleep, but as I load the papers and shoulder my bag and take off for the camp, one irrational question continues to pester me. *If Cocoa's right about the bomb, could the other stuff also be true?*

I should be warm from the exertion of the bike ride from home and hustling through the papers and building up speed again, but I feel a chill.

I'm halfway through my route when I arrive at Uncle Pete's barracks. A weak glow leaks through the windows. Trying to be quiet, I slip inside with the usual four copies of the *Journal* allocated to this building. I set them on a rickety card table and look around. Surrounded by sleeping soldiers, Uncle Pete's sitting on his bunk, taking off his boots. He nods in my direction and pads over, almost disguising his limp, and crushes me with a hug.

"What's up, Bobby?" he murmurs as he steps back. "Sorry I didn't call. I just found your note." He's in dusty fatigues, no hat. He's thirty-two, but he almost looks too young to be a soldier. Dark memories smolder beneath his pupils.

The big room buzzes with snoring. "I need to talk to you, Uncle Pete. It's important."

His eyebrows rise. "Short important or long important?"

"Long, I guess."

"Can it wait until I grab some sleep, pal? Been playing cowboy all night."

I picture him seated on a horse in the moonlight, his leg at the mercy of the big animal's broad-bodied anatomy and jostling. "Can you come to the house?"

"Why the house?"

"There's someone I want you to meet."

"*Someone*? You got a girlfriend, Bobby? You want your sophisticated uncle's approval?"

"Something like that."

"I think I can get a vehicle from the motor pool. Things have simmered down since yesterday."

"A lot of people left yesterday?"

"The goings outnumbered the comings."

"The radio said the explosion was accidental. So, why'd all those guys leave?"

Uncle Pete hesitates long enough to let me know something is up, something *was* up, which makes me think of Cocoa. Everything makes me think of Cocoa. "Loose lips," he whispers finally.

"Sink ships," I say.

"Exactly."

"Can you make it late this afternoon or this evening? She . . . my friend . . . has an appointment this morning."

"I don't have patrol duty until 1900 hours. I'll try to get to your place before your mom takes off for work so I can say hello to her."

"She'd love that."

"I might even say hello to your old man."

"Yikes."

"Yeah. Now on your way, kid. I need sleep, and you've got more newspapers in that bag." He yawns. Maybe he'd be more excited if he had a preview of the story. But that won't happen. Only Cocoa has a chance of making her yarn sound like the truth.

I deliver the rest of the papers. Talking to Uncle Pete has given me energy. It's good to have him close to home. For years, he was half a world away, and then in a Washington, DC, hospital, and then three hours up the road in Los Alamos, the top-secret facility in the mountains above Santa Fe. His transfer brought him here. I hope he'll stay. Someone has to guard this place after the geniuses and brass and worker bees leave.

Dad is the only one out of bed when I get home. He's just returned to the kitchen from milking the Andrews sisters and repairing a hole in the hen house floor. The robber-critter that made it got scared off before getting in, so Dad was able to collect the nine eggs now sitting in a bowl on the counter.

"Did Lolly get one?" I ask. He's stretched out under the table, but when he hears his name he rolls on his back, looking for a scratching. I kneel and oblige.

"Yeah, but I had to think about it. He didn't even whimper last night when the weasel or whatever it was came calling."

"I saw Uncle Pete. He said he'd come over this afternoon."

"Did you tell him I'll be here?"

"He likes you."

Dad presses the palms of his big hands against my cheeks and studies my face.

"What are you doing?"

"Checking your nose for sudden growth, Pinocchio."

When he releases me, I get up and sit at the table. I resist touching my nose. "The truth is, he said he might say hello to you."

"That sounds more like it."

"Don't argue with him, okay? I like having him around here."

# TEN

There's still no sign of Cocoa when Mom shuffles into the kitchen and goes straight to the coffee pot. Coffee is rationed, but we've done a good job of hoarding it. She's wearing her usual morning attire—nightgown, housecoat, slippers. Her hair has gone wild during the night.

"Tired, Mom?"

She takes a serious drink of black coffee before responding. "Someone was snoring most of the night. Then someone got up at four thirty and rattled around the bedroom while someone else was trying to sleep."

Dad smiles sheepishly and gets back to his newspaper, where an article reports on an accidental ammunition explosion. The article says windows fractured hundreds of miles away.

*An explosion of ammunition breaks windows hundreds of miles away?* I picture other noses growing—the reporter's, the Army spokesman who fed him the lie.

Mom brings a bowl to the table. While she fills it with Rice Krispies and milk, she begins the *Reader's Digest* version of last night's trip to town.

"I talked to the sheriff. I told him a little about Cocoa. He wasn't aware of a missing person report on anyone, but he'll check outside the county. He said he didn't see any harm in her staying with us until someone can figure out where she belongs, or until we get tired of her. I told him we won't get tired of her."

At Mom's words, I get a warm feeling in my chest. "Why would we?"

"Yes," Dad says. "Why would we? We might have to tell the hens to increase their egg production, though. For such a skinny thing, the girl can eat."

By nine thirty we're all in the car on our way to Socorro. Cocoa and I are at opposite ends of the back seat. I should've brought Lolly and stationed him at a window, compressing our usable space, but Dad wanted him home protecting the chickens. Like that would happen.

Doctor Kersey's office is stocked with furniture and paintings and magazines and a curvy blond nurse named Marla, who's at the reception room desk when we walk in. Behind the door to the inner office, I know, is modern X-ray and other equipment. Once, when Marla and I were waiting in the examination room for the doctor to come in and check out my raw throat, she explained to me what all the instruments were called. The names—stethoscope, otoscope, ophthalmoscope—were like fishhooks. They stuck in my brain, refusing to be dislodged.

Marla looks surprised at the size of Cocoa's fan club, but she smiles and buzzes the doctor and, in a moment, he emerges from behind the door and asks Cocoa and his nurse to step inside. He tells us we're welcome to take care of errands, because this is going to take a while. We find seats and magazines and settle in. Before the door closes, Cocoa gives me a look, but it's as foreign to me as whatever language she grew up speaking.

Cocoa didn't convince the doctor yesterday. *Can she do it today?* I wonder. *What's Uncle Pete going to make of her story? What will she have to do make believers of the people who matter?*

I've made my way through a whole *Life* magazine before Cocoa and the doctor reappear. Her expression is still incomprehensible, but he looks calm, as if he has things figured out. Uncle Pete told me once that this expression is something doctors learn in medical school. He saw it on a lot of them after he was wounded. It's part of what they call *reassurance*, and they use it when they're stumped, or a patient is unfixable—or dying.

"She's all set for today," Doctor Kersey tells my parents in a reassuring voice. "But can I talk to you briefly in the consultation room? Cocoa and Bobby can wait here."

"Actually," Mom says, rising from her chair, "I'm going to take Cocoa shopping for some real clothes. We'll be at Penney's. So, Chuck, when you and Bobby are done consulting with Doctor Kersey, can you meet us at the store? Young ladies' department."

*Chuck and me, consulting with the doctor?* Mom just made me feel about ten feet tall.

"Is that arrangement okay with you, dear?" Mom asks Cocoa.

"I keep no secrets," she says. "And Chuck, Robert, and me— we are tight."

*Tight?*

Doctor Kersey looks a little startled, but quickly recovers his composure. Dad and I say goodbye to the shoppers and follow the doctor into his consultation room, which at my last visit doubled as an examination room. For a moment, I wonder if sometimes, when the handsome doctor and his gorgeous nurse are alone in the office, it triples as something else.

"Anything new?" Dad says when we're seated on stools and the doctor is perched on the edge of his examination table. He looks comfortable there. I picture him with company.

"Nothing dramatic," the doctor says. "We have to wait for the chest X-rays to be developed and the blood and urine to be processed, but until then we're pretty much where we were yesterday. A young woman with some significant and apparently chronic deficits of her body's systems, cause or causes unknown."

"You can treat her, though?" I say. "Or she might improve on her own?"

"She's no longer being exposed to the source of her problems," Dad says. "The mine or whatever it was. Bobby could be right?"

"That's my hope," the doctor says, "because I don't have a knockout treatment plan. I can only prescribe rest, fresh air, good food, and moderate exercise. That doesn't mean I'm satisfied.

Once the results come back, I'll pick the brains of doctors I trust and come up with a strategy."

"She has an appetite," I say.

"A positive sign."

"And an imagination," Dad says.

"I'm afraid it goes beyond that, Chuck." The doctor's expression turns serious. "She stands by her story of time travel and a ruined world with no resources, and what she calls thermonuclear bombs and perpetual wars and Hitler winning this one to start the whole mess. She thinks she can do something to alter what she perceives as this *history*."

"You know about the explosion yesterday?" I say.

"An atomic bomb, she claims," the doctor says.

"I believe her," I say. "I saw it. Felt it. It was no accident. The engineers who were there, working around the clock for the last six months—they're leaving. They've finished their jobs."

"Maybe she's right about the bomb," Dad says.

"Maybe," Doctor Kersey says. "But the rest of it? Ludicrous. If I were to talk to government authorities about her claims, which she's hoping I'll do, I'd be ridiculed. She'd be institutionalized. And you, Bobby, if you publicly step beyond supporting the bomb theory, would be the butt of everyone's jokes."

I consider telling him I'm already the butt of everyone's jokes. "Where'd she come from, then?" I say instead. "Why is she sick, and telling us these things? Why the German accent?"

"Maybe she was born in Germany," he says, "or grew up in a German community in the US. Maybe she's faking it."

I'm not swayed. The accent isn't fake. There are no German communities around here. *And if she arrived from Germany or some other European country, why wouldn't she say that?*

"She seems sincere," Dad says. "Not irrational."

"I agree," Doctor Kersey says. "She's convincing. But she's also been through a major hardship of some kind, which could make her sincerely irrational. Or irrationally sincere."

At the risk of offending Dad, I decide to give the doctor something more to ponder. "Did she tell you she was naked when I found her?"

The doc blinks away a startled look. Dad doesn't react. *Mom must've told him.*

"She was standing like a yucca next to the road, not a stitch on and not very concerned about it," I say. "Almost like she hadn't noticed. When I pointed it out, she said her clothes had disappeared. 'Small loss,' she said."

"Naked!" Doctor Kersey echoes. "It's odd and disturbing, but what does it prove?"

"What would it take to convince you?" I say, wondering how far I am from being convinced myself.

He shakes his head. "I don't believe in fairy tales, Bobby." He hesitates. "But this morning she told me that something big is going to happen in the next few days. She said she doesn't recall what the event will be, but it will slow the Allies' progress toward ending the war and give Hitler and his Japanese friends new life."

Doc doesn't smile. He may not believe Cocoa, but the idea of Hitler rising from the mat darkens his mood. "If something significant really does happen, I'd be more inclined to think the world has tipped on its axis and Cocoa's claims contain some truth."

"So, if her prediction comes true, you'd believe that she's a time traveler?" Dad asks.

The doctor smiles, but it's brief and grim. "I said *some* truth. But you—all of us—should hope her whole story, including the Nazi resurgence, is fantasy. I'd much rather deal with a delusional girl than a madman."

# ELEVEN

**M**om must've broken into her piggybank. On our way home, two full J.C. Penney bags sit on the seat between Cocoa and me. She says thank you a million times before we get to the house and continues as she and Mom head for the bedrooms.

A pot of chili simmers in the oven. Dad and I get busy making cornbread. All the traveling and talking and shopping and anxiety have made us ravenous, just like the skinny girl down the hall.

I've just moved the chili to the stovetop and replaced it with two pans of cornbread when Mom and Cocoa appear. Mom's wearing a smile. Cocoa's wearing clothes that make her look like the girls at my school, many of whom turn up their noses at me because I'm the son of a coward. On her feet are white Keds and blue bobby socks, and above the spindly ankles and calves are a pair of girls' blue jeans, rolled to just below her knee. Above them is a lightweight pink sweater, tight enough to show off her small breasts, now encased in a brassiere, maybe one with lace and frills. The sweater is short-sleeved, displaying her bony arms.

She looks at me proudly, and when Mom takes her hand and slowly twirls her to show off her new look, Cocoa blushes. It's the first time I've seen her blush. For a few moments, she's forgotten—or at least set aside—her demons and darkness.

Dad whistles. I imagine a big band playing—Tommy Dorsey fronted by Frank Sinatra, maybe, and me asking Cocoa to dance, and having my arms around her, and her whispering in my ear that I'm a good dancer and strong to boot. But the real me can only smile and clap. I've never been able to whistle. I've never learned to dance.

After lunch, Cocoa winds down. Her eyes droop, her smile vanishes, her body sags. She heads off to her room for a nap.

I'm tired but not sleepy. While Mom and Dad clean up the kitchen I feed the Andrews sisters and the sow. I make sure she hasn't rolled over on one of her piglets, who remain nameless because of a promise I made to my parents about animals we raise to be sold or eaten. I freshen the hay in the stalls and pen, feed the chickens, clean their coop, check it for new damage. Always hopeful, Lolly tags along. I reward my pal with the biggest egg of the eleven the hens donate.

When we return to the house, Mom is in the shower, beginning her getting-ready-for-work ritual, and Dad is at the kitchen table as usual, typing. I slip behind him to see if he's working on a story about Cocoa, but it's something on mining rights. *Interesting?* Maybe to a newspaper editor.

Cocoa's still asleep. Aside from the sounds of the shower and typewriter, the house is quiet. I head to my room and *The Time Machine*. Then, remembering Doctor Kersey telling us what Cocoa said—that something big and bad is going to happen soon—I go to the living room and turn on the news.

I'll read H. G. Wells' wild-ass notions of time travel and listen for a sign that they aren't so wild-ass after all.

Just as Mom is ready to walk out the door, the sound of something more substantial than a car grows in the distance. By the time the sound has built to a nearby rumble, I'm at the window. An open-top truck, doorless, army-green, sits in our driveway, dwarfing the DeSoto the way the DeSoto dwarfed Doctor Kersey's MG. It's one of the Dodge half-tons I've seen around the base camp, sometimes with Uncle Pete at the wheel.

He gets out, dressed in civvies—a T-shirt and shorts. Angry scars mar his bad knee. He wears dusty government-issue boots, which don't go with the rest of his outfit. But he's been traveling light since December 1941, when he quit his job as a construction foreman in Albuquerque and signed up to fight the Nazis and Japs.

*Will the war be over before it's my turn?* A week ago, I thought so, but Cocoa's story makes me wonder.

While Uncle Pete's in the yard talking to Mom, I knock—and knock—on Cocoa's door.

"What?" she says finally. Door and distance and probably sleepiness muffle her voice.

"Uncle Pete's here."

"Open the door."

I do. She's sitting on her bed in her new clothes, looking dazed. "Is he waiting for me?"

"Saying hi to Mom."

She runs her hand through her tangled hair. "Give me a minute."

"Sure." I turn to leave.

"Robert?" Cocoa says.

"Yeah?"

"Is he cool?"

"Cool?"

"Nice? Is he nice?"

"Mom says that growing up he was sort of a hellion—getting in scrapes, chasing girls, skipping school. But he grew out of it, and he's always been nice to me. Better than nice. He'll be better than nice to you, too."

"I want him to believe me."

"He came home from the war quieter. *Introspective,* Mom calls it. He's seen lots of shit, and I know some of it is hard to comprehend. He'll listen to you. But believe? That's a stretch."

She looks at me like she wants something more. Reassurance.

"Be convincing. Nobody but me believes you." And I'm not even sure about *me.*

I turn off the radio. There's been no big news. I'm mostly

grateful. Now, the only sounds are the sporadic hailstorm of Dad's typing, flies buzzing against the screen door, and Mom and Uncle Pete's voices outside.

Mom's DeSoto cranks to life. Gravel crunches. I hear the kitchen door open, and Uncle Pete interrupting Dad's typing.

"Bobby asked me to come over."

"They're in the living room."

"Nice of you and Dottie to take her—the girl—in."

"It was the only thing to do."

"It's not the first time."

"Easy decisions. Both of them."

"Still . . ."

"Interesting girl. Fascinating story," Dad says.

"I should go hear it."

"Yes, you should, Pete."

On cue, Cocoa and Uncle Pete walk into the living room from different directions. I introduce them. Uncle Pete seems unfazed by her accent or appearance. On his long and deadly march up Italy's boot and into France he heard exotic languages and encountered starvation camp survivors. His letters home always glossed over his experiences, but even I could read between the lines.

We sit on the sofa and briefly make small talk before Cocoa gets to the point.

"I am from the future."

Uncle Pete almost smiles, but he sees the anguish on her face and catches himself. He glances at me. I try to look serious.

Gathering himself, he listens attentively as she rushes rapid-fire, but not crazily, ahead. She's from a place called New Dresden, formerly New Mexico—*our* New Mexico, but a century from now. The Axis powers—Germany and Japan—won the war with atomic bombs and threats of annihilation. They slaughtered and imprisoned and ruthlessly reigned for decades. But Hitler died, and the fist weakened, and countries rebelled. New wars began, and before long the wars were global and nuclear, and everybody and everything lost, including the planet, which is dying along with its remaining inhabitants.

Most of this I've heard, or guessed at. But Cocoa's gotten more specific and sure of her facts—or her story, at least—and herself.

She has me more convinced, but I don't know what Uncle Pete's thinking as he hears her irrational words tumble out in such a rational way. He wears the same noncommittal expression I've seen since he returned from the war.

"How did you get here?" Uncle Pete says.

"When Robert first found me, I had no idea. I thought I was dreaming, or dead. But as every hour passes, more comes back. My brain must be recovering from the shock of travel."

"*Time* travel," I say, so there's no misunderstanding.

"Time *slippage*," she says. "A gear in the clock faltered, and for a moment, my past and your future were thrown together. I believe now it was the atomic bomb test that brought me here."

"*Atomic bomb test*?" Uncle Pete says. He's been interested. Now she has his complete attention.

"I believe the force of it temporarily opened up a passageway between our worlds," Cocoa says. "I was drawn into it."

"No one—except the brass and brains and bigwigs—knows about the test," Uncle Pete says. "Officially, *I* don't know."

"It really *was* a test?" I say.

"Many people know," Cocoa says. "People who talk and whisper and spread rumors. There are spies."

"Spies?" I say.

"How did *you* know?" Uncle Pete asks her.

"For me it is history. I have always been fascinated with history, with what man has done to himself and the planet. How something so beautiful got so fucked up."

Uncle Pete doesn't even react to this girl saying *fucked*.

"I lived in a ruined library," she continues, "because the torturing sunlight doesn't penetrate its basement. The air is cooler and perhaps cleaner. Many of its books and newspapers and magazines remained. I devoured them. Some are in English, which I taught myself to read. Before the last of the batteries failed, I watched videos."

"Movies," I say.

"Yes," she confirms. "Movies."

"No schools?" I say.

"No schools, no teachers. Learn by surviving, and survive by learning."

Uncle Pete sighs. Dad appears at the kitchen entry. *How much has he heard?* He's a newspaperman, curious. "Can I get anyone anything?" he asks.

"When I am done speaking to Peter," Cocoa says, "maybe I will have some of your rhubarb pie, Chuck."

"I'll take some lemonade." I usually don't expect Dad to wait on me, but I'm not getting up. He exits. We stare at each other and the floor until he returns with a tray holding a pitcher of lemonade and three glasses filled with ice. He sets it on the coffee table and leaves again.

"It's a crazy story, Cocoa," Uncle Pete says at last. "But that doesn't mean *you're* crazy."

"She isn't," I say.

He looks at me apologetically, imploringly, like he's unconvinced and wants me to convince him.

"She knew about the atomic bomb test," I say. "Listen to the way she talks. Hear what she has to say. *Look* at her."

Uncle Pete shakes his head. He's been through a lot, but not this. "Time slippage," he says, like the concept is too much.

"I believe her." I feel Cocoa's eyes on me. *A vote of confidence, but what's it worth?*

"What do you want me to do?" Uncle Pete asks her. "I'm just an Army grunt."

"My memories continue to solidify," she says. "Since I arrived here I have had a feeling of dread, then the feeling became more focused. Something would change the course of the war if it didn't go unchecked. I have hoped that the sheriff or Doctor Kersey or you could talk to someone in the government and warn them. But until I woke from my nap today, I didn't have anything specific to warn them *about*."

"Now you do?" Uncle Pete says. "Even though it came to you in a *dream*?"

"It didn't come to me in a dream. Sleep seems to recharge me. When I awake I sometimes have a clearer picture of what has been hiding in my fog."

"I'm not on a first-name basis with anyone important," Uncle Pete says. "Doctor Bainbridge, who runs the base camp, makes it a point to say hello to everyone, and I've exchanged salutes with General Groves, an even bigger big shot, and some of his staff, but that's about it. Doctor Oppenheimer and the rest of the scientists work long hours. I've barely seen them. There's my boss, Lieutenant Bush, but he isn't very high up. And he's a realist. I'd have to convince him that what you're telling us isn't a tall tale, and then get him to talk to his bosses."

"Could you?" Cocoa says.

"People have already left," Uncle Pete says. "More are leaving. Already there aren't as many to listen. But what's the specific information you remember? What could I say that someone way above me—politicians and the military—would be willing and able to act on?"

Cocoa takes a deep breath. She pulls a scrap of paper from her pocket and glances at some notes. "Because yesterday's test was successful, your President Truman has given his approval to use the same kind of bomb to drop on Japan and a similar bomb to drop on Germany. Naval ships carrying the two bombs left California and Virginia today for an obscure island in the Pacific and Liverpool, England. The plan was—*is*—to load them on B-29 bombers and have specially trained crews conduct bombing missions within the next three weeks."

Uncle Pete and I stare at each other. If she's making this shit up, she's an amazing storyteller.

"That's pretty specific," my uncle says.

I picture blasts like the one I experienced, ripping apart Tokyo and Berlin and killing . . . *What? Thousands? Millions?* "What's the problem, though? What's Uncle Pete supposed to warn them about?"

"The problem," she says, raising her voice. Dad appears in the kitchen doorway. His curiosity has been pushed beyond its limit. "The problem is that German and Japanese submarines sink the American ships and their priceless cargoes. The course of the whole war reverses."

Her words are confident. I swallow them whole, but Dad looks unconvinced.

"When?" Pete says. If he thinks she's making this up, he's hiding it well.

"July 20. The sinkings are coordinated so neither ship can

be warned of the other's misfortune."

"Can you remember the ships' names?" Uncle Pete asks.

Cocoa taps her head. "I feel I have those memories in here. I had to sift through a century of history to recall what I have come up with so far. But have I not already given you enough?"

"Look, Cocoa," Uncle Pete says, "against all reason, this feels authentic. And scary. But I'm afraid my lieutenant wouldn't see it that way. I had to see a head doctor while I was in the hospital for my leg, so my credibility would be lacking to start with. Lieutenant Bush would most likely consider passing along such a crazy story even crazier." He grimaces. "Sorry."

"It's okay," Cocoa says. "This feels insane to me, too. But if your lieutenant realizes I know things I should not know . . ."

"That isn't necessarily a good thing," Uncle Pete says.

"Does she look like a spy?" I ask.

"No, but it might help if she knew one."

"What do you mean?" Cocoa asks.

"It would provide a realistic reason for you to have this information. You somehow heard a stranger talking, or you found a letter, or you were kidnapped and abandoned by men—Nazis—who are plotting against us. If I start talking about time *slippage*, they'll put me in a straightjacket and send me off to a rubber room."

"What can we tell them?" I ask.

"I don't know," Uncle Pete says. "Something believable. We're short on time." He turns to Dad, still frozen in the doorway. "Any ideas, Chuck?"

"I'm the pacifist, remember?" Dad says.

"And when it comes to confronting the bad guys, as useless as tits on a bull," Uncle Pete says. "You know what the world will be like if Cocoa's story's true? If Hitler wins the war?"

"It doesn't escape me," Dad says.

"Then *think*," Uncle Pete says. "All of us, including Dottie when she gets home, have to *think*. By tomorrow we have to have a reasonable—and convincing—story." He glances at his watch. "Find me in the barracks in the morning, Bobby, and we'll talk, but right now I have to go."

He gets up, hugs me, hugs Cocoa, and limps off. While the

three of us gaze at each other in silence, I try to conjure up an idea that will make this work. I expect Dad to be angry over the "tits on a bull" comment; I expect Cocoa to be disappointed that we have another hurdle to jump. But they're *thinking*.

Outside, the truck thunders awake and roars into the evening heat.

# TWELVE

D ad may be a pacifist, but he's never hesitated to declare war on a hen that quits producing. While Cocoa and I sit on the porch and brainstorm, he carries the unsuspecting victim to the back of the barn, where they can be alone. I try to ignore the whack of blade against feather and flesh and stump. Cocoa barely flinches. She's no stranger to mayhem.

A few minutes later Dad heads for the back door holding the naked carcass of the chicken, and soon we hear him rattling around the kitchen.

"Chicken soup for supper," I say. "Let's get some vegetables. Loosen our thoughts, maybe."

It doesn't take us long to pick green beans, peas, and tomatoes, and dig up some small onions and new potatoes. By the time we're inside, Dad has the hen doing the backstroke in a big pot on the stove. He thanks us for the vegetables and shoos us back outside. "Geniuses need solitude," he says.

Soon typewriter sounds reach the porch. And it's then that the junior genius has an idea. "Let's go bother him," I say. Dad gives me an annoyed look when we re-enter the kitchen, but I forge ahead. "I've got a plan."

"Let's hear it."

"We need you to find a letter in our mailbox tonight. It will be from some anonymous source written to your newspaperman self. The source—us, really—will claim to be in a position that's privy to intercepting information from both sides. Mom will type the letter at work in case somebody compares the type on the letter to the type your typewriter makes. In books, they call that a 'signature.'"

Dad unsuccessfully hides a grin, but I go on. "In the letter, we explain what Cocoa's told us—the bomb, the other bombs, the plans for Japan and Germany, the ships, the sinkings. Not Germany winning the war. Nobody could know that. In the morning, I'll take the letter to Uncle Pete and get him to show it to his boss or his boss's boss."

Cocoa nods. "It's a good plan, Robert."

While Dad digests my idea, I remain standing, my head full of excitement and worry. Cocoa shifts from foot to foot.

Finally, Dad passes judgment. "I don't see any holes in it, except the letter will be passed along by a pacifist."

"So, you'll call Mom?"

"It's still a long shot," he says. "Even without the time travel, the idea is still going to be hard to swallow. Whoever sees the letter—or hears the message—that Pete passes on is likely to dismiss it as the work of a crackpot. It's going to have to get high enough up the chain of command to reach someone who's aware of the Allies' bombing plans and the ships carrying the bombs. *If* the plans and bombs and ships actually exist."

"They do," Cocoa says.

"We have to try," I say.

He contemplates his nervous hands, Cocoa, me. "You're right, Bobby," he says finally. He removes the piece of paper from his typewriter and inserts a fresh one. We sit. "Before we call your mom we need the words, and they have to be good."

The soup smells like soup by the time we've perfected our message. My mouth waters. My stomach growls. But no one wants to eat before we call Mom.

Dad goes to the phone, makes sure the line is free of other parties, and dials Mom. When she answers, he explains the plan and her role in it. She tells him she'll have to call us back in an hour. Her boss is still there.

We eat our soup and bread and the remains of the rhubarb pie. As usual, Cocoa eats like she hasn't eaten before, which is both upsetting and pleasing. A couple of times I look up to see Dad studying her face, the face of a puzzle. And I don't blame him. *Who is she, really? Where is she from, really? How did she get here, really? How much of what she's said is true?*

We're doing the dishes when Mom calls back, ready to type. I read her the letter, pausing regularly for her to catch up.

*July 17, 1945*

*Dear Mr. Hastings,*

*I have hand-delivered this message to your mailbox under the cover of darkness because of the need for speed and secrecy. I chose you because I followed your columns and stories in the* Journal *and* Chieftain *over the years, and you seem to be reasonable and open-minded. This situation requires both qualities. It also requires you to recognize the gravity involved and convince someone to pass along this message to the ultimate authorities so that urgent steps can be taken to thwart the plot I will now describe.*

*I am aware that a successful test of an atomic bomb was conducted at the nearby government facility yesterday. I am also aware that its success triggered approval for similar bombs to be loaded on US Naval vessels awaiting orders to leave for foreign destinations. As of this morning, one ship has departed Norfolk carrying a bomb, destined for Liverpool. From there, the bomb will be transported to an Army Air Force base, where a B-29 crew awaits. That crew has orders to drop the bomb on a strategic target in Germany within the next three weeks. The other bomb—a twin of the weapon tested yesterday—was loaded on a second warship and left a California port this morning, bound for an island in the western Pacific where another B-29 crew awaits. That bomb will target Japan, also within the next three weeks.*

*Our commander-in-chief, the top ranks of the military, and other essential personnel are aware of the plan. What they are not aware of is that Germany is a step ahead of us, both in intelligence-gathering and atomic weaponry. The Germans and their Japanese allies intend to sink our ships, on July 20, to be precise, buying them time to finalize preparations for an attack with their own weapons while we scramble to replace the lost bombs.*

*Circumstances do not allow me to come forward in person. It is vital to the welfare of the US and its allies that you get this information moving through appropriate channels immediately. If you, or others, are unwilling or unable to act, the consequences will be dire.*

*Sincerely,*

*A Citizen*

"That's it," I say when the sound of Mom's typing dies.

"Scares the life out of me," she says. "But that's what we want, right?"

"Someone has to believe."

"I want to make sure everything's correct," she says. "Let me read it back to you."

She reads. It's perfect. She says she'll bring an original and carbon copy home, along with an envelope with Dad's name typed on it. I say goodbye and hand him the phone, and Cocoa and I take Lolly for a walk. Once outside, away from the letter and phone and reminders of what we've done and what might come, I can breathe.

The next morning Leo's waiting at the shack. He tells me my job may be history by the end of the month. When I arrive at the base camp I can see why. Equipment and belongings are piled in the backs and on the roofs of trucks and cars, men carry and load, farewells fade away in clouds of dust and exhaust.

Not that I can do anything about it, but I wonder how many of these preoccupied fellows will be skipping out without paying their *Journal* bill.

I find my uncle pacing outside the barracks door. When he sees me, he gives me a hug like we haven't seen each other in weeks, even though it's been maybe twelve hours.

"I've been thinking about you, kid," he says as I squirm out of his hold. "Word is most of us will be going back to Los Alamos."

"How soon?"

"Security will be the last to leave, and a skeleton crew might stay on if anything valuable is left behind."

"I don't want you to go."

"If my next stop's Los Alamos, we'll still see each other."

"Not enough."

"No. Never enough." He stares into the emptiness of the desert. "I've been thinking about your little girlfriend. You two gave me a lot to ponder while I was out guarding the cactus crop last night."

I don't bother denying the *girlfriend* label. I dig the envelope out of my newspaper bag.

"We have a plan," I say. On the envelope is Mom's typing: *Mr. Charles Hastings.*

I hand it over. "Don't open it yet. First let me tell you about it."

I try to stay calm as I run through the scheme. All he has to do is talk to his lieutenant boss or, if he's feeling extra brave, Doctor Bainbridge or someone else with enough power or brass to speed the letter or its content to the next level, and the next level, and so on.

"Your idea, Bobby?" he says as he opens the envelope, which Mom sealed and then sliced open with a letter opener before bringing it home.

"Mostly."

"Let's find some light."

We stand inside the door while he reads our masterpiece and I wait for him to say it's crap.

"If this doesn't get their attention, nothing will," he says when he's finished. I breathe. "I'll show it to Lieutenant Bush and ask him what he thinks the next step should be. Maybe Doctor Bainbridge, maybe someone farther up the lieutenant's chain of command."

"You'll call me?"

"Stick around the house. I'll give you the blow-by-blow."

"Thanks for doing this, Uncle Pete."

"Thank *you*. And thank Cocoa. If there's any truth to this—"

I hand him the newspapers and he follows me outside. "I think it's time for you to drop the 'uncle' formality. I call you Bobby; you're old enough to call me Pete."

"Sure . . . Pete." It doesn't feel right. It also doesn't feel right that I haven't told him everything. "Uh, Pete?"

Through the gloom, I can see a grin. "Yeah?"

"Monday, when I found Cocoa standing on the side of the road."

"Uh-huh?"

"She was naked."

"*Naked*?"

"Wherever she came from, she arrived with no clothes. They got torn off during her journey or whatever it was, she said. The time-slippage thing."

"Wow," Pete says.

"I gave her my shorts. Right away." I tug on my bag. "And this."

His grin widens. "So, you've seen it all now."

"It was still kind of dark."

"You can definitely call me Pete."

"I like her, Pete."

"I can tell. I'm glad you were such a gentleman."

At first, I don't know what to say to that. But I remember that morning like it was five minutes ago.

"She wasn't embarrassed. Not much. She's had a different life. I think she lived in hell."

"I think you're right, Bobby. Whatever she's been through, it was real. Whether the rest is real, I don't know. But we have to assume it is. We have to do what we can to make sure we—and our offspring—don't end up in Cocoa's hell, too."

"Call me," I say, and pedal away.

# THIRTEEN

When I get home, Cocoa's writing at the kitchen table. Our dictionary is open at her elbow. Lolly lies at her feet, under her spell. Last night he slept on her bed. He doesn't lift his head when I drop the *Journal* on the table.

"Did you talk to Peter?" Cocoa asks as I pour myself some coffee. A half mug, still steaming, sits next to the dictionary.

"He liked the idea." I sit, move my chair closer, look at her writing. It's a list—state names, with New Mexico at the top. The rest seem to be alphabetical. I can smell her—toothpaste, soap, coffee, and for some reason, barnyard. "What are you doing?"

"I woke up with my head buzzing like the flies buzzing over the unnamed pigs and their shit. All I could think about was the ships, what we could do to save them. If I could think of their names, my story—and the one we manufactured—would be more convincing."

"You think the ships are named after states?"

"Places. I started with states because there are fewer of them than cities."

"Battleships are named after states," I say. "The *New Jersey*, the *Missouri*, the *Iowa*, the *Indiana*, the *South Dakota*."

She glances at her list. "Did you say *Indiana*?"

"I'm pretty sure there's a battleship *Indiana*."

She shakes her head. "Not right. Will Peter show the letter to his superiors?"

"Lieutenant Bush and whoever else Pete—or the lieutenant—can get to."

"Two days," she says. "Little time for doubts."

"It has to be enough."

She goes on with her list, writing down names in her weird handwriting that's neat but, with its strange angles and curls, barely legible.

"Anything?" I say when she finally puts down the pen.

She runs her finger down the list, pauses at *Indiana*, and continues. "I would not feel comfortable choosing any of these."

"We've already provided specific details. Should be enough without a ship's name. Someone knows what ships are carrying the bombs."

"I hope you're right, Robert."

"How about we go see the animals?"

"Chuck was already out there. Up before me and then returned to bed. He fed them. He milked the Andrews sisters. He brought a small pig to the kitchen that had a scraped leg. I held the small pig while he washed and bandaged the wound. The small pig was very cute."

"Piglet."

"What?"

"Piglet. It's what they call a young pig."

"Piglet."

"So, did Chuck—Dad—bring back eggs?"

She shakes her head. "No naked headless hens, either."

"Let's go visit the chicken coop."

Once we're outside, Cocoa is spellbound by the stars overhead, fading but still fiery. Lolly and I wait while she stands in one spot and scans the sky, west to east, finally settling on the glow above the eastern mountaintops.

Franklin crows. He's late, getting old, derelict in his duties.

Soon he'll be swimming in the soup pot. I don't mention this scenario.

"I see them every morning now," I say. "The stars. I didn't think about them much. Before." *Before you came*, I almost say, but it would sound like something from a movie. Artificial and calculating.

"I never saw them. Except for my mother, no one I knew ever had."

"Not even the old people?"

"In my world, an old person has twenty years."

"*Twenty*?"

"Peter needs to be convincing."

"Twenty," I repeat, my way of agreeing that Peter needs to be convincing.

We visit the barn, then the chicken coop, where we collect fourteen eggs—thirteen for us, one for Lolly, who snatches it off the ground—cracked—after Cocoa under-hands it only halfway to him.

"You didn't have baseball where you came from?"

"We had rocks. Sticks." She plunges her hand in the pocket of her new jeans. "A few acorns from dying trees." She holds up an acorn that even in the dim light I recognize as being from a burr oak.

"Did you bring that with you?" I remember her dropping something in my bag the morning I first saw her.

She nods. "I found it before the rats did. It was going to be my breakfast. But you have these acorns here, too. I have seen them, still green, hanging on healthy trees."

"It's from a burr oak."

"Burr oak," she repeats. She pronounces *oak* like *awk*. Cute. "Yes. It's one I know."

We resume walking to the house. A light is on in my parents' bedroom. "You grew up speaking German?"

"German. English. Or a messy marriage of the two. Gerglish. I also tried to learn Japanese because many Japanese moved to the US after the Devil's War. Their language became widespread. But I didn't have a knack for it. The vocabulary was puzzling. The characters eluded me. The learning programs were on audio and video. Without power, they were garbage."

"I speak English," I say. "Barely." I wait for her to tell me I speak it well, but she's stingy with her praise, at least when it comes to me.

It's too early for Pete to call, but as we near the kitchen door, I find myself listening. Inside, Mom and Dad sit at the table. They eye us eagerly. I have a story to tell.

"Uncle Pete liked our plan," I say. "He's going to take the letter to Lieutenant Bush."

"It's a strong letter," Mom says.

Dad has the carbon copy in front of him, studying it for the zillionth time. "I don't see where we could have added anything."

"They might think the whole thing is a lie," Cocoa says.

"You did what you could, dear," Mom says.

"Pete's supposed to call," I say. "Can everyone listen for the phone?" I go to the counter and set down the basket of eggs.

"I'll be here working," Dad says. "But if I leave, I'll make sure one of you is within earshot."

"My other news came from Leo," I say. "He says I may not have a job after this month because so many people are leaving."

"Makes sense," Dad says.

"I won't be bringing home any money. Maybe I could do odd jobs for the Unsers."

"You could," Mom says, "but then your dad would lose the jobs he's doing for them."

"Maybe another ranch would hire me."

"Let's not worry about it for now," Dad says. "The Lord will provide." He avoids Mom's skeptical gaze. She's almost always on his side, and she's not against asking the Lord for help, but when it comes to money matters, she's from the *Lord-helps-those-who-help-themselves* school.

The radio is muffled background noise, but now I turn up the volume, anxious. In theory we have two days. *But what if it happens early?*

So far, there's no earth-shattering news on the radio. And nothing dramatic in the pages of the *Journal*. No sinkings, no Maydays, no failures to arrive, no lost contact, no unexplained debris or oil slicks in far-off waters.

*If whoever winds up with the letter isn't willing to take action, what will the news be on the twentieth? Or the next day? Or the day after that? Will it be that the bad guys have new life? Will the good guys wait in shock for the next boot to fall?* I try to calm my thoughts.

While Mom and Dad read the paper, Cocoa and I come up with a breakfast menu—scrambled eggs, toast, Cream of Wheat, strawberries. We go to the garden. Her face hasn't shed its worried look, but it's alive with early-morning sunlight as we pick the berries.

We return to the kitchen and get busy. I catch Mom glancing at us now and then. *Does she think we're a cute couple? Are we a couple?* I've gotten no sense of that from Cocoa. A brother, maybe. A little brother, possibly. Neither makes me happy.

"You're good at this, Robert," Cocoa says as I turn down the flame under the eggs and add salt and pepper and chopped onion to the thickening yellow soup.

"Necessity," I say, surprised at the unexpected compliment.

"When Mr. Trainor offered me the job at the bank," Mom says, employing her super-hearing, "and I worried out loud about how Bobby and his dad would get by at suppertime, he reminded me about all the men who make meals for a living. And he was right. I provided the lessons and recipes, and hunger gave these two the incentive."

"I know about hunger," Cocoa says. None of us reply. I avoid looking at her body.

Halfway through the morning, just as Cocoa returns from a bath and a change into more of her new clothes, the phone rings. Partly distracted by her appearance and smell, I snatch the phone off the wall.

It's only Mr. Unser. One of his mares is foaling and having problems. Dad rushes out the door, leaving the house full of expectation and the useless chatter of the radio.

An hour later the phone rings again, and this time it's Pete.

"What happened?" I say.

"So far, so good. Lieutenant Bush was skeptical, but concerned enough that he's already taken the letter to Doctor Bainbridge. How much Bainbridge knows about the bombs and ships is anyone's guess, but he'll know who to talk to."

"You think the lieutenant can convince Bainbridge?"

"I think Lieutenant Bush's uneasiness over the threat will infect anyone he talks to, up to a point. It's a convincing letter, and if the military information in it—the bombs and how they're being transported—is accurate, that should be enough to keep it moving along."

"Only two days."

"Pray, Bobby."

When Dad returns, he hauls a bike from the DeSoto's back seat. It's an old Schwinn—faded blue paint and flat tires and a layer of dust—that's been taking up a space in the Unsers' barn, which now belongs to the newborn colt. With Cocoa in mind, Dad asked about the bike, and Mr. Unser told him to take it, that the time of kids and grandkids is past.

*Time.* I've never before thought so much about time.

Cocoa and I spend the next few hours in the shade next to the barn, cleaning the bike, patching a tube, pumping up tires. When we're done, it looks good—nothing bent, no dents or rust. It's a boy's bike, but I wonder if Cocoa even knows the difference.

"Have you ever ridden one?" I ask as we admire our handiwork.

"Where I come from, there is no fuel. Bicycles give us a way to get around."

I attempt to imagine her world. Or her imaginary world. But my disbelief is mostly gone. I no longer have to stretch to picture what she's said about where she came from. I can visualize war. Ruined earth. Ruined air. Lawlessness. Loss. Disease. Death.

It's harder to imagine the stuff she's left unsaid. *What was it like* for her *to lose her parents? To have no one? To be at the mercy of anyone who wanted to harm her? To go hungry? To struggle to breathe?*

*In how many ways did she suffer?*

I find myself praying that the *people who matter* accept our letter's wild-ass claims. "Give it a try," I say, balancing the bike for her.

She swings a leg over, but she's pretty much a regular-height girl—five-four, maybe—and the seat is too high. Once we lower it, she climbs back on and takes off across the yard and down the long driveway. She picks up speed, her skinny legs churning and blurring, her fine blondish hair flying. When she gets to the mailbox she turns around and starts back, and as she gets near, she stops concentrating on the ground and looks up—at me— and smiles.

Dad steps out on the front porch. "Thank you, Chuck!" she yells above the rattles.

"You look good on it, Cocoa!" he yells back. He glances in my direction and winks.

The rest of the day passes, Mom leaves, evening comes, supper, nightfall. No word from Uncle Pete. *No news is not good news,* I think, *but it's not bad news either.* If someone up the line ridiculed the information, and Pete heard about it, he would've called.

Cocoa goes to bed. I decide to also. But Dad stops me on my way to my room.

"You know what we've done will most likely turn out to be us simply humoring Cocoa, right, Bobby?"

He's surprised me. "You still think so?"

"Because of how convincing she's been, and how high the stakes are, it's worth going through the exercise, but think about it. While we're pounding the snot out of the Nazis, they develop a super bomb, they manage to sink the two ships that are carrying our super bombs, and a skinny shell-shocked girl is the only one who knows about it because she's come here from a future world via *time travel*?"

His words hit me hard. We're *humoring* her. *Does everybody believe that?* Anger rises to my throat. But he either believes or he doesn't. Cocoa will either be right or wrong.

"I just don't want you to get your hopes sky high," he adds.

"Time *slippage*," I say, and head for bed.

Dad stays up, nursing his skepticism and waiting for Mom. From my room, I hear him clacking away at the typewriter, working on something that faces worse odds than our letter.

It feels like I've just gone to sleep when I have this dream about walking through our yard in the dark and hearing a girl screaming, and the screams get more terrified, and terrifying, and familiar, and they're coming from a rusted-out car sitting on flattened tires at the side of a potholed road.

When I wake up, the screams don't stop. They come in bursts, like distant sirens. But they're not distant, and I leap from bed and race down the hall toward Cocoa's room in my Navy-issue boxers. When I get there, Mom is already at Cocoa's bedside, holding her. An instant later Dad arrives.

He and I stand motionless in the light from the hallway.

*Tits on a bull.*

Cocoa's screams have become whimpers. Mom gives good hugs. But I should be the one doing the hugging.

Cocoa's first words are foreign: "*Verzeihung. Ein alptraum.*" I imagine a ruined library, rubble, rats, a low, sickly sky. "Sorry," she says, opening her eyes. "It seemed real. I felt as if I were in the water, or hovering above it." She shakes her head, gulps air. Her nightgown is sleeveless, and a deep shade of pink, showing off her bony white shoulders.

"Where?" I ask.

"An open sea. Waves slick with oil and blood. Sailors in the water and on ruined rafts. Sharks everywhere, circling, churning, slashing. Jaws like vises. Teeth like razors. Picking and choosing, picking and choosing. Men trying to ward them off or helping their comrades. Or giving up. A nightmare. But not."

"Is this something you read about, Cocoa?" Mom says.

"A *video*?" I say.

Cocoa hesitates. "I suppose."

"Is it one of the two ships?" Dad asks, not sounding skeptical. "The survivors?"

"Can you remember the names now?" I say. "This nightmare ship, anyway?"

She scratches at her skull, as if she's trying to dig something out of her wispy hair. Her forehead is glossy. Mom gives her breathing room. "The name is in my brain, but hiding. It fucking refuses to come out."

"It doesn't matter, honey," Mom says, not even blinking at Cocoa's use of one of our household's forbidden words.

Apparently, the rules of the present don't apply to this girl from the future.

Dad doesn't react much either. But even in the scarce light I can see the light pink of his face deepen to the shade of Cocoa's nightgown.

"Where do sharks live?" Cocoa whispers. A shudder moves through her when she names the beasts.

"Almost everywhere," Dad says.

"Wherever a ship sinks," I say, and I picture the knife-like fins and the shadowy bodies, tubular and gristly and fast like torpedoes. I picture the bloody water and the teeth and jaws and the men waiting to die and I tell myself that Cocoa's vision wasn't an experience or a prediction, it was just a garden-variety nightmare. And then I promise myself that when the time comes for me to go to war, I'll enlist in anything but the Navy.

# FOURTEEN

I 'm barely asleep when my alarm wakes me, not from a dream but from the haunt of Cocoa's screams, her words, her expressions. My bed is cozy and I have a long, chilly bike ride ahead of me, but I have no trouble getting up and heading for the bathroom. Without Lolly in my way, I have a clear path. Almost everything I have and want is within these walls, but part of me is glad I'll be leaving the house and its chilling echoes of the night.

At the base camp, there are more signs of people moving out. I find Uncle Pete, but he's on his way to bed and has no news. Doctor Bainbridge is busier than usual and hasn't gotten back to Lieutenant Bush.

I'm tempted to tell Pete about Cocoa's nightmare. Sunken ships. Sharks. Blood in the water. *What could be more important than preventing the nightmare from coming true?*

But he's done his part. And returning to his lieutenant with a tale of a strange girl's scary dreams won't add weight to the contents of a letter that has nothing to do with her.

Back home I find Cocoa in the kitchen, standing at the wall calendar holding a cup of coffee. She nods distractedly. My best friend, Lolly, his big head resting comfortably on her feet, grants me two sweeps of his tail.

"Tomorrow," she says as I drop the *Journal* on the table. She stares at the calendar, as if she's willing today's date to slip backward the way she claims she did.

"Maybe not," I say. "Maybe some big shot will do something. Maybe you're off on the date, or maybe you're all the way off. On everything."

"Thanks for having so much faith in me, Robert."

"Those would be *good* things."

"Me being *all the way off* is not a good thing."

"It's the one we should hope for. Who could blame you?"

"It is not true. And I am afraid you are going to find that out."

"You've been through some shit."

"If we don't stop this, your world will be going through some shit."

My stomach growls. I pour myself some coffee, open the refrigerator. On a bottom shelf, Mom has left a mixing bowl full of peanut butter cookie dough. I take a three-fingered scoop. It's cool and smooth and nutty and sweet, perfect for a pre-breakfast snack.

I excavate another blob and carry it to Cocoa, resisting the temptation to toss it. There's a good chance her catching resembles her throwing.

"Thank you," she says, and takes a nibble. Her eyes light. She pops the rest in her mouth and chews slowly.

"You like?" I say.

She swallows. "Kick-ass," she says, which I take as a yes. Her eyes go back to the calendar, and I sit with the newspaper. I'll look for something more likely than days slipping away in reverse order: American ships sunk; German bombs wiping out an army, or a country, or the world.

Franklin the rooster greets the new day belatedly. Cocoa and I tend to the animals. We ride our bikes to the road and back in speedy loops. If the phone rings, I want to be there.

After breakfast, when it finally sounds off, it's not Pete. It's the doctor, telling Mom that he'd like to see Cocoa again, today preferably, to go over the results of her tests. Which fits in with

Dad's plans. He's finished an article for the *Chieftain* that he wants to drop off at the newspaper office, and he has a noon meeting with his conscientious objector group. On Saturday, groups from all over New Mexico are marching for peace in Santa Fe.

It's a coordinated effort; in nearly every state, marchers will descend on capitals, carrying their signs and making their voices heard. Trying, anyway. Since Pearl Harbor galvanized nearly everyone's thinking on the war effort, the pacifists' demonstrations seem to drive more people away than they've drawn in. Families and friends and loved ones of fighting men want them to come home, but not if it means letting Germany and Japan off the mat.

The frequency of the national marches has steadily increased—up to once a month now—which only annoys people more. Many cities attract countermarches and letters to the editors of their newspapers. Instead of *peacemakers,* the letters refer to them as *sympathizers* and *collaborators* and *traitors.* The government—the FBI, mostly—has taken notice, bringing in COs and pacifists for questioning. Dad had his turn. A day after two agents came to the *Journal* offices and hauled him off for an afternoon of interrogation, he lost his job.

Mom makes an appointment for ten thirty. While the three of them get cleaned up and dressed, I sit in the living room and listen to the radio. *Somebody* has to stay focused.

After a while Cocoa emerges, showing off a summery, peach dress and brown-and-white saddle shoes and bobby socks and a grin. I wouldn't think she had enough hair to pull back, but it's tied behind her head with a red ribbon. She wears lipstick to match and something on her eyelashes that makes them darker and longer. Mom's handiwork.

Under the clothes Cocoa's still skinny, of course, and under her skin there's other stuff going on, but this is the best I've seen her look. Pulse-quickening. I have second thoughts about choosing the radio over good grooming.

"What do you think, Robert?"

I get up and switch off the radio. She's put me on the spot. "Nice," I manage.

"Is that the same as beautiful?"

Mom and Dad walk in, rescuing me. They're also dressed in their going-to-town clothes, leaving me as the only country bumpkin. I might as well put on a battered straw hat and stick a weed in my mouth and smear cow shit on my shoes.

I casually brush breakfast crumbs from my T-shirt and shorts, get in the back seat with Cocoa, and listen to Dad go on and on about today's meeting and Saturday's demonstration and how it doesn't matter if public opinion and the government are against them. That big movements usually begin with small, unpopular first steps.

I wish he'd be like other dads and drop out, especially now that Cocoa's told us about the fate of the world if Hitler gets his way. *Pay attention to which way the wind's blowing, shut up about the war, go to work, come home, don't be a target, don't make your family a target. You might have a job. Your son might have a friend.*

But that's not him. *And if it were, would he still be the dad I care so much about?*

Mom doesn't share his enthusiasm, but she hasn't discouraged him. In theory, she believes in pacifism. But she also believes in the value of jobs and earnings and neighbors who don't hate you. She believes her brother and her husband should respect and like if not love each other. She believes Hitler is the supreme asshole of all assholes and Emperor Hirohito and his crew will take over the entire Pacific if we allow that to happen.

Cocoa gazes through her dusty car window at puffy white clouds moving across the blue; I gaze out my open one at unspoiled desert stretching to the mountains in the distance. I picture German tanks rumbling over yucca and mesquite and Nazi soldiers goose-stepping behind them and the sky gray with ash and death. Instead of Dad's drone, I wish for a radio voice assuring everyone that the trend of positive stories from the war is continuing.

But there's only Dad and the grumble of the engine and the

wind rushing through my open window and the hiss of tires on baked pavement.

There's no radio in the old DeSoto. And no good news.

It's a Thursday morning in July, and Socorro is quiet. On the sidewalks are a few kids, a few women, a couple of older men. The younger men are gone to war.

Doctor Kersey is ready for Cocoa. Marla the blond nurse shows the patient and Mom into his consultation room, or whatever he's calling it today. Dad and I sit. His undersized chair creaks with his bulk.

"I wonder why the doc wanted to see her again," he says.

"To go over the test results, supposedly. I don't know why he couldn't just call."

"Maybe he wanted to examine her again."

"Maybe she'll be better," I say.

"Definitely looks better. Don't you think so, Bobby?" He gives me a sideways glance and a grin.

"Mom did a good job of helping her pick out clothes and stuff," I say, dodging the gist of his question. "But we need to feed her more. She weighs less than one of your arms."

"Mom's taking you to lunch while I'm at my meeting. Finish it off with some ice cream. The *Chieftain* is actually paying me for the article I'm dropping off."

"It's not about the peace movement, is it?"

"Not much demand for peace movement articles," he says. "The war movement gets all the ink. It's about the scenic wonders of New Mexico."

"Not controversial."

"Even rabble rousers need to earn a living."

I don't have a response, but I wonder if it's something he's heard Mom say.

"We have a baseline now," Dr. Kersey says as he and Cocoa emerge with Mom on their heels. "So now, Dottie, I'd like to see Cocoa once a week to evaluate her progress." Marla checks the calendar and sets up an appointment for a week from today—Thursday the twenty-sixth.

Mom has described Marla as *voluptuous*. When she does, Dad resists commenting. In nearly twenty years of marriage, he's learned. But now, as the nurse turns her rear end to us and bends to write the appointment in the appointment book and Mom's attention is elsewhere, he raises an eyebrow and gives me a look. And in spite of all that's going on, I chuckle. Quietly.

After Mom assures Dad that Cocoa is doing okay, he heads off to his meeting at the Quaker worship hall and the rest of us go to lunch at Slim's Diner.

Mom must see the questions on my face, because as soon as we sit in our booth she gives me a summary of what Doctor Kersey said—no surprises from the lab tests and X-rays, which mostly confirmed what he'd found earlier. There are some irregularities in blood counts and blood chemistry, but he feels the numbers will improve with better nutrition and clean air. He still doesn't accept her story of coming from a ruined future earth, but he can't explain how she has the lungs of a seventy-year-old smoker.

His prescribes healthy eating, exercise, sleep with an open window so the desert air can come in, and, last but not least, cod liver oil daily.

"You'll love it," I tell Cocoa. "Nothing better than rancid fish oil in the morning."

"It's not that bad, Bobby," Mom says.

"Hold your nose and pretend it's honey," I say. "Just don't think about the ocean."

Cocoa ends the discussion. "At least it's not shark liver oil."

"I wonder if Pete's heard anything," I say.

"He'll call, one way or another," Mom says.

"Doctor Kersey listened to my story more closely this time, Dottie," Cocoa says. "Did you notice?"

"He seemed to, dear. And even more encouraging was when he said he may call his Army buddy at Los Alamos to get his reaction."

"Do you think he will?" Cocoa says.

"He brought it up," Mom says.

"How's that going to fit with our mysterious letter story?" I ask. Maybe the Los Alamos Army guys won't talk to the base camp Army guys.

"I told him about my nightmare, Robert."

"Any advice?"

"No. But he asked about the date of the sinkings. I told him. He told me I'll sleep better when tomorrow passes uneventfully."

"I hope he's right," I say.

# FIFTEEN

From the road, we spot an Army truck parked next to our house. Uncle Pete's sitting on the front porch. My heart stalls.

When we get out of the car, I study his face, but he doesn't tip his hand.

Dad nods in Pete's direction and heads to the barn. Mom hugs Pete and invites him in, but he says he'd rather inhale the desert where the best inhaling is. Cocoa and I bookend him, close enough that he can put his arms around our shoulders.

Mom comes out with a pitcher of lemonade and three glasses and heads back inside. Lolly, ignored, goes looking for Dad. We sip. Finally, Pete speaks.

"I wanted to see you, but I don't have anything positive yet. Nothing negative, either, though."

"Has Lieutenant Bush talked to Doctor Bainbridge again?" I ask.

"He's trying not to be a pest, but he's been making himself visible."

"Do you know who Doctor Bainbridge talked to?" Cocoa says.

"He was going to try a couple of options, General Groves or someone on his staff, as well as somebody at the War Department. If not Secretary Stimson, then one of his assistants. Patterson or McCloy. Someone with clout. And an open mind, I hope."

"Tomorrow is July 20," Cocoa says.

"Believe me, Cocoa, I know it," Pete says. "Could you be off on the date, though?"

"I do not think so. It is the date the ships sank, the tide turned, the Nazis seized an opportunity to cause death on an even wider scale." She stares off into the desert. "Widest."

I can practically hear her thinking, remembering. Imagining.

No. I don't believe she's making up shit. *What about Pete? He passed on her warning, but was he, is he, humoring her like Dad? Going along because the stakes are too high* not *to?*

"For anyone who pays attention to history, it is a memorable date," she says. "For a while, after time slipped backward, it escaped me, but I have it back."

"I was hoping you'd say *yes*," Pete says. "Failing that, we'll have to pray that the right people make the right decisions in time, or—"

"Or that she's inventing everything?" I say.

"She's been through a lot."

"I am a survivor," she says, "with no reason to be devious."

"Not devious," Pete says. "Mistaken."

"I guess we'll see," I say.

"Yes," she says. "On July 21, I hope all of you will be able to say 'I told you so.'"

I do hope she's wrong, but I don't like being lumped in with all the skeptics. The last thing I'd tell her is "I told you so."

"Can you relate your story for us once more, Cocoa?" Pete says. "I've got time, and Bobby and I would like to hear it again."

I would like to hear it again. But I'm pretty sure his reason for asking doesn't have much to do with me. One of his former duties was interrogating German prisoners, and the main thing he looked for was consistency. Is your story the same now as it was an hour ago? Yesterday?

Cocoa's is. Between sips of lemonade she recounts her existence in a ruined civilization a hundred years from now. She tells of genocide and political upheavals and nuclear wars and killer pollution and the depletion of resources and government failures and anarchy and the collapse of infrastructure. She describes the invention and eventual demise of innovations I can barely comprehend. She talks about lack of food and unbearable heat and disease, about survivors being lucky to reach sixteen and facing old age at twenty.

If she's making this up she's got an imagination that goes way beyond *devious*.

She recounts the day it happened. An ordinary morning, until an odd cloud suddenly appeared and there was a crack like thunder and the sky opened up and she was sucked away and found herself lying on a desert floor, naked and alone. For the first time, she was breathing clean air and seeing stars and smelling plants and watching a *rabbit* look at her curiously and then duck behind a *yucca*, names she knew only because she'd seen pictures of the small animal and the spiky plant.

After that, she walked. She found me. The rest is shared history.

When she's finished talking, she slumps back in her chair. I go inside and get soda crackers and cheese and hurry back. Cocoa and Pete are still sitting silently. Cocoa digs into the cheese and crackers. Pete nibbles.

"They *have* to warn those ships," he murmurs finally. He gets up, and Cocoa and I stand, too. She looks unsteady on her feet, exhausted. He gives her, then me, drawn-out hugs, and heads down the porch steps.

"Call if anything happens?" I say.

"The minute I hear."

He climbs in the truck and drives off, trailing a cloud of dust. Once again, I'm reminded of seeing another cloud, only three days ago, and how, in that short time, that cloud and that morning have changed everything.

# SIXTEEN

I lie awake most of the night, thinking doomsday thoughts and listening for Cocoa's screams, which don't come. I wonder if she's stifling them in her sleep.

I'm up before the alarm sounds, beating Leo to the shack. When he arrives, he's in a talkative mood. Although he's well aware of my dad's beliefs, he rambles on about pacifists who accomplish nothing but giving comfort to the enemy.

When I steer him away from that subject, he switches to his wife and how deprived he is. I listen to his complaining until I can't anymore. Before the papers are rolled, before I say something harsh, I take off.

At the base camp I find Pete, but his news isn't calming. According to Lieutenant Bush, Doctor Bainbridge spent a good deal of time on the phone trying to get the message across, but whether he did is anyone's guess.

I finish my route and race home. By the time I start up the back steps, I stink from exertion and nerves and not having showered in two days, and I wonder who will notice.

Nobody.

I've barely opened the door when Dad traps me in a hug that I know means something awful has happened. Mom and Cocoa are at the table, slack-jawed and teary. And on the radio a newscaster relays the story of a Mayday in the far reaches of the Pacific, and an American ship—a cruiser—being torpedoed and sinking almost immediately, and many of the officers and men going down with it, and survivors in life rafts and in the water awaiting rescue.

In my brain, a neon sign flashes: *Loose lips sink ships!*

Dad lets go, and then it's Mom's turn. When she finally slips away, I wait for Cocoa to follow my parents' example. I wait for the chance to hug her back, because I know we'd both feel better. But she doesn't, and I don't, and we don't. Even though she's the only one who was sure this was going to happen, she seems to be in shock.

I take advantage of her distracted condition and stare at her. I can't help myself. Any remaining doubts I might have had about her and her story vanish. Swept away by the truth.

She's not mistaken or mentally ill or devious. She's a time *slipper*. Practically a superhero. To her, what's happening now, what's going to happen in the days ahead, really *is* history. Until the past few days, she really *has* lived her life in the hellish place she described.

Which makes me want to hug her even more.

But I don't.

While the newsman continues talking, I get coffee, add some to everyone else's cup, and sit. Mom holds my hand. Cocoa's hands are in her lap. She's in a white robe over her pink pajamas. Her hair is a mess, her face tortured.

A cruiser is a large ship, the newscaster says, typically named after a US city. In this case, the *Indianapolis*.

A haunting name. I remember Cocoa using the list of states to try to prompt her memory, pausing on *Indiana,* saying it's not quite right. But it was close enough to get her attention. Indianapolis is the capital of Indiana. The name *Indianapolis* is a cousin-word to *Indiana*.

In Cocoa's eyes is a question. What if *Indianapolis* hadn't eluded her?

"You gave them plenty to go on without the name," I say.

A hint of a smile, but I wonder if she believes me.

"Of course," Dad says. "There was no need to tell them what they already knew."

Mom nods. The newsman goes on. The *Indianapolis*, the first cruiser to be sunk since the July 1943 sinking of the *Helena*, had a crew of approximately twelve hundred officers and men. It was on a *routine mission* when it was apparently attacked by a Japanese submarine. Rescue vessels and aircraft have been dispatched, but the ship is in a remote area, and getting to the survivors will take time.

I recall Cocoa's nightmare, the men doing a death dance with the beasts of the deep. I think about the next sinking. *Will the next ship be on a* routine mission, *too? Has it already happened?* Cocoa said the sinkings were *coordinated*.

The phone rings. I know who it is, but when I say hello I want it to be someone from the War Department, calling to say that the news on the radio is part of a secret plan to sucker the Axis powers.

"Have you been listening to the radio, Bobby?" Everyone's eyes are on me.

"Is it true, Pete?"

"Afraid so. Are you okay?"

"No."

"Sorry. Sorry the brass dropped the ball. Is Cocoa there?"

"Upset. Why didn't they listen?"

Silence.

"Is it too late for the other ship?"

"I haven't heard anything," Pete says.

"Has anyone talked to Doctor Bainbridge?"

"Lieutenant Bush is trying. The camp's in an uproar. By now nearly everyone knows what the *Indianapolis* had in her hold."

"Cocoa told the truth," I say. She shuffles over, holding out her hand.

"I know," Pete says.

Cocoa takes the phone. "Peter?"

I hear him respond, "Yes," then, "Sorry, Cocoa."

"My feelings don't matter," she says. "What matters is that

there will be more of this . . . this *shit*. If the assholes do not start listening, we will experience the ultimate shit."

She's trembling. I take the phone back. "They have to listen," I say to Pete.

"By the end of the day, you're going to have visitors—Army brass and government bigwigs—and your dad is going to be in the spotlight. He's not going to be able to keep up the ruse. The government will be watching your house, and listening to your phone calls, and there won't be an opportunity for a mysterious stranger to deliver warnings in the middle of the night."

"What do we do?"

"Cocoa needs to tell her story, outlandish or not, and if she can detail the coming trouble, she needs to do that."

Mom stands at my shoulder, eyeing the phone.

"You have time to talk to Mom?" I ask.

"Put her on."

From the table I listen to her end of the conversation and the news throbbing out of the radio and wait for the other shoe to drop.

She hangs up and comes back. "Tell them, Bobby," she says. "What Pete told you, I mean. He had to go. He says he gave you his thoughts."

I tell Dad that getting another mystery letter isn't going to work—that everything he does from now on is going to be under a microscope. I tell Cocoa that when the government guys show up, she needs to tell her story, crazy or not, and if she can recall anything else about the future actions of the Axis powers, she'll have a rapt audience.

"It was worth a try," Dad says. "The letter. But Pete's right. If Cocoa has more to tell, she should tell it."

Mom sits, takes Cocoa's hand. "Do you, honey?" she says. "Do you have more to tell?"

Cocoa looks even paler than usual. She nods. "During the night, I awoke and could not get back to sleep. I kept thinking about the ships and the men, that I could do nothing to help. But the thinking, and the images, led me to more images, and memories."

"Enough to be useful?" I say.

She shakes her head. "Blurry impressions. But that's how the memories seem to start. I once read that people who have seizures often have a sensation first—an aura. This morning I have the aura. Later on, who knows?"

"Would a nap help?" Mom says.

"I couldn't sleep. Your radio has me all hyper. The words echo in my head while I wait for the next words. And think about the government men coming to pick our brains."

*That's. Couldn't.* In close proximity, she's used examples of what my English teachers call *contractions*. A weird thing to notice. *But what if dropping her charmingly formal speech means she's even more upset than she appears?*

Or maybe we're rubbing off on her. I'll go with that.

Dad starts a pot of coffee. I turn up the volume on the radio and help with breakfast. We're all focused on the newsman's voice. He seems on edge. The war has been going our way lately, and now, suddenly, it's not. Now a Japanese submarine has sunk one of our ships and sharks are eating our men, and if those things can happen, anything is possible.

Just before noon there's an ominous pause in the broadcast. Outside, the sun shines on the green and brown of yard and desert, and part of me wants to be out there.

Most of me wouldn't be anywhere but here.

"With regret," the newsman murmurs, "we bring you news of another sinking. A second cruiser, the USS *Augusta*, has been torpedoed, presumably by a German U-boat, in the international waters of the North Atlantic. The *Augusta* was on a routine mission, on a heading toward port in England, when attacked." He sighs. "Because the vessel was unaccompanied, the survivors of its crew of approximately eight hundred are still in lifeboats, awaiting rescue. More complete news of this sinking, and the nearly simultaneous sinking of the *Indianapolis*, will be forthcoming as soon as particulars are available to CBS News."

Another routine mission. We all expected this. *Cocoa knew it.* She's propped up against the refrigerator, but with every word from the newscaster she seems to sink lower, until finally I grab her arm and steer her to a chair.

Two years since the last sinking of a cruiser. And now two

of them—and two thousand men—go down in one day. *Routine missions? Coincidence? Nah.*

On the table is a bottle of cod liver oil, unopened. I put it in a cupboard on a high shelf. We've had enough torture for the day.

# SEVENTEEN

The big engines shift from four-part harmony to dissonance. They sputter. Gasp. Die. One by one, the props rotate to a stop. In the pilot's seat, Colonel Tibbets grins and gazes through the windshield at Tinian Island's North Field. Another flight in the books. He has no use for overconfidence, but he's pleased that all the studying, planning, flights, practice drops, debriefings, fine tuning, repeat, repeat, repeat has paid off.

Today's trial run went particularly well. Even with a full load of fuel, and the five tons of rebar simulating the weight of the bomb, the big warbird lifted off smoothly and reached safe flying speed well before panic set in. And the climb to thirty-one thousand feet was uneventful. *Uneventful* is exactly what they'll need once the real cargo—precious, fragile, and beyond dangerous—comes aboard.

He grabs a notebook and jots down a few notes for the debriefing. All the pieces of this morning's rehearsal—loading, positioning, arming, sighting, opening, double-checking, releasing—went off like clockwork, and the B-29, not known for its agility or the reliability of its engines, responded like a champ when he goosed it and banked away from the imaginary descent path of the imaginary bomb dropping toward its imaginary target.

Soon, none of this will be imaginary.

Tibbets and Captain Lewis, his co-pilot, have barely gotten their boots on the ground when a familiar figure approaches. General Lemay. A fine day ruined.

Waves of heat rise from the tarmac, thinning the general's fleshy body and making him shimmy like a drunken bar girl. His shoes appear to be suspended a foot off the ground, giving false credence to his overinflated ego.

Tibbets offers the general a half-assed salute, and Lewis follows suit. By the time Old Ironpants has returned their greetings, they've come to a halt, an arm's length apart. The general radiates the pleasant aroma of Old Spice, but he looks unhappy.

"Get lost, Lewis," he growls. "I need a word with Colonel Tibbets."

"Yes sir," Lewis says. He manages another salute, gets a dismissive grunt in return, and hurries off.

"What is it, General?" Tibbets says when the captain is out of earshot.

"Bad news, I'm afraid, Tibbets. You're going to have to put off the heroics for a while longer."

"The special delivery?"

"Suddenly there's nothing to deliver."

"The *bomb*?"

"The fucking bomb. A Jap sub sank the *Indianapolis* on its way here. Fat Man—your surprise package for the Emperor—and the ship are at the bottom of the Pacific. A thousand or more sailors might be dead. At approximately the same time, Little Boy, on its way to England, suffered the same fate. A U-boat sank the cruiser *Augusta*. Ship and cargo are lost. Lots of dead sailors. No one believes the timing was coincidental."

"How could they know?" Tibbets's mind is crowded with images: fiery explosions, oily waters, panicked crews, fighting ships turned into great gray coffins—for men and bombs.

The general fixes Tibbets in a glare. Almost accusing. "Loose lips, Colonel."

"What now?"

"We continue pounding the hell out of 'em with our conventional stuff. And wait. Word is, more super-bombs are in the pipeline."

"My men are ready *now*."

"They'll have to maintain readiness. Your job is to make sure they do."

"The same thing could happen again."

"Listen, if the Navy can't get the job done, I'll go back to the states and fly the bomb here myself, and there's not a fucking Jap or Kraut alive that can knock me out of the sky."

Before Tibbets can get off a salute, the general turns on his heel and heads off, leaving the colonel to ponder how a good day suddenly went so bad. Two ships' crews dead or dying or fighting for their lives. No bomb. No bombing run. The war effort that seemed all but over has taken an about-face. And now he'll have to deliver the news to his crew. *But that's my job, isn't it? If anyone has doubts, they need only ask Old Ironpants.*

Tibbets senses someone approaching. When he turns, he's not surprised to see Colonel Oliver, his wingman. He glides to a halt in that irritating civilian-like way of his. He grins his easy grin. Underneath the casual façade, though, Oliver is driven. And right now, curiosity lights his eyes.

"A visit from the old man," he says. "How'd you get so lucky, Paul?"

"I wish he were that quick to pass along *good* news," Tibbets says. He needs to tell Oliver what's happened, but he'd rather shit barbed wire. The delay will give the wingman more time to stew and sour over what he considers the general's poor decision—giving Tibbets the lead role in this drama.

But there's nothing to be gained by putting off the inevitable. Motioning for Oliver to fall in next to him, Tibbets resumes his trudge to the shack. "I'm afraid we've had a setback," he says. As he explains, he keeps his eyes ahead, on the shimmering airstrip, and the metal buildings, and the ocean beyond.

# EIGHTEEN

**W**hen I answer the phone, Cocoa is still sitting silent, Mom at her side.

"Bobby?"

"Yes?" I say, remembering not to say *yeah*.

"It's Doctor Kersey. Mom or Dad home?"

"Just a moment, please." Manners again. I hand Dad the phone. "Doctor Kersey." I fear he's calling with bad news about Cocoa: a test result, a diagnosis.

Dad says hello, nods. "I understand. Dottie may be gone, but the rest of us will be here."

After listening, he hangs up and explains what's going on. Doctor Kersey talked to his Los Alamos buddy. The buddy didn't swallow the time travel aspect of Cocoa's story, but everything else intrigued him. He spoke to his superiors. Now the events of the day have meshed with Cocoa's tale, causing a giant stir, and the doctor has been requested to meet officials from Los Alamos at our house, this afternoon at four.

"Our invented story is in shreds," Dad says. "But don't worry about it, Cocoa. I'll tell them it was my idea. What they'll care about is what else you know."

"Why is the doctor required to be here?" she asks.

"They want him in on the conversation," Dad says. "Get his viewpoint on your health."

"My mental health."

"Everything," Dad says.

"But they will be willing to listen to me."

"More than willing."

"I need a nap," Cocoa says, and Mom ushers her out of the kitchen and down the hall.

I'm drying dishes when the phone rings again. I beat Dad to it. He doesn't make much of an effort, and I suppose it's because he figures it's Pete this time.

It is. "The lieutenant just officially notified me that you can expect a visit from a delegation of bigwigs, Bobby. They're coming from distances—Los Alamos is the closest—so they won't be there until four o'clock or so."

"We've heard," I say, as I picture a bunch of big shots invading our small house. I relate for Pete the gist of Doctor's Kersey's call.

"Figures. Lieutenant Bush says the government guys have doubts about the letter."

"Did you say anything about it?"

"Bullshitting a superior officer could get me court-martialed. I played dumb. Which means I've left you and the family, including the newest member, to go it alone. But being a civilian has its advantages. If you explain what's behind the letter, I think they'll be understanding. If they haven't already, the Army brass and politicians are soon going to realize that Cocoa is a prized goose bearing golden eggs. They won't want to do anything to upset her."

"You'll be here?" I say. Dad wanders toward the living room.

"Unofficially. But I can answer questions, vouch for your character. All of you. Even though it might hurt."

The living room radio comes on. Bad news in both ears. "You're talking about Dad?"

"Kidding, Bobby. Your dad has too much character. It's what makes him a pain in the ass."

# NINETEEN

**M**om and Dad clean house while I tend the animals, mow the lawn, pull weeds, and wash the DeSoto. It's my chance to drive it a few feet, maneuvering back and forth until I'm on a perfect grassy spot where I won't create red mud. If Dad weren't so preoccupied he would've raced outside, lecturing me on the scarcity of gasoline and Mom's need to get to work. But he is preoccupied, and nervous.

Doctor Kersey arrives at three thirty. I'm still outside. His little MG fishtails off the road and kicks up dust heading down our driveway.

"Mr. Hastings," he says to me as he climbs out. "Am I first?"

"You're early."

"You don't show up late when the king throws a party. Expecting a big crowd?"

"More like a pack of wolves."

"Is Cocoa inside?"

"Napping. Trying to recharge. Afraid she won't be able to help."

"She tried. People—some people, anyway—didn't listen. You were the exception."

"There's more coming, she says. More bad stuff."

"I know. I hope she . . ." His words trail off. He's staring over my shoulder.

When I turn, I spot a horse and rider in the distance floating toward us. In front of them, heat rises in shimmering waves, making the pair seem like ghosts, or temporary moving parts of a mirage. As they get closer I can make out a twisting white stripe, roughly the shape of the Missouri River, on the chestnut brown of the horse's long face. It's a mare named Big Muddy, one of the sentry horses from the base camp.

And then I recognize her rider. Pete.

"You know my uncle?"

Dr. Kersey nods. "Is that how Cocoa looked? All alone?"

"It was the same feeling, kind of; the same desert. Except it was daybreak, and I was riding my bike, and she was standing. And she was naked."

"An indelible memory, I'm sure."

Pete rides into the yard and pulls up a few feet away. Sweat glistens on Big Muddy's hide. "Okay if I hitch her to something in the shade, Bobby? And give her some oats? Shortage of vehicles today."

"You know where they are," I say. "But if Cocoa's awake, can I tell her we've got a visiting horse? I think she'd like to see Big Muddy."

"Tell her," he says. "We'll wait in the barn."

"Handsome horse," I hear the doctor say as I hurry off.

When I get inside, Cocoa's in the living room putting on her shoes. She looks tired and nervous. "Uncle Pete's here," I say. "He rode in on an Army horse. Want to see her?"

She springs to her feet with surprising energy. Her hair is brushed, her clothes—jeans and a white blouse—are clean and ironed. Suddenly she looks revitalized. Lolly tries to follow us, but I shut the screen door on him. He's good with animals, but I don't know how good Big Muddy would be with him.

Doctor Kersey tags along as we head to the barn, throwing glances Cocoa's way. Maybe now that he knows she's not crazy and making up shit, he wants to see her without all the preconceptions clouding his view.

We detour to the garden, where Cocoa and I pull up handfuls of carrots. When we get to the barn, Pete's holding Big Muddy's reins, feeding her oats. She stares calmly at us. She's been in every kind of situation—sentry, transport, tomfoolery. She and Cocoa lock eyes, and then she spots the carrots in Cocoa's hand and tosses her big head. An invitation.

"Can I touch her, Peter?" Cocoa says.

"She'd love it," Pete says.

Cocoa doesn't hesitate, even though the horse is tall and broad and muscular and Cocoa is barely the size of one of her legs. She moves one hand slowly over the velvety brown coat of Big Muddy's neck, working her fingers into the slightly darker mane, and offers her a carrot. The horse chomps it down and looks for another.

"In my world there were no horses," Cocoa says. "No cows. No pigs. Nothing bigger than a rat."

I join in. We feed and pet and admire until we hear a car approaching. By the time Pete has Big Muddy hitched to a railing and the four of us are outside, a Buick sedan is pulling to a stop behind the DeSoto and MG, and Dad and Mom are on the front porch.

As the four doors open, another black sedan, a Chrysler, comes racing down the road and turns into our driveway, trailing red dust. It lurches to a halt behind the Buick. More doors open. I try to see who's inside, but all I see is glare. Finally, as if they choreographed it, eight men get out of the two cars simultaneously. The drivers and the front seat passenger in the first car are in uniform, and even though Pete isn't, he snaps to attention next to me. The five other men are wearing dark suits and ties. They blink into the sunlight, glance in Mom and Dad's direction, and see us coming.

"Groves," Pete says under his breath, and I realize he's right. The Buick's front-seat passenger, the stocky older guy with the brass and ribbons on his uniform and the stars on his garrison cap, is General Leslie Groves, who's only one small step down from God. He even tells Doctor Bainbridge when and how high to jump.

And speaking of Doctor Bainbridge, he's here, too, the front-seat passenger getting out of the Chrysler. The rest of the men I don't recognize.

Mom and Dad come down to greet the arrivals. Mom looks okay; Dad looks uncomfortable in a fish-out-of-water kind of way. By the time introductions begin, I'm trying to remember my own name, but I manage to catch some of theirs.

Besides General Groves and Doctor Bainbridge, there are two scientists from Los Alamos, Doctor Robert Serber and Carl Addleman. General Groves describes Serber as Doctor Robert Oppenheimer's right-hand man. Oppenheimer, who isn't here, might take his orders from General Groves, but according to Pete he's the brains behind whatever's going on at Los Alamos and the base camp. I've seen him a few times. He's one of the engineers whose minds always seem to be in the clouds. By now I've figured out he's not an engineer. He's a physicist, and mostly responsible for that giant cloud ripping and roaring through the sky four days ago.

The men are polite but their faces grim. And their eyes keep going back to Cocoa. Whatever Doctor Kersey said to his Los Alamos buddy, it's gotten through.

As we go inside, Lolly goes out, carrying my hopes that he'll avoid Big Muddy's hooves. There are thirteen of us, an unlucky number. The visitors stand around the living room while Mom drapes her arm protectively over Cocoa's shoulders and tries to get a conversation started and Dad, Pete, and I bring in more chairs from the kitchen. A pitcher of ice water and several glasses sit on the coffee table.

Except for the two drivers—both wearing captains' bars on their collars—we sit. On the sofa, Mom is on one side of Cocoa, I'm on the other, Dad is next to me. Around us, in a ragged half-circle of chairs, are Pete, Doctor Kersey, Serber, Addleman, General Groves, Bainbridge, and the two fellows in suits. I sense urgency, but nobody seems to know how to kick off this get-together.

Mom's curiosity surfaces. "What do you gentlemen do?" she asks the two nameless guys wearing suits and dour expressions. Their fedoras sit on their laps, covering their hands, but their fingers are restless. The hats shift and twitch. At Mom's question, they turn to General Groves, who nods.

"We're agents, ma'am," the shorter, thicker one says. "Federal. He's Browning, I'm Swan."

"FBI?" Dad says.

"Yes," Browning says. He's Dad's age, probably, but his unlined face makes him look younger. City life.

"Do we need them here?" Dad asks General Groves. His experiences with the FBI have soured him.

"They're here to take notes and pass along a baseline of information to their superiors in case circumstances deteriorate," the general says.

"They *will* deteriorate." Cocoa's *will* comes out *vill,* making me leery of reactions in the room. "If nothing is done, they *will* deteriorate."

Doctor Addleman says something to her in what sounds like German, but she responds in English. "I grew up speaking German."

"In Germany?" he says.

General Groves interrupts. "Is that how you came to have this knowledge? Someone in Germany passed the details of the plot on to you?"

"My home is New Dresden," Cocoa says. "Formerly New Mexico. Germany is an uninhabitable wasteland, a cesspool. We all suffered for its sins, but in the end Germany suffered the most."

All eyes go to Doctor Kersey. *Is this girl crazy?*

"Since the day of my initial meeting with her," he says in response to the stares, "Cocoa's story has remained consistent. She says she came here from a bleak time in the future, almost a hundred years from now. She believes her journey—or whatever you want to label it—was caused by a vast disturbance in the atmosphere and a disruption of what we accept as nature's laws, caused by an atomic bomb detonation."

"I'm going to speak candidly here, young woman," the general says. "We don't have time to be circumspect." His attention flits back to the doctor. "Do you feel she is mentally ill, Doctor Kersey?"

"She's been through a lot, obviously," the doctor says.

"Yes." General Groves glances Cocoa's way. "But is she *mentally ill*? Or is it possible she's competent and telling the truth?"

"Your two cruisers are sunk," Mom says. She's mostly held her tongue, but I've sensed her energy surging. "Cocoa told anyone who would listen that it was going to happen. She said that it would happen today, that an atomic bomb would go down with each ship. I don't *know* that you lost your bombs, but since you're here I'm assuming you did. So why are we discussing mental illness?" She stands, fire in her eyes. "I need to leave. But I trust you gentlemen will treat Cocoa with kindness and respect. She's trying to save the world."

Mom throws Dad and me a *you-better-take-care-of-her* look, grabs her purse, and leaves before anyone responds, before anyone stops her, although Addleman frowns in the general's direction. Like he thinks she shouldn't be allowed to go. The general is smart enough to ignore the scientist. I hear her start the DeSoto and maneuver back and forth to get around the other vehicles, and then the sounds fade away.

Doctor Bainbridge asks a question. "Why the letter, Mr. Hastings? I believe Sergeant Blakely gave it to Lieutenant Bush thinking it was authentic, and when I passed along its contents I certainly thought that."

"My idea." My words come out strangled. "We—my parents and I—didn't think anyone would believe Cocoa's story. And someone needed to believe it."

"Bobby's idea, Doctor Bainbridge," Dad says. "But his mother and I enthusiastically participated in its execution. Unfortunately, the plan didn't accomplish its main objective. Someone *didn't* believe. But if the warning had come from a time-traveling girl, would it have even gotten past you? If we'd told Pete—Sergeant Blakely—the real story, he wouldn't have even bothered his lieutenant with it. None of you would be here now." Dad gives Pete a glance.

"It's a ridiculous story," Addleman says.

"Yes," General Groves says. "But I'm going to tell you something that must stay within the confines of your minds; Cocoa's story is essentially true."

While the conversation halts, another layer of certainty forms over the unshakable belief in my head. *Cocoa was right.*

"How far did it get?" she says.

Everyone looks to the general. "Doctor Bainbridge provided the substance of the letter to my office and the office of the secretary of war," he says. "Doctor Kersey's message detailing this young lady's history also reached my office. In each instance, the information was shortstopped by well-meaning but unimaginative staffers who are now tortured with guilt."

"Where are you from, really, young woman?" Addleman asks.

"Hasn't Doctor Kersey already covered everything you need to know about her?" I say.

"Do you have identification?" Addleman says to her, ignoring me, the kid.

She doesn't look interested in answering him. There are higher-powered fellows in the room. I have a feeling she's saving her energy for them.

"She came with nothing," I say. *An acorn.*

"How long—" Addleman begins.

But Doctor Serber interrupts him, and I'm left guessing his question. *How long have you been here? How long have you known? How long will you put up with an asshole interrogating you?* "Enough, Carl," Doctor Serber says. "This isn't an inquisition. Cocoa here obviously knew something that could have saved two ships, hundreds of lives, and two precious weapons that in turn could have saved millions of other lives."

"I no longer care where you're from or how you got your information, Cocoa," General Groves says. "You don't look like a spy to me. You look like a frightened but brave girl. What I want to know is what more you can tell us. Beyond the sinkings of the *Indianapolis* and *Augusta*, what do our enemies have in mind?"

"So far, I have nothing useful," Cocoa says. "Feelings. Apparitions. But that is the way the concrete memories have begun. So I am hopeful." She taps her temple. "I am hopeful that the knowledge is in here but needs time and maybe some prodding to materialize."

"We don't *have* time," Addleman says.

"Being reminded of that is not helpful," Cocoa says.

"Can you tell us something about yourself, Cocoa?" Doctor Serber says.

She nods, and goes on to give an account of her day-to-day existence in her former life. The devastation, the hardships, the love affair with the ruined library and its antiquated, depleted treasure of books and periodicals. She speaks of her curiosity about how the earth and its inhabitants were damaged beyond repair and where the missteps happened and how she found answers to questions that no one else was asking because they spent all their time figuring out how to stay alive or how to die or were caught in the stranglehold of indecision.

Her story puts another hush on the room. Addleman rolls his eyes, but he gets no backing. Frowning, General Groves looks at his watch. He goes to the window and gazes out. The sun has dropped lower, silhouetting his bulky shape.

"Nothing, General?" Doctor Bainbridge asks.

"Not yet."

"Expecting someone else?" Dad says.

General Groves returns to his chair. "The secretary of war has given one of his assistants—the man who squelched the contents of the letter—a chance to redeem himself. He was scheduled to land at Kirtland Field an hour ago and come here posthaste."

"Is he willing to listen now?" Cocoa says.

I jump in. "Is he on our side, or just coming here to make excuses?"

"He'll either have his hackles up," the general says, "or his tail between his legs."

"Just what I need," Cocoa says. "Another fucking flea biting at my shins."

I stifle a snicker but can't hide my grin, and neither can Dad. General Groves doesn't hold back; he laughs deeply, and immediately the others, with the exception of Addleman, join in. Even the two soldiers lose their military bearing for a moment and let themselves chuckle. This isn't a meeting of the unimaginative bureaucrat's fan club.

"Without turning ourselves into fleas," Dr. Bainbridge says, "is there anything we can do, Cocoa?"

"She likes being outside in the fresh air," I say.

"Doctor Kersey?" the general says. "Should we be worried about her health?"

"Cocoa and I and her new family have discussed her condition," Doctor Kersey says. "Her previous living environment has resulted in compromised health, possibly chronic in nature. But there's nothing acutely threatening. With rest, proper diet, exercise, and, as Bobby indicates, clean air, she has a chance to improve significantly."

"We have to keep the lab rat alive," Cocoa says.

"That would benefit all of us," the general says.

And I agree. Keeping Cocoa alive would benefit all of us.

The next half hour consists of uncomfortable small talk and Cocoa and I escaping to the kitchen to make popcorn and General Groves getting up and down and pacing.

Finally, through the screen door and the open windows comes the growl of a car hurrying down the driveway. Once again, the general gets to his feet and peers out. An engine shuts down. Doors slam.

"Beware the flea, Cocoa," he says with a grin, and goes to the door.

When he opens it, a man in a rumpled brown suit is first in, followed by another captain. I wonder if the Army will soon run out of them. The suit shakes hands with the general and takes a vacant chair across from the sofa. Cocoa glances at General Groves.

"For those of you still in the dark, this is Assistant Secretary of War John McCloy," the general says. "He's well aware of the contents of the letter and he's been briefed on the fact that the warning originated with Cocoa. He flew all the way from the nation's capital on one of our fastest bombers to be here, so we shouldn't complain about his tardiness. Secretary of War Stimson asked him to make the journey to talk to Cocoa in person and assess the situation."

Cocoa sits on the edge of the cushion. She's already told her fantastic story in this room and mostly escaped ridicule. *But what will this guy, who's already scoffed at the warning once, think of it now? What will he think of Hitler and the Axis powers rising from the ashes, and time slippage and a future without hope and this skinny girl who knows it all?*

Pete, who's been quiet in the face of all the power and brass in the room, moves from his chair to Mom's vacated spot next to Cocoa. If there's going to be an inquisition, she and the remaining members of what the doctor called her "new family" are going to meet it together.

"I take it you're Charles Hastings?" John McCloy says to Dad, whose faded shirt and jeans and boots give him away.

"Chuck," Dad says, trying to be cordial.

"Whose idea was it to make the warning in the form of a letter to you, *Chuck*?" McCloy spits out Dad's name like it's something he found stuck to his dentures.

*Another asshole.*

"My idea." This time my words don't come out strangled. McCloy has a title and a suit, but I know a bully when I see one.

He yawns through my explanation and Dad's attempt to shoulder some of the blame, and then tries to turn his attention to Cocoa.

But Dad isn't done. "I'm disappointed by your lack of imagination, Mr. McCloy. But not surprised. You and your War Department cronies can't even imagine a world without war."

*Uh-oh.*

"We didn't start this war, Mr. Hastings. Remember Pearl Harbor? The Nazis overrunning Europe? *They* declared war on *us*."

"I've interviewed people who endured those hardships," Dad says. "Unimaginable brutality. Unforgettable people. But I also remember all the missteps that led up to the war."

"You're advocating appeasement."

"No," Dad says. His face is redder than usual. If he were still writing for a newspaper, this is where his editor would steer him back to moderation. But this isn't an article or opinion piece. There is no editor. These are airborne words, unmoderated. "I'm not talking appeasement. I'm talking communication and cooperation, and I'm not talking the weeks or months while everything was going to hell. I'm talking years. I'm talking before war became inevitable."

"My sources tell me you're a pacifist, Mr. Hastings. And a writer. A dangerous combination."

"I am. And I—and my family—pay for it constantly. What have your choices cost you, Mr. McCloy? Before the war, you underestimated the threat from Japan. After it started, you lost focus on the real enemy and wasted the country's time and resources and years of innocent people's lives by locking up 120,000 Japanese Americans as potential collaborators. But we really know why they were treated like the enemy, don't we?"

McCloy's jaw clenches. My armpits flow. "Ironic you should mention the Jap internees," he says. "You're not in a position to be shooting off your mouth. Drawing attention to yourself is the last thing you want to do."

"What's that supposed to mean?" Dad says.

"Pray you don't find out." McCloy glances meaningfully at the FBI guys and, now that he's given Dad something to think about and me something to be frightened about, he finally gets back to Cocoa.

"Do you really expect us to believe you came from the future?"

"Some people already do," she says.

"Me, then. Do you expect *me* to believe it? It would be infinitely more reasonable for me to believe you're a spy."

"A *spy*?" Cocoa says. "I'm sure you're embarrassed, but your bluster is clouding your judgement. I'm sixteen. I'm ill. The only government people I've ever talked to are in this room. And *I* am giving *you* information. And asking for nothing in return."

"And where does this information come from?"

"From my memories," Cocoa says. "Not whispers in the night or cryptic notes on scraps of paper. I'm the farthest thing from a spy."

"It doesn't matter where she's from, McCloy," General Groves says. "Or how she learned what she knows." He looks amused, as if he enjoys the exchanges between the good guys and the suit. "She had exclusive knowledge, it was amazingly accurate, and she was willing to share it. And you failed to act. If that was because you're overly involved in another matter, your priorities are pure shit.

"Now you may get a second chance, and if and when Cocoa has more information for us, you're to refrain from putting a lid on it. You need to pass it on to Secretary Stimson and General Marshall immediately."

"That has already been made clear to me, General."

"Let's keep our minds open," General Groves says. "Let's give Cocoa some breathing room, and pray that she can recall the kind of detail that will help us get back on the road to victory."

I should stand up and shout *Amen!* But I'm content to sit next to Cocoa and stew about McCloy's narrowmindedness. And while I stew and hear the asshole ask her questions that are more courteous and reasonable, I also wonder what he knows that we don't.

Cocoa is patient. She doesn't call him a fucking flea. When he's done with his questions he flashes a phony smile and thanks her and gives her his direct phone number as well as the phone numbers of two of his top aides and Secretary of War Stimson himself.

After a flurry of farewells, McCloy and his driver are gone like a passing hailstorm, heading back to Albuquerque for the night before returning to Washington. The rest of us sit and wait. *For what? Something from Cocoa?* Nobody stares at her, but she's the center of attention anyway. An encyclopedia. A time-bomb. A secret weapon harboring secrets not even she knows.

Dad turns on some lamps. He goes to the kitchen and returns empty-handed, his way of pacing. The presence of all these military and government men has him on edge. Without Mom to hold his hand, he's not himself anyway.

General Groves gets to his feet, so everyone else does. "Most of us are returning to Los Alamos," he tells us. He gestures toward one of the captains, the taller, younger one, who was driving the general's car when they arrived. "But Captain Nelson here is to remain billeted at Trinity—the base camp—for as long as necessary. We'll drop him off there."

He hands Dad a slip of paper. "Thanks to Doctor Bainbridge, this phone number has been assigned solely to the captain. He'll check in with Cocoa by phone three times a day, and in person daily. He'll know how to reach me at all times. In the event that you recall anything at all, Cocoa, your first phone call should be to him. He'll make the decision on whether or not to call me, but I'm encouraging him to freely do so. My job will be to assess the information and if necessary make the next call."

He gives Pete, Dad, and me a quick once-over.

"I expect that if Cocoa needs any support, you three and Mrs. Hastings will be there for her. And your country. And, Sergeant," he says to Pete, "at my request, Doctor Bainbridge has spoken to Lieutenant Bush. For the duration of Captain Nelson's stay at the base camp, your primary duty will be assisting him with his responsibilities—manning the phone when he has to be elsewhere, getting him access to what he needs, driving him where he has to go. A car will be at your disposal." He pauses. "I notice you have a limp that you're doing a fine job of disguising. I assume that you're fit enough for this assignment?"

"Any assignment, sir," Pete says.

"Thank you for your steadfastness," the general says. "And your sacrifice."

I half expect Pete to say it was nothing, but it wasn't nothing, and he just nods.

Near the door, the general turns back. "Thanks for your hospitality, Chuck. Please thank your wife for her words of wisdom. And thank you, Doctor Kersey, for your insights." He aims a grim smile at the doctor. "Keep her healthy."

The general's entourage files out. Lolly, halfway in, handles the doorman responsibilities.

"Can we give you a ride back to the base camp, Sergeant?" Captain Nelson says to Pete once we're outside.

"Appreciate the offer, sir," Pete says. "But I got here on a horse. Big Muddy. They're expecting her back with me in her saddle."

Captain Nelson grins. "Sounds like more fun. But when you get back look me up. We'll get acquainted." He turns to Cocoa, his grin even warmer, and I can see why the general chose him to babysit us. "You've got my number and I've got yours, Cocoa. We'll talk soon. I'll stay within shouting distance of the phone— and the sergeant here—at all times." He slips on his garrison cap and hurries to catch up with the rest of his party.

# TWENTY

After the crowd leaves, Dad promises us grilled cheese sandwiches and Campbell's tomato soup if we get some fresh air while he cooks. And while we're at it, he says, we can see Doctor Kersey and Pete off, tend the animals, and pick raspberries for dessert.

Cocoa is glowing. She's made it through the inquisition, and now she gets to see Big Muddy again. On our way out, she grabs a couple of sugar cubes. I don't have the heart to tell her sugar is rationed. We let Lolly come along. He's been around the mare for hours, unchaperoned, and he's still standing.

Before Pete, Cocoa, and I head to the barn, we say goodbye to Doctor Kersey. I'm sure he never imagined something like this as part of his small-town doctor duties.

Big Muddy greets us with a toss of her mane. "We'll have an easier going than coming, girl," Pete murmurs as he swings into the saddle. She backsteps toward the open barn doors. "Go ahead, Cocoa," he says. "You have something for her?"

When Cocoa removes her fist from her pocket and unfurls her fingers, her acorn is sitting on her palm with the two sugar cubes, attracting Lolly's interest. He's always been a fan of anything resembling a ball. Cocoa lets him sniff the acorn and then slips it back in her pocket, a souvenir of the creepy carnival ride that she calls *home*.

Big Muddy laps up the cubes, gives Cocoa a horse-nuzzle, and gazes up at Pete as if to say *Let's head home, pardner*. Then they're off, cowboy and horse, silhouetted by the falling sun.

Hounded by Cocoa's version of the future, I picture a different desert landscape with different occupants. But I put the picture away before it gets too detailed. Maybe she can uncover more memories in time for General Groves and Henry Stimson to do something. Which could be the start of changing her story, and mine. If she can't remember, or the bigwigs can't act in time, or it turns out that the fate of the world is set in stone, the death throes and the dying will begin right here and now.

We feed the nameless pigs and chickens and the Andrews sisters. Cocoa wants to try milking, so I demonstrate on Maxine, the pushover, and then let Cocoa take charge. When the first spurt makes the pail sing, her smile lights up the barn.

We head into our desert surroundings—red dirt and sand, flats and mounds, gopher and snake holes, jimsonweed and creosote bush and prickly pear cactus, spindly yuccas standing among the scrub like lost girls. Lolly leads the way, avoiding the snake holes. He's never been bitten, but he has a natural aversion. He's been known to bark at coiled rope.

Cocoa stares at the clear blue sky and drops her gaze to the distant mountains.

"Some people call them the Mockingbirds," I say.

"In my time, they have no name."

"They do. It's just been forgotten."

"What if this all goes away, Robert?"

"It won't be your fault."

"I—my story—wasn't convincing enough."

"You were convincing back at the house, with all those hotshot politicians and brass and brains."

"McCloy is a prick."

"Next time he'll listen."

"Truman, Churchill, Stalin—they think they have Hitler

cornered, but he has something he's been preparing for them."

"Bombs."

"Yes, but when do they start? Where? How are they delivered?"

Lolly brings me an egg-shaped chunk of wood. When I ignore him, he drops it in front of Cocoa. She kicks it into the scrub and he bolts away.

"Maybe the answers will come easier if you get away from the radio and newspapers and commotion," I say. "Maybe if you're out here breathing in all the good oxygen and good smells and peacefulness, you'll remember."

"I'll try."

"You've got your own bike now," I say. "Feel like getting up tomorrow, early, and doing my route with me?"

"The newspaper shack?" she says. "Leo? The base camp? Peter? Captain Nelson? All of it this time?"

"The thrills won't stop."

Lolly races back. We ignore him and turn back to the house. Lit up by the setting sun, it smolders.

"Don't let me sleep longer than you," she says.

Lolly shadows us, staring up at Cocoa, begging. She takes the soggy chunk of wood from him and flings it, and as he zooms off in a cloud of dust I realize I was wrong about her arm. She may not throw accurately, but she doesn't throw like a girl.

# TWENTY-ONE

Cocoa is dressed and sitting on her bed. Her eyes spark in the light from the hallway. "What took you so long, Robert?"

"Couldn't sleep. When I finally did, I was dead to the world. Including my alarm clock."

"In my other life, I tried to sleep as much as possible. Sleep and read, sleep and read. It kept me from dwelling on my situation. Repetition. Sameness. Inevitability. But here, I'm too curious. And anxious. There is unspoiled countryside, and interesting people, and animals, and a chance to help, and surprises in store. I try to stay awake for all of it."

"You're sure you're okay to go?"

"Did you not just hear my speech, Robert?"

On our way out, we cut off hunks of homemade bread and plaster them with butter that Dad churns himself. Twice a week he loads crocks of butter and cans of milk into the trunk of the DeSoto. Mom drops them off at the co-op. The proceeds barely cover upkeep on the Andrews sisters, but we have as much butter and milk as we want, despite rationing.

Cocoa is wearing jeans, so she has no trouble hopping on her bike and pedaling into the starlight, and I stay as close as I can without trading rubber. The morning air intensifies the desert smells, but I'm able to pick out hers: shampoo, soap, deodorant. A hint of bread and butter, maybe. A sweet combination. I'd like to bottle it and keep it next to my bed. But, for now, I'm content having it drift back to me, making me almost forget that it's early and we have a long way to go and a day of uncertainty ahead.

She knows the way to the shack, which we passed when we visited the base camp. So I'm happy to lag behind and watch her shadowy outline. I don't need to be reminded that she's got the lungs of a miner. The last thing I want to do is push her.

Cocoa and I are sharing the bench when Leo's Ford crunches to a stop. He pops out. He's killed the motor but left the lights on, allowing me to glimpse his not-so-insightful grin.

"Got help today, Bobby?" he says, opening the back door.

"This is Cocoa. My bodyguard. Cocoa, this is Leo. My boss."

We get up from the bench and Leo does a double take. *My bodyguard* was a joke, of course, so I'm glad he doesn't remark on her lack of bodyguard characteristics. They shake hands. "Any friend of Bobby's," he says. "I like your name, Cocoa. Live around here?"

"Thank you, Leo," she says. "I do live around here. Kind of."

He gives her a curious look, but luckily she doesn't explain *kind of*, and he doesn't give her an accounting of how many days it's been since Mrs. Leo let him have his way with her.

"Helluva thing about the ships going down, huh?" he says. "It's all in here," he adds, holding up a *Journal*.

Cocoa gives me a look, like it's *not* all in here. But explaining that to Leo would take half the day. And fall under the heading of *loose lips*.

We grunt to show him we're listening.

"Some good news, though, Bobby," he says. "For some reason, they're not emptying out the base camp. In fact, my boss told me the population may increase over the next few months. So, you'll have your job for a while."

"That's great," I manage, even though the reason for the improvement in my employment prospects is anything *but* great. Two of the most powerful weapons in the history of the world lie at the bottom of the ocean. They have to be replaced. Quickly. And that won't happen without more scientists and support people and long hours and, once in a while, a *Journal* to provide news of the outside world.

Soon Leo's back in the car. He gives me a conspiratorial wink and Cocoa a *nice-to-meet-you* nod. I watch his taillights for a moment, afraid he's going to realize he didn't give me his marital-relations update. But the old Ford rattles on.

I show Cocoa how to roll the papers, and she catches on quickly. Soon we have the bag stuffed and we're heading for the base camp.

*What did General Groves call it? Trinity? As in* holy?

Again, the sentries near the camp entrance aren't bothered by the presence of my sidekick. As we continue, two civilian cars and an Army truck roll by. A sign that Leo's right: the loss of the cruisers has changed some high-level minds about the fate of Trinity.

The newspaper route goes faster with Cocoa helping, even though the renewed urgency means more people are in our way. She gets to use her arm—infrequently accurate but always strong—and I have more time to gaze through the gloom, hoping to spot Pete or Captain Nelson or even Dr. Bainbridge.

But I don't see any of them, not even when I peek inside Pete's barracks.

When we get back to the house, the car is gone. At first, puzzling. But then I remember. "Dad's on his way to Santa Fe," I say as Cocoa and I lean our bikes against the barn.

"His march." The word makes me anxious.

I picture him there, pissing people off. I recall John McCloy's not-so-subtle threats. I wonder what he meant and whether he was just being an egomaniac and not used to a small-town reporter in worn jeans and boots giving him shit.

"He thinks he's doing the right thing."

"It *is* the right thing," Cocoa says. "If only everyone believed it."

Inside, the house is quiet. We sit while the coffee percolates. I unfold the paper. Cocoa scoots her chair closer, and I find myself wishing I'd showered off the sweat from the bike ride and the anxiety that's been pestering me for days. It wouldn't have helped with the anxiety I'm feeling at her nearness, but I pretend it doesn't affect me, and she pretends I don't stink.

Leo was half right. The headline *TWO US WARSHIPS SUNK* accompanies an article that follows what we've heard on the radio—two cruisers and hundreds of crewmen lost, rescue efforts ongoing, routine missions. The word *coincidental* is in there, but what isn't in there is any mention of cargo, bombs, a local connection.

What isn't there is the whole truth.

Whoever wrote the article made up for the missing facts with a shitload of chest-thumping—boasts about how vermin are no match for an eagle, that the German and Japanese forces will pay for their treachery ten times over.

"It makes you wonder about the bullshit ratio in all these war articles," Cocoa says.

"Beyond wonder." Dad has often hinted at below-the-surface mischief. "An unhappy but convenient marriage between the government and the fourth estate," he calls it.

At the bottom of the front page a smaller headline catches my eye. *STATE'S PACIFISTS TO MARCH TODAY.* I've just begun reading when Cocoa lets loose with a punctured-tire hiss. When I look up she's staring at the headline. "What is it?" I ask.

"Not good," she says.

"What do you mean?"

"I have seen this headline before. One like it, anyway."

"So?"

"McCloy. What he said yesterday wasn't an empty threat. Something happens."

"To the peace marchers?"

"Marchers. Conscientious objectors. Religious groups that preach peace."

"*What* happens?"

She gets us coffee and returns. "If you could open up my skull, the answers would be in there, cut from old stories, pasted into the folds of my brain, where shadows and time obscure them. The Nazis, the Japanese, the peacemakers. Not Chuck's name, but Chuck's people."

"When?" I say.

"Soon. But overshadowed by a bigger event."

"That's all you know?"

"This is maddening, Robert. This fog."

I don't push her. We get through most of the day doing laundry and other routine stuff and thinking about Dad and whatever's buried in Cocoa's head. Captain Nelson calls twice, but beyond her anxiety over the *bigger event*, she has nothing to tell him.

Mom tries to be cheery. But as the afternoon wears on, she spends more and more time glancing through windows that give her a view of the car's usual parking space and the approach from the road.

Finally, we hear the sounds of the DeSoto rolling down the driveway. Pretending not to be relieved, we're slow to look up when Dad steps through the kitchen door. But, when we do, we gasp.

He tries to smile, but his right cheek is puffy and bandaged. The eye above it is swollen nearly shut and surrounded by reds and purples. His glasses are lopsided. The right lens is missing.

Before he can take another step, Mom is there. "I was afraid of this," she says, fingering his cheek.

"How do you know I didn't just fall down?"

"Did you?"

"After the cursing and spitting and rocks."

Mom pushes him to a chair. Up close, he looks worse.

"This *movement* will come to no good," Cocoa says.

"What do you mean?" Dad says.

Cocoa tells him what she told me.

"What can they do to you?" Mom says. She sets a bowl in front of him. In it is a glob of red Jell-O crammed with canned fruit cocktail. For some reason, one of his favorites. She peeks under the bandage, frowns, hurries off before he can answer.

"You're a citizen," I say.

"Not in good standing," he says.

Mom returns with the first aid kit. She yanks the bandage away with more force than necessary, revealing a nasty scrape.

She sets on the table her instruments of torture—cotton swabs and alcohol and iodine—and goes to work on the wound. "No more marching." She intends it to be an order, I'm sure, but it sounds like a plea. It would've been more effective delivered in a German accent. Cocoa should've done it.

"We'll see," Dad says. Mom replies with extra alcohol, extra iodine.

After we finish supper, Pete and Captain Nelson show up. Following a question and answer session about the origins of Dad's wounds, we go to the living room for coffee and tea. Even if Cocoa has nothing to tell them, they'll get something for their trouble.

Before he sits, Pete takes a closer look at Dad's face under the glow of a floor lamp.

"My first war wound, Pete," Dad says.

"I hope it's your last, old man," Pete says. He finds himself a chair next to the captain, who has a notebook on his lap and a pen in his hand. An optimist.

"Have you thought about shelving the activism for a while, Mr. Hastings?" he says. He's young—still in his twenties, probably— but his bearing makes him seem older. "There's a lot of anger over the sinkings and, if our setbacks continue, it will overflow. Anyone who's seen as acting against the war effort could get drowned."

"I've heard that before, Captain. But I appreciate your concern."

"He thinks God's on his side," I say. "Or Jesus. Or somebody."

"The Constitution," Dad says.

"None of those is going to pay for your glasses," Pete says. "Or your next hospital visit. Or your funeral."

"Peter," Mom says.

"It's true, Dottie," Pete says. "He needs to think of you and Bobby. And Cocoa, now."

"Something bad is coming," Cocoa says.

"What?" I say. "What kind of bad?" Her *somethings* are getting annoying.

Captain Nelson fingers his notebook and pen.

"If I knew, Robert, I would say. I only want Chuck to be careful."

"Yes, honey," Mom says. "We all do."

"Are you listening, Dad?" I say.

"Both ears," Dad says. "There's nothing else planned, anyway."

"And if there were?" Mom says.

Dad focuses on the view through the window. Desert twilight. "It's good to be home."

Although Cocoa's admitted she doesn't know anything specific, the captain asks her if there could be even one hazy image in her head that might be contributing to her worries.

She says no but tells him that her journey to enlightenment isn't necessarily a steady process. The memories could materialize out of the constant stirrings of a gentle breeze or the sudden violence of a tornado.

Captain Nelson puts his notebook away. When our small talk ends, the two soldiers head for the door.

Before we go to bed, the captain calls again. Just checking in.

# TWENTY-TWO

**W**himpering—a girl's whimpering—pulls me from sleep. Cocoa, wrestling with another nightmare.

I lie in my bed and listen. Breathe. Clear my head. I hear nothing. *Maybe this was* my *nightmare.*

Maybe not. Dressed in only my shorts but sweating, I head for her room.

She's not there. Lolly is gone, too. I walk back down the hall. Light spills from the kitchen, and when I get there Cocoa is sitting at the table studying a pad of paper. She's wearing her pink pajamas. Her hair is pressed flat to her head on one side. I stand at the door and clear my throat, but it takes her a moment to look up. Lolly, stretched out at her feet, doesn't bother.

"Robert," she murmurs.

"Another nightmare?"

"Yes, but riddled with memories. Before the last of our library's video players died, I saw old newsreels of the first Nazi atomic bomb, wiping out a city." She jots something down. "I'm chronicling my impressions before I lose them again."

"What city?"

She shakes her head. "No interruptions."

I can take a hint. While she writes and sighs and stares, I get the coffee pot going and settle at the table, silent. Lolly lifts his head, and I give him a scratching.

The kitchen clock says one-twenty. In three hours I'll need to be on my way, and the lack of sleep will be even more noticeable on a Sunday, when the papers are twice the size of dailies. But compared to what Cocoa's going through, that kind of burden seems insignificant. I'll keep her company until she tells me to get lost.

I fill two mugs halfway with cream and top them off with coffee. Brain food. Cocoa takes a sip, thanks me, and gets back to her notes, which now fill close to a page. But soon she's doing more frowning than writing. She exhales hoarsely and lays down her pencil.

I raise my hand like I'm in school.

"You may interrupt now, Robert. There is no longer anything to interrupt."

"Should we call Captain Nelson?"

"You decide," she says, and pushes the notebook over to me.

I've seen her penmanship before, but still it takes me a few seconds to realize she's written shorthand descriptions of images she's seen in her nightmare, her awakening: *Massive harbor city, boats and ships adrift, sinking; water blazing with burning fuel; vast stretches of smoldering land surrounding the harbor; scores of docks in shambles and sunk; low waterfront buildings, roofless and turned to rubble; a ruined ferry boat high and dry against a burning warehouse; standing water, thick with bodies, where the harbor has erupted and pushed ashore; taller structures inland, toppled and crumbling; vehicles overturned in streets and parking lots; fire licking out of demolished buildings; smoke everywhere; more bodies lying in the street and on the sidewalk under a movie theater's marquee advertising a Noel Coward movie; women and children running from a waterfront area where an inferno rages; their clothes and skin hang from them in shreds, their hair smokes; a church the size of an entire city block, collapsed except for its bell tower; streets and bridges unusable; cars, trying to leave the city, piled up at intersections and waterways; panic; chaos; a huge airfield littered with broken planes; more docks, more sinking ships; dead bodies everywhere, most in uniform; buildings surrounding the field on fire or blown apart or both; a huge fighting ship, its superstructure twisted above a flat deck, lists at the remains of a dock; more bodies, sliding into the burning water; flashes of lightning; a roiling cloud; no sounds, but I can imagine them all; no smells, but I breathe them in with every breath; I don't know the date; I don't know the place; I believe it is one city but it might be more.*

"We can't keep this to ourselves," I say. "Even for tonight."

"How will it help?"

"It's a city. It's on a body of water. If there's a fighting ship moored at a dock, the Navy probably has a base there. The scenes shocked you awake, so you're probably describing America. An atomic bomb, somewhere in America."

"I can't remember where. Or when."

"This narrows it down, though. It doesn't mean much to us, but maybe it will to the captain, or the fellows he reports to."

She sips her coffee. "Call them."

Captain Nelson answers on the second ring. A minute later he's done listening to my *Reader's Digest* version of Cocoa's notes. He promises to get "Sleeping Beauty" out of bed and be on the road in ten minutes, and before hanging up tells me that a cup of strong coffee sure would hit the spot.

We have time to step outside. Lolly stays put, confident we're not going far, and we don't. But, even shirtless and barefoot, it feels good to be out in the cool, breathing in desert smells.

We move away from the lights of the house. The stars come alive. Cocoa stares up at them for so long I begin to think she's hypnotized.

"It's like a giant blanket, Robert. Millions of tiny holes. Light shining through them."

"Shooting stars are the best. On a night like this you don't have to wait long to see one."

"Meteorites?"

"A rancher found one nearby. Size of a grapefruit. They say

it traveled through space for millions of years. It's in a museum now."

"We should look for one," she says. "When this is over."

"Ours will be the size of a watermelon." I follow her gaze upward, hoping for fire in the night. But nothing appears, and we return to the kitchen.

The coffee has just finished perking when car sounds get our attention. I grab a T-shirt, half expecting to see a light under Mom and Dad's door, but there's no sign they're awake. Recent events have caused me sleepless nights, but all the excitement and worry and shit must be having the opposite effect on them.

We sit at the kitchen table, voices hushed. Cocoa slides her list to the captain and Pete. I study their faces, waiting for reactions, but Pete's not exactly demonstrative, and when Captain Nelson's only response is a mild frown, I decide he got chosen for this assignment because of his ability to keep a level head.

"Distinctive handwriting, Cocoa," he says finally, grinning.

"I taught myself, mostly. You can read it okay?"

"Perfectly." He glances at the phone. "Your dream prompted this?"

"So vivid. Tied to memories. Books. Photos. And movies I saw when I was younger. The memories survived the dream. I had to preserve them."

"I found her here, writing everything down," I say. "She wouldn't talk to me until she was done."

"I was not done. I simply ran out of images."

"There's nothing here we can use to pinpoint location or time," Captain Nelson says.

"Sorry," Cocoa says. "Robert thought we should call you anyway."

On the table, Pete's big hands make fists and open, make fists and open. "Robert was right," he says.

"This gives us way more than we would've had," the captain says. "But can I ask you a few questions?"

"Maybe they will be ones I have not asked myself."

"I won't guarantee that. But we'll see."

Cocoa nods. I'm feeling helpless; everything they want to know is in her head or already on the notepad.

"The big ship," Captain Nelson says. "It was probably an aircraft carrier. Do you recall seeing a number? If you do, we'd have a chance to pinpoint its current location."

Cocoa closes her eyes, breathes deep.

We wait.

Finally, she shakes her head. "The metal, all of it was battered. Part of it was missing. I don't remember a number, or even part of a number."

The captain is taking his own notes. "Was there anything else that might set this ship apart from others?"

She doesn't think as long this time before shaking her head.

"Planes on the deck?"

"No planes. Bodies."

"Anything about the city you don't have in your notes? Unique buildings? Bridges? Waterways? Signs? Billboards? Statues?"

She opens her eyes. She's trying. But she shakes her head no.

"The terrain, Cocoa," Pete says. "Flat? Hilly? Mountainous?" The questions aren't unfriendly, but they're coming too fast. I want to take her hand, but of course I don't.

"Flat," she says after a moment. "Everyday."

"Could it have been tropical?" Pete says. "Hawaii? Pearl Harbor again?"

"Regular clothes . . . regular trees . . . no beaches . . . no ocean surf. Not tropical. Temperate, perhaps. I am almost certain it is the United States mainland."

"The movie theater," Captain Nelson says. "Did it have a name?"

Her head takes a break from its back-and-forth. "It did," she says. "A short name, beginning with an *L*. Or perhaps something—another sign—masked part of it, or perhaps it was partially blown away."

"What about the words on the marquee?" the captain says. "Aside from the actors' names—Noel Coward and the rest— which would likely be the same no matter the location, were the words in English?"

She stares up at the space where ceiling meets wall. Imagining, maybe. "Probably," she says at last. "Anything else—even German—would have struck me as foreign. Or at least different."

The captain and Pete are quiet while she continues to think. I get the coffee pot and refill our cups.

As I sit back down the head-shaking starts again. "Sorry," she says. "I can't be sure of the language. And making something up would be fruitless."

"You've done fine, Cocoa," the captain says. "I'm going to call General Groves and give him what you've given us. Anything else you can think of?"

"The Nazis have the atomic bomb. They are going to use it."

"Thanks for the reminder. But we believe you. Now. And what you've told us is way too big to forget. Or ignore." Captain Nelson carries the notes to the counter. "Bobby, this conversation may take a while. Tell your folks they'll be reimbursed for the cost of any calls I make."

"Sure." My parents love this country, but they aren't rolling in dough.

He reads the operator a number. In no time, he's telling General Groves that Cocoa has remembered some vivid, though not clearly helpful, details of what appears to be an atomic bomb detonating in a large American seaport. Then he methodically reads through her notes and the few he's made, giving the general time to digest, or write, or shit his pants.

Even from ten feet away I can hear the bark of the general's voice, and when Captain Nelson doesn't respond I realize the general has people with him and he's giving them orders: *Do this, do that, look up this, find a map, call this number, tell them this, ask them that. Move!*

At last the conversation ends. The captain comes back to the table. "He asked me to thank you, Cocoa. He's serious about responding to what you've told us. He's making calls to other important people, happy to get them out of bed. Assistant War Secretary McCloy, War Secretary Stimson, generals, admirals, anyone who might have the insight to figure out where this place might be and the power to stop what you've described from happening."

"You've made believers out of them, Cocoa," I say.

"Not McCloy. Narrow minds like his are what doomed the world."

"He'll be outvoted," Pete says.

"Or muzzled," she says. "How many ports are there?"

The captain frowns. "Dozens. The question is, how many of them have a Navy presence? But someone will know the answer, so you've already whittled it down."

"Not enough," Cocoa says. "I should be able to remember more. Then we would have a chance."

"We *have* a chance," Pete says.

For a while we're quiet, waiting for another lightning bolt of inspiration to strike her. But she looks empty, and the captain and Pete get up and say their goodbyes.

Cocoa and I are about to head back to bed when Dad shows up, and we have to explain what he missed. When I finally make my way to my bedroom, I realize I have to be back up in less than an hour. It's going to be a long day.

# TWENTY-THREE

I'm practically on top of the base camp before I realize that all of its exterior lights have been extinguished. Blackout curtains cover every window.

Somebody's taking precautions.

With the lack of light added to the condition of my sleepless body added to the extra weight of the Sunday papers, I struggle through my route. I don't spot Pete or Captain Nelson.

Nobody, including Lolly, is up when I get home. I'm tempted to return to bed, but as I lay Dad's *Journal* on the table, the headline catches my eye.

*HUNDREDS MARCH, THOUSANDS JEER.* Below it is a photo of a Santa Fe street crowded with sign-carrying peace marchers. Surrounding them on the street and sidewalks and hoods and roofs of cars and even clinging to light poles is an unruly mob. Scowls, mouths twisted with rage or some other poisonous emotion.

*Are they worried that a negotiated peace will allow Hitler to continue his dirty work? Or that these people promoting peace will jeopardize their sons' or grandsons' chances for glory, or the privilege of being buried in the cold, wormy ground of some far-off hellhole?*

Above the street, people lean from windows. One man has his arm cocked, poised to throw something. *I don't see Dad, but was he the target?*

Halfway through the article comes mention of a rumor that the government is considering action against those in the peace movement. I recall John McCloy's comments. His linking Americans working for peace to Japanese Americans who have been locked up behind barbed wire since early in the war. It sounded like a threat then. It feels more like a threat now.

Dread grips me. The feeling is intense but not new. It's exactly what I felt when I accompanied Dad to the government office in Albuquerque and sat on the edge of the wooden chair while the old guy with the thick glasses and drifts of dandruff on his brown suitcoat's shoulders shook his head with disapproval over Dad's conscientious objector papers.

To our great relief, he signed them. He gave Dad the names of people to contact for CO jobs, although, in the end, Dad didn't qualify. Created for healthy and draft-age *conchies*, the jobs weren't routinely given to the remanded—the old and nearsighted or otherwise lacking. Dad didn't mind. He was still at the *Journal* then. He hadn't yet gotten entirely under the skin of his coworkers and bosses—and the government—and been shown the door.

The meeting with the asshole official happened more than three years ago. But I still recall Mom's concern over it, despite Dad's advanced age and bad eyes. She was so apprehensive that she couldn't bear the prospect of attending the hearing.

Which worked out nicely. Because I thought I could somehow prevent anything bad from happening to him, I was planning on going along anyway. So, I volunteered to stand in for her. I didn't expect to get rewarded, but afterward Mom was so grateful that she offered to do my chores for a whole week. I accepted.

It seems like only this morning that she greeted us in the

front yard, tears in her eyes, and hugged Dad tight, as he told her his CO status had been approved.

I'm finishing the article when the kitchen door opens and Dad walks in, blanketed in the sweet-sharp smells of hay and cows and milk and manure. I've been picturing him in bed, but he's obviously been outside, taking care of our animal friends.

"Bobby," he says. "Why aren't you back in bed?"

"In a while."

He gets coffee and sits, and I slide his newspaper across to him, front page showing. Up close, his face looks worse. Beneath the bandage, the cheek is just as swollen, and above it the eye is purple, going black. His lids form a slit.

It doesn't take him long to read the story. "There were some hate-tainted people there, Bobby," he says, "but I think underneath they're mostly good folks. They're simply blindfolded by their own prejudices and unwilling to look at another point of view."

"The government is on their side, Dad."

"Oh?"

"You heard McCloy. He was threatening you. Cocoa has a bad feeling. Now this article."

"I'm not about to become less vocal," Dad says. "Which doesn't mean I can stomach the thought of a Nazi victory. I'm happy that Cocoa and the generals and politicians are trying to prevent her bomb story from coming true. And if she shows us that a huge piece of history can be altered, maybe we can keep this smaller piece you're talking about from coming true, too."

"Smaller, but not small. You have to back off." I point at the photo. "You see these faces?"

"I saw them up close. But me backing off would be like a prickly pear shedding its spines."

"A prickly pear doesn't have a choice."

"Besides," he says, "it's probably too late."

"Too late?"

"If something's in the works, it's in the works."

I don't like his response, but I'm tired of the conversation and just plain tired. Before I head to bed, I spot a smaller headline near the bottom of the page. *SEARCHES FOR SURVIVORS*

*CONTINUE.* The article that follows rehashes the *Indianapolis* and *Augusta* stories and covers the latest on rescue efforts and the numbers of missing. It doesn't mention secret missions or bombs or the derailment of the chance to end the war or what Hitler and Hirohito have up their sleeves.

I sleep through breakfast and lunch and get up to find Cocoa and Lolly in the kitchen. The radio is on, a low murmur but loud enough to catch any change in content or emotion. The clock says one-forty. Once again, Cocoa has a pad of paper in front of her. I feel her eyes on me as I go to the refrigerator, half-starving, and open it. Someone has made liverwurst and Velveeta sandwiches on homemade bread and stacked them on a plate under waxed paper. I love liverwurst and Velveeta sandwiches.

I take the plate to the table and wait for Cocoa to acknowledge my presence. She's dressed nice—yellow blouse, red shorts. Her hair is brushed. She smells good, not like a barnyard. Her paper is blank.

"Robert," she says finally. "You do not have to be ridiculously silent. You can't distract me. My mind is constipated."

"Sandwich?" I say, diving in.

"I have had my fill," she says, but an instant later grabs a half and goes to work on it.

"My parents?" I say. I mumble the words through a mouthful.

"Town. Chuck went to church. Dottie is visiting a soldier's pregnant wife. They will be back by three."

"Heard from Captain Nelson?"

"Twice. I had nothing to tell him. He had nothing to tell me. He's sure people are working on it. He and Peter will be here this evening."

I nod. The *Albuquerque Journal,* looking more well-read, is on the table. "You saw this?" I say. "The article on the peace march?"

"McCloy has more ammunition," she says. "As if he needs it."

"Still have a bad feeling?"

"Feelings, Robert. And frustrations. But am I fooling myself, thinking I can do something to alter what has already occurred?"

"You *have* done something."

"Too little, once. And maybe again."

"Maybe not. Everywhere should be on alert by now."

"How can they prepare for an attack *everywhere*? *Everywhere* the people will think it is happening *somewhere else.*"

Although we both would rather be outside under a blue sky, we turn on the living room radio and settle on the sofa. Lolly stretches out on top of Cocoa's feet. She has her paper and a pencil in case she gets inspired, but she's probably not counting on me for the inspiration. I still haven't figured out what she thinks of me, and maybe she hasn't figured it out, either. Painful to consider, but maybe she thinks nothing at all. From the morning we first met, her mind has been on more important things. And people.

Mom and Dad come home. They listen to the radio for a while, then head outside. They make us promise to get them if the news we're dreading becomes a reality.

Despite my prayers and crossed fingers and lucky socks, at five-twenty a network announcer interrupts the local weather report.

"I have shockingly dreadful news to convey," he says in an undertaker's voice.

My heart stalls. I can't breathe.

"We have just learned that the war's devastation has reached the shores of the United States." He pauses, and I'm certain it's not for dramatic effect. I'm certain it's because he's swallowing his emotions, struggling for composure.

"Minutes ago, at approximately 6:55 eastern daylight time, the city and port of Norfolk, Virginia, were all but obliterated by a huge explosion. According to a pilot flying high overhead, the blast originated in the harbor but instantly sent ripples of destructive energy in every direction, sinking ships, launching a tidal wave toward the city's shoreline. The force of the explosion raced inland, incinerating and knocking down buildings, destroying bridges and other structures. A giant mushroom-shaped cloud rose over the city. Tens of thousands of Norfolk residents and military personnel are feared dead."

*Dead* launches me to my feet, running. Through the house, into the yard. I'm screaming "Mom! Dad!" and sprinting for the barn. But already they're on their way out. We race back to the house, and all I can manage is "Norfolk! Norfolk! Norfolk!"

When we skid to a halt in the living room, neither Cocoa nor Lolly has budged. Cocoa's face is in her hands. Her shoulders are heaving. "Norfolk." The name spurts from her lips like something bitter—a double dose of cod liver oil. "Of course," she murmurs. "Why couldn't I remember? I'm sorry. I'm so sorry."

I don't care what anyone thinks, I sit next to her and put my arm around her and try to let her know that it's not her fault and this family still loves her and, no matter what, it's going to be okay. Still mostly bones and skin, she kind of melts into my side and we both just sit while she swallows air and tears.

The announcer is still going, and we're all captivated, even though we know better than almost any other listener what's happened in Norfolk. *What caused the blast? Who is responsible? Who tried her hardest to stop it?*

"You did everything you could, honey," Mom says, sitting on Cocoa's other side and taking her hand but not interfering with my arm, which is not going anywhere.

"Government personnel in Washington have asked news organizations to refrain from speculation about the bomb," the man on the radio says. "But I can tell you that calls for help have been sent out by the Virginia governor and mayors of neighboring cities to military, police, fire, and medical personnel, and qualified volunteers. As I speak, those calls are being answered.

"We will give you updates on this heinous enemy attack as the information becomes available, but for now we return you to regular programming."

The regular programming, a local agriculture show hosted by a guy who is obviously distracted, has barely begun when the phone rings. I pull away from Cocoa and run to get it.

It's Captain Nelson. Once I tell him that we're all aware of what happened, and none of us, especially Cocoa, is doing very well, he asks to talk to Mom.

I give her his message, watch her hurry off, then sit back down next to Cocoa. Dad perches on the edge of his chair, the *Journal* and its headline prominent on his lap.

Cocoa stands, begins pacing. "You thought those people

were pissed off before, Chuck," she says. "Now they will greet you with pitchforks and whips. You need to stay away from demonstrations."

"Thanks for your concern, Cocoa," Dad says. His way of saying *Don't count on it.*

Mom returns. "Captain Nelson and Pete are coming over," she says. "The captain has asked permission to bivouac in our yard. Use our facilities. Eat here, if it's convenient. The government will pay all expenses."

"The government," Dad says. As in, *The pig shit drying on the sole of my boot.* "You tell him yes, Dottie?"

"They want to be as close as possible to Cocoa."

"You couldn't tell him no," Dad says.

"They're bringing a trailer. Food from the camp storehouse. Supper for tonight."

Cocoa returns to the sofa. "They will expect me to know something. About what comes next."

"Pushing you won't be helpful," Dad says. "They know that."

"Someone—Groves or McCloy or maybe even Stimson—will be pushing *them,*" I say.

"McCloy," Dad says. *Pig shit,* part two.

"We won't let it affect Cocoa," Mom says.

Once again, a news bulletin interrupts regular programming. As the announcer begins speaking, Mom sits down and takes Cocoa's hand. *Why didn't I think of that?*

"Although our leaders have asked that news sources be cautious in releasing information," the guy begins, "it appears likely that the explosion in Norfolk's harbor this evening was due to the detonation by an enemy country of a devastating weapon of war heretofore only imagined by readers of scientific journals and science fiction. Science writers are speculating that someone—most likely Nazi Germany—has appropriated the work of Albert Einstein and other physicists in the field of atomic energy and concocted a way to harness that energy for evil purposes.

"That is only speculation. But fueling it is a report that National Guard and Coast Guard units have established check points around the perimeter of the city and harbor. They are allowing survivors to leave, but no civilians are being allowed into the area of the blast or even under the shadow of the mushroom cloud, which is now dissipating and moving out to sea. Besides the dangers of crumbling buildings and downed electrical wires within a two-mile radius of the blast's epicenter, there is talk of poisonous air and water.

"The government remains tight-lipped. But if the conjecture on the part of our civilian sources proves to be true, if the Nazis have such a weapon, the so-far favorable course of the war may have changed in the blink of an eye."

None of the bomb talk is news to us, but still, coming over the radio in the newsman's authoritative voice makes it seem more ominous. This wasn't a test. This wasn't an uninhabited stretch of land in the New Mexico desert. This was an unbelievably powerful weapon used in a real-life situation. This was a real city. These were real people.

This was us, taking one in the balls.

And on the other side of the Atlantic, Hitler and his crew of sadistic Nazis are no doubt raising their steins, smirking and giggling and pulling on their wienies like nasty little boys cheering on the schoolyard bully.

*What's next? When?*

The announcer goes on, mostly repeating himself. At one point, he mentions the possibility that a U-boat was involved, a U-boat on a suicide mission.

"Stay tuned," he says.

But I'm ready to spend some time around our animals. I get up, hoping Cocoa will follow me outside.

She does.

I hope she'll take my hand.

She doesn't.

Someday I'll do more than hope.

An hour later we're in the kitchen and my stomach is growling nonstop when the sounds of an approaching vehicle grumble through the screen door. I step outside. Coming down the driveway is an Army truck towing an Airstream trailer. Low rays of sunlight glint off the rounded corners of the trailer's aluminum shell as Pete maneuvers it to a spot near the house. For at least part of the day it will be shaded.

Cocoa comes out and helps me supervise Pete and Captain Nelson while they unhitch and level the trailer. Then all of us, including Mom and Dad, inspect the inside—bunks, sink, icebox, table, all arranged to save space. I could live in it, but two grown men?

"I hope they like each other," Dad says.

"Better than a tent," I say.

"Or a dumpster," Cocoa says.

In the truck bed are several sturdy cardboard boxes filled with canned goods, coffee, sugar, flour, bread, corn on the cob. In a big wooden box, under a layer of dry ice, are packages of ground beef, ham, and bacon, and in another is a baking pan. Pete lifts the lid, revealing a huge pot roast surrounded by assorted vegetables, swimming in brown gravy.

"Courtesy of Doctor Bainbridge, and our fine Army cooks," the captain says. I picture Eddie and Lard-Ass, the two cooks I met on the morning of the test. *Have they heard the news and put two and two together?*

Cocoa's fears about the captain or Pete pressuring her don't materialize while we're putting away the food or setting the table or eating or cleaning up. Nobody brings up Norfolk or the bomb or the direction of the war. Someone has turned off the radio, and we leave it off.

Finally, we all move to the living room with a big bowl of popcorn and a pitcher of lemonade. Cocoa raises the subject that everyone has been avoiding.

"I am sorry I could not—" she begins.

Captain Nelson cuts her off. "Look, Cocoa, you don't need to apologize. There isn't one person who blames you for what's happened. Nobody will blame you for anything that may yet happen. When they're not feeling overcome with wonder, everyone is completely impressed with your knowledge and your willingness to share it. We're certain you've done your best and you'll continue to do so."

I'm back in my spot, sitting close to Cocoa on the sofa. It feels comfortable. And it's nice to have Mom sandwiching her from the other side. Saturdays and Sundays are the only days Mom is home with us in the evenings, and tonight I'm extra grateful. Dad is sitting next to her, and Pete and the captain are across from us. The captain is in Dad's chair. Pete knows better.

"I'm still trying," Cocoa says. "Too late, memories are returning. I recall that a Nazi submarine delivered the bomb. I recall that it was a suicide mission, because the crew of that submarine are—will be—famous war heroes in Germany. I know more attacks are coming. My problem—everybody's problem—is the fucking details."

"The captain and I have been talking, Cocoa," Pete says.

This time it's Cocoa's turn to interrupt. "Chuck's situation is the same," she says. "I know something bad is going to happen to him and his peace movement friends. But I don't know what."

Neither Pete nor the captain says anything, and I wonder if they know something.

"I already lost jobs over it," Dad says. "I've been bruised and bloodied. What else can they do?"

*Plenty*, I think.

"Anyway," Pete continues, "we thought there might be ways to help you remember."

"And he's not talking about browbeating or torture or anything disagreeable," the captain says with a half-formed smile.

"We'd like to drive to Albuquerque tomorrow, visit the library, and study photos and maps of coastal cities and states," Pete says. "See if something jogs your memory. Also, we've called the owner of the biggest movie theater in town. He's agreed to let us view his collection of newsreels. He'll close down the theater long enough to show us any we want to see."

"How does that sound, Cocoa?" Captain Nelson says.

"Can Robert come with us?" she says, turning me warm all over and bringing a grin to Pete's face.

"Of course," the captain says. "We were planning on inviting him."

"Good," Cocoa says. "Yes, that will be good."

# TWENTY-FOUR

Monday, July 23

I'm pulling on a T-shirt and shorts when I hear someone in the bathroom. A moment later there's a knock on my bedroom door.

"Is it okay if I go with you this morning, Robert?" Cocoa asks. There's only one dim lamp on in my room, but I decide she looks troubled. *From yesterday*, I tell myself.

"Sure." I try not to sound too enthusiastic. "The customer count is back up, so I can use the help."

A spark of amusement flickers in her eyes. And I know why: I'm a bad liar, and the real reason I want her to come along isn't the increased customer count. But I'm only slightly embarrassed that she's seen through me so easily. More important is that for an instant, at least, the troubled look disappears.

Outside, Cocoa turns to me. All that's left of the moon is a faint glow above the western horizon. Her face is nearly invisible.

"During the night, I woke up with a memory, Robert." We're a good distance from the house, but she keeps her voice to a murmur. "No longer cloudy."

"The next attack?" I say, matching her volume.

"The government's plans for people in the peace movement," she says. "For Chuck."

"You remember what happened? What's *going to* happen?"

"They call it 'relocation,'" she says. "'Internment.' What they did to the Japanese Americans. They're going to round them up and ship them off and lock them up. Concentration camps, although they don't call them that."

Fresh in my mind: Dad and John McCloy butting heads and Dad mentioning Japanese Americans getting locked up and McCloy saying it was ironic Dad should bring up the Japs.

McCloy's words made me fear something like this, but Cocoa saying it with such conviction and sadness makes it real. "How can they?"

"Truman has signed an order."

"Effective when?"

"Today is the twenty-third?"

My head is a wasps' nest, buzzing angrily. "It is."

"Tomorrow," she says. "The roundup starts tomorrow."

"I should warn him."

"Let him sleep. A few hours won't matter. Maybe I'll be wrong."

I have no faith in her being wrong, and she's right about letting him sleep. *What difference will it make?*

The trip to the shack seems to go faster with my mind elsewhere and Cocoa riding beside me, even though we barely talk. Maybe it actually does go faster, because Leo doesn't show up until we're there for several minutes. He angles his car so the headlights are on the shack, and us. He gets out holding a newspaper.

"Hello, Cocoa," he says, handing me the *Journal*. His voice is friendly but serious, an unsettling combination. "Big news, Bobby," he says. "You've gotta read it. Now."

"We heard all about it on the radio last night," I say. "Nazi skunks."

"Open the paper, Bobby," Leo says.

I do. Giant headlines shout *NORFOLK BOMBED*. An aerial photo—buildings turned to rubble, smoke rising, boats tossed ashore—and an article take up the rest of the space.

"Page two," Leo says. "Any other day, front page stuff."

Cocoa squishes closer as I turn the page. I can sense her anxiety. Part of me wants to go back and read about the mayhem.

At the top of page two is another, smaller headline: *TRUMAN SIGNS ORDER TO LOCK UP PEACE MOVEMENT ADVOCATES.*

I swallow. I try to fight off the chill.

Cocoa was right.

McCloy's threat was more than a threat.

In the glare of Leo's headlights, we begin reading. There are words—*disloyal, dangerous, cowardly, unpatriotic, inflammatory, seditious, subversive*—that I race past, seeking the meat of it—*when? Is Cocoa right about that, too?*

Leo paces. Cocoa takes my hand, which should make me melt, but I'm focused. Finally, I get to where the article mentions *detainment* and *relocation* and *internment.* I get to the part where it says *The actions are being taken for the safety of those involved in the peace movement.* I get to the part where it says *President Truman's Executive Order 9598 will be implemented beginning Tuesday, July 24.*

Tomorrow.

Cocoa wasn't wrong. About anything.

I re-read the article, searching for who and where and how long. But all it says is that relocation centers already exist, inhabited by people interned earlier in the war.

"Sorry, Bobby," Leo says, giving me a slip of paper. "My home phone number. In case you need to talk to someone. You know the work number."

"Thanks, Leo," I manage.

He opens his door and hands me my stack of papers. "Sorry," he says again, then gets behind the wheel and drives off.

With the headlights gone, darkness has returned, but the stars and a hint of dawn over the hills make it easy to sit on the bench and roll papers.

"The relocation option has been considered for a long time," Cocoa says. "The concentration camps are occupied, but room remains, and they can be enlarged. The sinkings, and the public reaction to the marches, and now the bombing, have provided the government with an excuse to imprison another class of citizens."

"You're remembering more stuff?"

"Continually. Like acorns dropping from dying trees."

"They'll arrest all of them?"

"Anyone who has made their stand public," she says. "The FBI has records. Conscientious objectors and members of religious groups like Quakers and Mennonites are the easiest to finger. Some conscientious objectors are already in work camps and workplaces, performing alternative public service. Sitting ducks. But everyone who has been vocal or marched or written an article or letter to the editor is in jeopardy."

"Dad's done it all."

"As McCloy said, he's vulnerable."

"What about me? Mom? You? If they send us away, what about *you*?"

"I don't recall if families went. Japanese American families did. But almost all members of the Japanese American families have one troublesome thing in common. Their race."

She hasn't said anything about herself, *but how would she know?* "I can hardly imagine Dad behind barbed wire."

"He will have company. The camps will be crowded. It will take time to build more shacks. But at least the groups will be compatible. Chuck's church, and others, have worked to ease the burden on Japanese Americans."

They have. I wonder if Dad ever thought he'd end up in the same boat as the internees he was helping.

I shoulder the bag. We head out. The breeze is cool, but I sense heat coming. And heartbreak.

"You think Leo would get me a bag so I can help carry?" Cocoa says.

"Probably. But we may not be here much longer."

"They won't put me in a camp. I am the precious goose. So far, my eggs haven't been golden, but only because they arrived late. The general and the assistant secretary of war and the men above them are going to continue keeping close tabs on me. Why do you think Captain Nelson is living in your yard?"

"You're all they have."

"They will want to keep me happy, Robert."

An early-morning wind kicks up. I can taste the desert. "You're right."

"Which means you're not going anywhere."

Maybe the wind is playing tricks with her words.

"What?"

"You're not going anywhere," she repeats. "They have a bone to pick with Chuck, but not you. So, I will tell them. Robert stays, or I will be unhappy."

I don't know what to say. I can feel water in my eyes, but I tell myself it's just the wind. I've been trying to decide what she thinks of me, and now—

"Unless you want to go with Chuck, and maybe Dottie, too."

"No." The word doesn't come fast enough. "I want to stay here." *Should I say "With you"?* "With you."

She's pedaling a couple of arm's lengths off to my left, and darkness is still fighting the arrival of dawn, but I sense a smile.

The sentries wave us through. We ride into the dark camp.

Cocoa insists on throwing half the newspapers. Luckily, her accuracy has improved. We whip through the route, leaving extra copies where new arrivals have begun working or eating or sleeping. There's a lot of activity—walkers hurrying from place to place, lamplight edging past blackout curtains, voices behind the locked doors of the ranch houses and newer buildings. Until today, the slapdash structures have never reminded me of people living their everyday lives in backcountry prison camps behind plywood walls and barbed wire fences.

Light shines through the kitchen window of our house. Even though I'm only bringing home two copies of the *Journal*, suddenly my bag is heavy.

I resist the temptation to wake up Pete or Captain Nelson to be my backbone when we walk through the door and I hand Dad his paper. *I can do this.* If I blubber, I want as few people as possible to see the tears.

Dad and Mom are at the table. Steam rises from their coffee cups, but it doesn't begin to mask their expressions—bravery, false cheer, despair—and I know they know. Lolly is lying at Dad's feet. He doesn't move. He has a job to do.

I set the papers on the table. The one Leo gave us is open to page two. "You've already heard?" I feel the tears building up in the back of my throat. I swallow them.

Mom slides the paper closer to her. I'm looking at the headline upside down, but it hasn't changed: *TRUMAN SIGNS ORDER TO LOCK UP PEACE MOVEMENT ADVOCATES.*

"A fellow from church called," Dad says. He glances at the headline. Mom is already reading the story. Her head is already shaking. "He heard about it from a cousin who's with the FBI."

"When?" I say. "The article says the relocation begins tomorrow."

"'Start packing,' my friend said."

"What about Dottie and Robert?" Cocoa says.

"They're not involved," Dad says.

"How can you say that, Chuck?" Mom says. "The last time I checked you were my husband. Bobby's father. They're going to lock you up and we're *not involved*?"

Dad answers her with silence, with his big fingers tightening around his coffee mug until they lose some of their color.

"Maybe the radio will have more information?" I say.

"I'm beginning to hate that radio, Bobby," Mom says. "But turn it on."

I do. At first all the news is Norfolk. Dad unrolls the second copy of the *Journal* and starts reading the article under the familiar headline: *NORFOLK BOMBED.*

Cocoa and I sit. The news from Norfolk is chilling. The city is still off limits to civilians, and nobody's saying much, but some word has leaked out. A four-mile-wide circle of ruin. Tens of thousands dead and dying. Tens of millions of dollars in property loss. Infrastructure ruined. Leadership gone. Naval facilities destroyed. Personnel decimated. Countless Navy and merchant vessels sunk.

President Truman has declared a heightened state of emergency. National Guard units are on alert everywhere. Those closest to Virginia have been mobilized to help.

Cocoa's face is haggard with guilt, and I want to tell her that this isn't her fault. I wonder if just mentioning it makes her feel even more guilty.

Finally, after the story has been repeated and the newscaster has run out of statements and opinions and wild guesses, the broadcast switches to the page two news.

Once again, the words roll out. *Pacifists. Truman. Executive Order. Relocation. Internment. Anti-war. Collaboration. Morale. Disloyalty. Public outcry. For their own safety.*

Missing are the important words: *Where? Who goes? Who stays?*

"I am not going," Cocoa says. "The government men will want me here."

"You're right, Cocoa," Dad says. "There's no reason to drag you into my troubles, anyway."

"Robert is also not going." Cocoa says it in a way that doesn't leave room for disagreement.

"No," Dad says, allowing himself a small grin. "I'm the only one who's going anywhere."

"You don't know that, Chuck." Mom fingers the internment article. "There's nothing in here about who has to go or can't go or can go if they want."

"Who would *want*?" he says.

She levels her gaze at him, letting him know who would want, and he drops his eyes and peers into his empty coffee cup, and the small grin returns.

"We'll see," he says finally. "But based on what I've learned, and what happened with the roundup of Japanese Americans, I have a feeling this is going to happen quickly. As close as we are to sensitive military facilities, for me *quickly* could mean tomorrow."

"Cocoa knew," I say. "She told me before we left for the route. The specific stuff. The scheme. The date. We decided not to wake you."

"I appreciate it," Dad says.

"When did you remember the details, honey?" Mom says.

"During the night, I woke up with the memories gnawing at me. I tried to go back to sleep, hoping for more, but I couldn't. I decided to tell Robert and go on his route with him." She flashes me a look. "With so many new customers, he needs the help."

"I'm sorry your sleep is so troubled," Mom says.

"If I can be useful," Cocoa says, "it will all be worth it."

Dad puts on a fresh pot of coffee and goes back to his newspaper while the rest of us take stock of our new wealth of food. It's good being distracted, even for a few moments, by something that doesn't cause heartache.

While we're organizing breakfast, Pete and the captain knock and walk in. They say good morning to the group but otherwise ignore the actual Hastings family and our long faces and focus on the golden goose.

While she uses her skinny arms to whip up a bowl of pancake batter, she tells them that she hasn't come up with anything. "Sorry," she says. But she does tell them about Dad's problem, how she woke up remembering the history of the United States putting pacifists in concentration camps. Dad tells them about the call from his friend. We give them the papers to read.

Pete is quiet, biting his tongue. He doesn't tell Dad "I told you so."

"How soon, Chuck?" the captain says.

"The paper says it begins tomorrow."

"What are your options, Dottie?" the captain says.

"We don't know," she says.

"She's staying here," Dad says. "She's got Bobby and Cocoa to look after."

Cocoa stops stirring. She looks at the captain, maybe waiting for him to say something about where he expects her to be, but he doesn't. So far, he doesn't have any reason to.

After breakfast, Cocoa and I are outside weeding the garden when an approaching car puts an end to the quiet. By the time we walk around the corner of the house, the sheriff's car is turning into our driveway.

The dusty Ford comes to a stop behind the DeSoto. When Sheriff Wally opens his door, we're standing a few feet away. "Hey, Bobby," he says. He puts on his Stetson and pulls it down snug. The hat's white, but I'm not fooled; he's up to no good.

I tell him "Hi" while he gives Cocoa the once-over. Instantly I wish that both Pete and Captain Nelson hadn't gone to the base camp to meet with important people and make important phone calls having to do with the bombing and Cocoa and the impact of the relocation order, all lumped together in what I've heard them call the *situation*.

At the base camp, Trinity, they're also trading the truck for a car for our trip to Albuquerque, which is going on as scheduled. Pete said he'd call if they were going to be more than an hour, but an hour hasn't yet passed and now we have this *situation* right here.

"This the mystery girl?" the sheriff says.

"Cocoa," she says.

"Right," he says. "Cocoa."

"This is Sheriff Wally," I say.

"Good to meet you, Cocoa." He stalls.

"Your dad in, Bobby?" he says finally.

All evidence points to him being in. *Why lie?* "In the kitchen. Working on a story."

"I won't take much of his time."

Feeling like Judas or Benedict Arnold or some other asshole, I lead him inside.

Dad's at the table with his back to us, facing a mostly blank page spooled up in his typewriter. He turns and eyes Wally like a condemned rooster. His battered face looks better, but not much. "Wally," he says.

For a moment Sheriff Wally is speechless as he eyes Dad's face. Maybe he's thinking about asking what happened. Maybe he'd rather not know.

"Got something for you, Chuck," he says. He glances at the newspapers on the counter. "You've read the news."

Dad waves me away, but I pretend not to notice. From the bathroom, the sound of the shower tells me where Mom is. I'm glad she's missing this.

"The roundup," Dad says.

Sheriff Wally nods. "The FBI came around this morning. They're shorthanded for this operation, and they kind of deputized me. No choice."

"That's fine, Wally," Dad says.

"They gave me some instructions to deliver." Sheriff Wally removes a thin stack of envelopes from his jacket pocket. He hands Dad the top one and puts the others back. Dad's name is typed on the envelope: *Charles Robert Hastings*. I recall the other envelope with Dad's name on it, the one that contained the fake letter we gave Pete. It seems so long ago.

This envelope is barely sealed. Dad pops it open and removes a sheet of paper. Sheriff Wally and I wait, as still and silent as yuccas on a calm day, as Dad unfolds it and reads. Slowly, like the words are written in some foreign language.

"Tomorrow morning?" he says. It's a rhetorical question, and the sheriff doesn't answer.

"One suitcase," Dad says, his eyes still on the letter.

"Somewhere warm, I hear," the sheriff says.

"It says families are eligible to accompany the miscreants."

The sheriff frowns at *miscreants*, possibly struggling to pluck its meaning from the context. Finally, he nods. "You'll need to make that decision before the agents arrive."

"I can't ask my family to go," Dad says, ignoring me. I hear a *click*. Cocoa's standing at the screen door.

"Wouldn't be an easy life," the sheriff says.

Dad goes back to staring at the letter. I sense the tears again and I try to distract myself: *bike rides, walking in the desert, watching the sun come up. With Cocoa.*

In the distance, the shower shuts off.

"I best be going, Chuck," Sheriff Wally adds. "You're only the first."

"Lucky me."

"You'll be fine." The sheriff extends his hand. "Sorry."

"Not your fault," Dad says, swallowing the sheriff's hand in his own. "Fear and flag waving make for an ugly—but formidable—marriage."

I don't know that Sheriff Wally follows what Dad is saying, exactly, but he nods once more and hurries through the door, tipping his hat to Cocoa as he brushes past her.

Mom walks in. Her hair is wrapped in a towel. She is wrapped in a robe, and barefoot. "Did I hear voices? A car?"

Dad hands her the letter. "Sheriff Wally. New errand boy for the FBI."

Mom sits beside Dad and takes his hand while she reads.

She tries to keep her face neutral, but her shoulders move with a silent sigh.

"Tomorrow morning?" she says. It's the same question Dad lobbed at Sheriff Wally, but this time there's an answer.

"Won't take long to pack. I'm going by myself."

She shakes the letter at him. "This says you can bring your family."

"You've seen photos of places where they've stuck the Japanese Americans, Dottie. Tarpaper shacks. Communal bathrooms. Crowded mess halls. Wind and dust and mud. What kind of life would that be for you?"

"We'd be together."

"I'd hate myself," he says. "It's all my doing. My fault."

"It's not your fault," she replies. "It's your life."

# TWENTY-FIVE

From outside come the sounds of another car, and Pete and Captain Nelson walk in.

Pete knows us well enough to know something's happened. He glances at the radio.

"What now?" he asks.

Mom picks up the letter by a corner, as if it's poisonous. "It's official."

Pete reads it and passes it on to the captain. "Not much time to decide, Dottie," Pete says.

"Hours," she replies.

We talk about what the letter means. Dad fights to hold himself together. His eyes water, his voice quivers. This isn't another attack on the country, but it's an attack on him, and his family, and countless other pacifists and their families, and the Constitution. The captain doesn't say much besides offering his regrets, and once again, Pete keeps his thoughts to himself. This isn't a time for lectures, or quarrels.

"You'd have to give up your job to come with me," Dad says to Mom. Apparently, he's been rehearsing.

"We'll look after the place," Pete tells Mom. "Including the critters. And Cocoa, of course."

"The government will have no problem backing up Pete in the role of her custodian and caretaker," the captain says. "Food, clothing, personal needs, medical care, education, transportation, anything."

"Robert will also stay," Cocoa tells him.

Mom looks on the verge of saying something, but Pete beats her to it. "Makes sense." He winks at me. "Loneliness averted. And no harder for the captain and me."

"I get the impression that Robert is very self-reliant," the captain says. "Besides, who would bring us our newspaper?"

"And do the chores?" Pete says.

Despite everything, Dad chuckles. It's rare that Dad chuckles at anything Pete says.

"I can't imagine it," Mom says to me. "Dad, all alone. Or me with him, but you and Cocoa here by yourselves."

"We'd have Pete," I say. "And Captain Nelson. And Cocoa and I are *both* self-reliant. She's raised herself, for God's sake."

"Don't I get a say in this?" Dad says.

"No, Chuck," Mom says. "I won't blame you for what's happening, but the rest of us have to figure out how best to deal with it." She eyes me. "You'd really want to stay, Bobby? Whether or not I go with your dad?"

"I might be able to help." It's the least hurtful—and embarrassing—reason I can think of.

Mom goes quiet, head in her hands, while the rest of us sit or hover nearby.

"I have no idea what I'm going to decide," she says at last. "But I have the rest of my day here, and then my work time, and then the night, to think. And pray. And in the morning, I'll know."

A half hour later we're on the road to Albuquerque; Pete drives, the captain rides shotgun, with Cocoa and me in back. Mom has packed us sandwiches, which we're inhaling. Once we've passed Socorro, everything's new for Cocoa, and she spends most of the time gazing through her window. Like mine, hers is rolled down a couple of inches.

She smiles with her eyes. "So many plants. Fertile hills. So much blue above them. The air tastes like rhubarb pie."

"We're going to try to keep it that way, Cocoa," the captain says.

Our first stop is the library. I've visited it a couple of times with Mom and Dad, and once, before the war, with my schoolmates. It always impresses me with its size and design—towers, beams, nooks and crannies and places to hide from impatient parents, the countless books sitting on endless shelves.

Once inside, Cocoa's eyes dart everywhere—books, magazines, newspapers, high ceilings, art on the walls. I can feel her itch to explore.

But the librarian—a woman Mom's age, but skinny like a stovepipe—is expecting us. When she looks up from her desk and sees two soldiers and two kids walk in, she hurries over.

"Can you show us where to locate the atlases and maps first?" Captain Nelson asks. "Miss Lang, is it?"

"You can call me Trudy, captain. I've already set aside materials I thought you'd find interesting."

The captain tells her thanks and gives her an appreciative smile. She responds by blushing, then leads us to a small room behind a door that says *MEETING*. In the room is a long table and eight chairs. On the table is a stack of atlases surrounded by maps, some folded, some flat, a couple framed. She leaves after telling the captain to be sure to let her know if she can be of any additional help.

Eyes flashing, Cocoa circles the table, studying the maps— United States, Eastern states, Southern states, Alaska, Hawaii. She sits and opens an atlas and finds the pages that show in detail the Hawaiian Islands. She begins taking notes. The rest of us open other atlases, locate coastal areas in the US and Alaska and even Europe, and bookmark them with scraps of paper.

She's through the atlases and into the maps when Trudy and a high-school-age girl show up pushing carts loaded with a set of the *Encyclopedia Britannica*—I count twenty-four volumes—and a variety of magazines, including *Life, Look, Collier's, The Saturday Evening Post, National Geographic.* When Cocoa glances up and sees the onslaught, she doesn't look overwhelmed. She looks excited. She puts her head down and gets back to work.

Trudy and her helper leave. Captain Nelson, Pete, and I remove the encyclopedia volumes and magazines from the cart and replace them with the atlases and maps Cocoa's already seen. While she continues to study them, the captain and Pete comb through the encyclopedia set and I attack the magazines. Like Pete and the captain, I'm looking for photos, and when I find one I think might be worthwhile, I bookmark it.

While I'm paging through a *Collier's,* I find something that isn't a photo but might still be useful. It's an article on a Nazi death camp in Poland. *Shocking. Sickening. Hate, boiling over.*

I mark the article for Cocoa, but I think of Dad. I tell myself he could be worse off.

She's almost through the maps when she pauses at a map of the Northeastern states. She zigzags her finger down the coastline, into and out of harbors. She goes to the cart and retrieves an atlas and stands over it, turning pages.

The rest of us hold our breath. The room is dense with heat. Pete opens the only window.

She stops. *Maine.* Moves on. *Massachusetts. Boston* and its harbor. Fingers drift along the tiny shoreline. Pages turn. *New York. New York City.* Rivers and harbor. More fingering. Note taking.

"Can I help?" Afraid to break the spell—if one exists—I barely breathe the words.

"The encyclopedia, Robert. The volumes containing Boston and New York."

Heart thumping, I bring them to her.

She opens the *B* volume. We've all drifted closer, looking over her narrow shoulders as she locates the entry on Boston. There are photos. *Beacon Hill. The Old North Church. The waterfront.* She stares, taking in the images, perhaps trying to lodge them in her brain to cast light on the shadowy things stored there.

She opens the second volume to New York City. Again,

there are photos. *Liberty Island* with its inspiring statue. The skyscrapers of *Manhattan*. *The Bronx, Brooklyn, Queens, Staten Island. Coney Island* with its famous amusement park. Ships and ferries everywhere. She lowers her face to the book, as if she's trying to conjure up a third dimension, a smell.

She closes it. "Can we visit the movie theater now, Captain Nelson?"

"Of course." I know he has questions. We all do. But we walk wordlessly out of the small room and across the big one. As we pass Trudy's desk, the captain lets her know how much we've appreciated her help. She tells him it was nothing. Anytime. I can feel her eyes on us—on him—all the way out the door. *Motherly*, I tell myself. Smiling.

At a phone booth near the library entrance, Captain Nelson makes a call. Then we head out. In the front seat, he and Pete talk baseball, and in the back, Cocoa sits taller, closer to me, studying her notes and sketches. I feel the presence of something positive.

There's a lineup, mostly kids, outside the Ranch Theater when we pull up to the curb. Marie and Theresa, two girls from my class, notice me getting out of the Army car but pretend they don't. They giggle, study the movie posters on the building wall, gaze at the ground.

Once they learn that my dad is going to be locked up, I'll be even more of a pariah.

They don't look back toward me until Cocoa slides out, notebook and pencil in hand, and joins me on the sidewalk. Then the captain emerges, all uniform and ribbons and upright bearing and strong jaw. Pete walks around the car, favoring his bad leg but also impressively handsome, and gives Cocoa and me a smile.

A man hurries over and introduces himself—Mel, the theater owner—and tells us he booted out the kids so we'd have the place to ourselves. His high forehead and unruly fringe of hair make him look like Larry of *The Three Stooges*. Marie and Theresa watch open-mouthed as he escorts us to the door.

Popcorn. In the lobby, the smell is thick. My mouth waters. Cocoa swallows. Mel tells the kid behind the refreshment counter to bring us four bags of freshly popped and four Cokes.

"What we'd like to see," the captain says, glancing in Cocoa's direction, "are any newsreels you have that would give us a look at the northeastern US, particularly Boston and New York. Also, any Naval vessels anchored or docked in a northeastern harbor. Especially anything that shows ships' numbers."

"Does this have to do with yesterday?" Mel asks. He looks anxious, an expression I've noticed on lots of faces today.

The only answer Mel gets is an intense gaze from the captain, so he swallows his question. "Sure," he says. "I have our collection practically memorized. You folks go find yourselves the best seats in the house while I go up to the projection room and get things rolling. If you want to see something twice, wave an arm and I'll backtrack."

"Thanks, Mel," the captain says as the owner makes his exit. A moment later we all thank the refreshment counter guy when he beckons us over for our hot popcorn and icy Cokes.

We find seats. The lights go down. Under other circumstances, this might feel like a date. Cocoa and I would lean into each other. We'd eat popcorn and drink Coke, but we'd be sharing. I'd hold her hand, and she wouldn't let go.

But it doesn't feel like a date. It feels like the world is spinning out of control and flying apart and we're trying to slow it down and hold the pieces together.

For the next hour, images parade across the screen. Some are unhelpful. Admiral Nimitz gets honored. Nazis retreat in Russia. Hitler and Mussolini smile and wave and probably argue over the claim of worst human ever. The Allies invade Normandy under an October 9, 1944, sunrise, finally, after a four-month-long series of weather and strategic delays.

But Cocoa might find other scenes useful. A convoy of supply ships leaves New York Harbor escorted by a pair of destroyers. Jewish refugees land at Ellis Island, skyscrapers and waterfront and bridges and then the Statue of Liberty visible in the background. Truman makes a speech on the steps of the New

York Public Library. Military supplies leave the South Boston Army Base by train. An aircraft carrier with the number four clearly showing on its flight deck, accompanied by two smaller ships, steams into Boston Harbor. Crowds gather at a Red Cross rally in Boston. Naval ships take shape in the Newport News, Virginia, shipyards.

*Would Virginia be hit again?*

Three times Cocoa waves and Mel backs up the film to scenes featuring Ellis Island refugees and Red Cross workers and the aircraft carrier.

"I'm ready," Cocoa announces.

The projectionist/owner/snoop meets us in the lobby. "I hope it was helpful," he says, glancing from face to face, settling on Cocoa's.

Fishing. I can't blame him. *Was* it helpful?

"We really appreciate it, Mel," the captain says, and again the theater owner has to bury his curiosity.

Once we're in the car and moving, Pete breaks the silence, and the taboo. "You know you're keeping us on the edges of our seats, right, Cocoa?" Next to me, she writes something in her notebook and closes it.

"I was waiting for fewer ears," she says. "Loose lips and all that."

"So?" Pete blurts.

I study her expression—guarded relief, a pinch of excitement. "Boston," she says. "Three or four days after Norfolk. Another U-boat. Another Nazi hero and his submarine full of martyrs. New York next. Two days after Boston, while chaos still reigns and defenses are spread thin. Still another U-boat." She breathes. We all breathe.

Pete whistles, almost drowning out the whistling wind.

"That's wonderful, Cocoa," the captain says. "Not that Boston and New York are in jeopardy, of course, but that you've given us a chance to respond. You're terrific."

"Unbelievable," Pete says. "You're gonna be a hero, future girl."

"I wouldn't like to be looked at as a hero, Peter. But *Future Girl?*" She doesn't want to be a hero, but it's a superhero's name.

"I like Future Girl."

We all laugh, and then the captain says, "Sergeant, we need to make a detour."

"To?"

"Kirtland. Thanks to Future Girl, we have urgent news to share. Face-to-face would be best."

"Yes, sir." Pete takes a right, then a left, setting a new course.

Kirtland Field is a place I know. It's a huge Army Air Force base at the edge of Albuquerque, home to hundreds of planes and thousands of personnel. Dad once marched outside its gates with his pacifist friends. A week later he took me to the scene of the crime. Although, at the time, it wasn't a crime. They marched, and nobody bothered them. Hardly anybody—except the MPs watching for trouble—even saw them.

If there's interesting stuff going on at Kirtland, it must be far beyond the gate and fences. When Dad and I drove along the perimeter of the base, all I saw were distant buildings and hangars and row after row and swarm after swarm of big airplanes. Parked and taxiing and taking off and landing and circling overhead.

A novelty for a hick kid from the desert countryside. But to the residents of Albuquerque, the activities at Kirtland Field had become ho-hum.

Cocoa fidgets as we approach the gate and stop to show credentials to the MPs and Pete and Captain Nelson explain where we're going. At the mention of General Groves, the conversation ends.

The captain directs Pete to a low building surrounded by other low buildings. Like everything else here, they look like they've been tossed up in a hurry.

Beyond the buildings, the runways are alive with activity. A huge plane—a B-29, is my guess—lifts off and banks into the sky heading south. I wonder if it's headed for the Alamogordo Bombing Range—the site of *Trinity*—where not many days ago a mushroom cloud climbed into the morning sky and all of this began.

We park and get inside before Cocoa and I attract stares.

"General Groves in?" Captain Nelson asks the attractive

young woman behind the reception desk. She's wearing a uniform. *A WAC*, I decide. Her nameplate says Corporal A.E. Lewis. She returns the captain's smile but saves a bigger one for Pete. Although he's normally shy around women and we have bigger fish to fry, he smiles back. It looks good on him.

"He's in a meeting, sir," Corporal Lewis says.

"He needs to see us right now," the captain says. "Captain Nelson. Sergeant Blakely. Bobby Hastings. And Cocoa."

"It's Pete," my uncle says. Cocoa gives him a grin that he pretends not to notice.

"I hate to interrupt him, sir," the corporal says.

"Trust me, he'll thank you."

"Yes, sir." She goes to a closed door and knocks tentatively. A familiar voice barks out an "Enter!" and she does. A moment later a colonel walks out with his hat in his hand, eyeing us curiously. The corporal ushers us into the general's office.

He's up, pacing, chewing on an unlit cigar. His eyes are on Cocoa as he waves us into chairs. He sits behind his desk and opens a notebook. "Speak to me, young lady."

She does. While he takes notes, she recounts her afternoon in Albuquerque, poring through maps and atlases and encyclopedias, reclaiming her memory of incidents through images and drawings and descriptions. Just being in the library helped, she says. "A catalyst," she says.

She tells him about her first visit ever to a theater, seeing moving pictures of the cities and harbors of the Northeast, how the movies cemented what she'd already seen at the library, how they connected to similar movies she calls videos, ones she saw before her future world ran out of electricity for good.

"Boston," she says. "Then New York. Not much time."

She gives him her notepad. He frowns. "I'm glad I have my own notes," he says with a grin.

"Three or four days after Norfolk, sir," Captain Nelson says.

"So, two or three," the general says. "Not much time, indeed." He fixes Cocoa in an unwavering gaze. "You're reasonably sure about this, young lady? I'm not about to stand by and witness another gutless assault on our country, but I'm also not interested in letting some doubting prick in Washington beat me up like a piñata for sounding a false alarm."

"McCloy," I say.

General Groves nods in my direction. "Even after what she's done, there are still naysayers back there."

Cocoa looks eager to answer the general's question. "More than reasonably sure."

"Good enough." The general gets up and asks Corporal Lewis to join us. In an instant, she's there with a notepad.

"First, get me Secretary Stimson," the general orders. "Try his office, then his home. If you can't reach him, call his aide, Robert Patterson, and if you can't get him, John McCloy. After that, I'll need to speak to Admiral King, chief of naval operations in Washington. They're all in DC, for Christ's sake. Where nothing gets accomplished. They're all in the directory. Remember the two-hour time difference. If they're eating dinner, even if it's with Truman or Churchill or Jesus himself, tough shit. Got that, Corporal?"

"Yes, sir."

He eyes the phone on his desk. "Leave the door open. If anyone gives you the runaround, I'll come out there and reach through two thousand miles of phone line and ream them a new asshole."

Corporal Lewis tries unsuccessfully to rein in a grin. "Yes, sir."

"Speed is essential, Corporal Lewis."

"Yes, sir," She does an about face and hurries to the door, allowing herself enough time to throw a new version of her grin in Pete's direction.

Nothing escapes the general's gaze. "You making eyes at my secretary, Sergeant?"

"No, sir. Not exactly."

"You'd like to, though?"

"If the circumstances were right."

"'If the circumstances were right?' The circumstances are never right. You outrank her, for Christ's sake. On your way out, ask her for her phone number."

Pete glances through the open door at the corporal. She's on the phone, concentrating. "I'll do that, sir."

"Good. Captain Nelson, there's no reason to keep you hanging while I spread the word. Get these folks home, then call me. I'll let you know where we stand."

The general halfheartedly returns a couple of salutes and shakes my hand, rearranging my bones. With Cocoa, he's gentler, and he holds on. "I can't thank you enough, Cocoa," he says. "In a war full of heroes, you might just rise to the top."

I wait for her to say she doesn't want to be a hero, but I have no ability to predict the future. "Thank you," she says. Her eyes are glassy.

We follow her out of the general's office just as Corporal Lewis says, "I'm transferring Secretary Stimson, sir. As soon as you're done, I'll try Admiral King."

"Good, Lewis. But don't *try*. *Do* it."

"Yes, General."

She transfers the call. The captain, Cocoa, and I head for the door, but Pete lingers at the receptionist's desk. Glancing back, I see Corporal Lewis smiling, handing him a slip of paper.

Cocoa is ready for him when we get in the car. "'If the circumstances were right?'"

Pete turns and gives her a look. He's grinning. "Shut up, Future Girl."

# TWENTY-SIX

**M**om has decided to sleep on it. She's listened to us and talked to her boss and prayed for inspiration, but still she's torn.

*Stay or go?*

After she got home from work, and learned of Cocoa's predictions, and had a little time to mesh that news with everything else that's unsettling her life, she banished Dad to the sofa. She announced that she had a giant decision to make and she didn't want him distracting her.

The good news: Her boss told her she'd have her job whenever she returned, that he'd bring in temporary help if she chooses to leave.

The bad news: She'd have no income, and Dad was quick to point that out. Even with the government's promise of what the letter called a *Basic Allowance for Separated Dependents*, and food from the captain and Pete, money would be tight.

When I finally headed off to bed, Cocoa was in her room, Mom was in hers, Dad was on the sofa, and Pete and the captain were in their trailer. When we returned from Albuquerque the captain talked to General Groves, who told him that a massive operation was underway to secure Boston and New York Harbors. He asked that we talk to no one.

Loose lips, and all that.

By then, of course, Dad was in on it already, and Mom soon would be.

It's after midnight. Mom might be sleeping. She might be deciding. I open a book, *A Bell for Adano*, and try to read, because that's how I like to end my day. It's a good book, but all I can do is roll the uncertainties around in my mind.

I close *Adano* and turn off my lamp. The images from the library and movie theater run through my head. The aircraft carrier cruising into Boston Harbor, its waterfront and buildings, the skyscrapers of New York, ferries crossing the water, bridges, the Statue of Liberty, people everywhere.

Dad's predicament is also on my mind. *Where will they send him? For how long?*

At supper Cocoa offered to speak to General Groves about getting Dad out of it. The general wants her happy, she reasoned. Ditto the War Department bigshots. But Dad wouldn't hear of it. He wouldn't consider getting special treatment while others are sent away.

I picture Dad, behind barbed wire in some godforsaken concentration camp, sleeping on a cot, eating crap, armed soldiers in guard towers watching his every move like he's a criminal.

Except for Dad's steady snoring, the house is quiet. I go to my parents' room and knock.

"I'm awake," Mom says.

She switches on her bedside lamp as I enter the room. "I need to talk to you, Mom."

She sits up and pats the bed next to her. She's wearing one of Dad's white undershirts. There's no sign of sleep on her face. I sit.

"What is it, Bobby?"

"I don't know if you've decided."

"How *can* I?"

"You have to go."

Unconvinced, she waits for me to present my case.

"If you don't go with him, he'll just have his fanatical friends. And a bunch of trigger-happy soldiers."

"His friends aren't exactly fanatical."

"Ask Pete."

"Pete has an opinion. So does your dad. So do I."

"Boring, then. Annoying."

She smiles. "Probably."

"Dad needs you."

"What about you, Bobby? Don't you need me?"

"I'm almost sixteen. Pete and Cocoa and Captain Nelson are all living here, for Christ's sake."

"You don't need to use that language to show me how grown up you are. And you're not almost sixteen."

"I keep thinking of him all alone, Mom. Will they even let him have a typewriter? Paper? A pencil? Will they censor everything? He'll die of a broken heart. You have to go with him."

She takes both of my hands and closes her eyes. "What if we're gone a long time? Years?"

"I'll be even older. I bet they'll let me visit."

She goes silent. Dad's suitcase, packed but open, sits on the floor next to the closet door. He has more to add, probably. A toothbrush. Shaving gear. A photo or two.

Hopes. Dreams. Principles.

"On the high shelf in the closet," Mom says, "is my suitcase. Put it next to your dad's." She gets up. She's wearing a pair of Dad's boxers. They look like a skirt on her. She hugs me and I hug her back and we don't let go for a long time.

"I'm going to miss you terribly, Robert Hastings."

"I'll miss you terribly, too."

She opens a dresser drawer. "One suitcase. How am I going to do it?"

"Maybe they'll let me send you things."

"Maybe."

She pulls out some items—underwear and socks, mostly—and puts them on the bed. "More decisions," she says. "This could take all night. You don't have to be here."

"I know."

"Promise me you'll listen to Pete. He's become wise, and he loves you, and he'll do anything for you. Captain Nelson seems like a good man. I know he'll help if you need it."

"Okay."

"Swear you'll write?"

"I swear."

"There's one more thing I need to say, Bobby. I don't know what time we'll leave tomorrow, so I want to say it now."

"I doubt the FBI gets up early."

"Regardless." She pauses. "I've seen how you look at Cocoa."

"Cocoa?"

"You know, that skinny, mysterious, delightful girl from the future you found in the desert not long ago?"

"Rings a bell."

"I know you care for her, but while we're gone, you need to *care* for her. Watch out for her. And you need to be a gentleman, even if the memory of seeing her without her clothes on still haunts you." Her smile is slight enough to tell me she's not kidding. "She's mature beyond her years," she continues, "and she knows a million things we'll never know, but she's also unwell and vulnerable. And the world, literally, is being asked of her."

"I'll make sure nothing happens to her." I mean it as much as anyone can mean anything, but Mom isn't wrong about me being haunted. *Am I that transparent?*

"I'm sure you will." She studies my face. There's something else on her mind. "But don't let anything happen to yourself, either."

"Like?"

"Love is a double-edged sword, Bobby. She'd never mean to, but don't let her break your heart."

I barely sleep before Cocoa and I get up to do the route. Her nearness brings back Mom's words. I've never had a broken heart, but it doesn't sound like a good thing.

*How do you prevent it, though? Do you not give your heart*

*away? Is that possible, when your heart has yearnings of its own?*

We don't hurry. We small-talk Leo, sit together close, but not close enough, on the bench and roll the papers methodically, pedal distractedly to the base.

Cocoa has her own bag now—a big help, you'd think—but we plod through the route. We have new customers, and it takes time to decide where to deliver their papers, and a lot of preoccupied workers are scurrying around, getting in our way.

But slow is okay. When I think about what's coming—Mom and Dad leaving, and maybe more bombs—I can't think of a reason to hurry.

When we get home, two suitcases rest on the front steps. On Dad's is his brown fedora, on Mom's her gray roundish hat with the brim that keeps her forehead from wrinkling. Lolly, figuring something's up, watches from the porch. When we head for the back door, he tags along at Cocoa's heels, nosing at the pocket of her shorts. She takes out the acorn and lets him sniff it.

Everyone is up, sitting around the table. Pete and the captain are dressed in civvies, Mom and Dad are dressed for a visit to town. But they're not going to town.

"There they are," Pete says. His voice is full of fake cheer.

Mom's eyes are red and puffy. She's holding Dad's hand. Maybe she should be holding mine. I drop two copies of the *Journal* on the table. I glanced at it briefly in Leo's headlights. The front-page articles continue to cover the Norfolk disaster. Rumors flow, real information is scarce. The evacuation of pacifists is relegated to a page-two story. *Evacuation* makes it sound like they're being rescued. *From what? Their freedom? Their happiness? Their rights?*

"Anything exciting at the base camp this morning?" Mom asks. More fake cheer.

"A shooting star on the way there," Cocoa says. "A nearly full moon. Shadows on the desert sand. A galloping horse. All breathtaking."

"Busy," I say. "Lots of people up early, going places. New customers."

"Robert's throws were off target," Cocoa says. "Mine were

accurate." She gives me a grin. Everyone is trying to lighten the mood.

"Cocoa dreams a lot," I say. I hope it continues.

She and I are barely through the breakfast dishes when an unwelcome sound reaches us. A car on the road. Mom and Dad are outside, wandering, saying goodbye to the animals. I haven't even thought about Dad's chores, but Cocoa and I should be able to handle them. Another thing I haven't considered is how we'll get the Andrews sisters' milk and butter to town.

Least of our problems.

Everyone, even Lolly, meets the strange yet recognizable car near the front of the house. Pete and the captain are back in uniform. If the FBI guys are inclined to give my parents any shit, it won't be easy in the presence of two soldiers, both of whom have given and taken on fields of battle.

The front doors of the familiar car open and two familiar men get out. Browning and Swan. From the day of the bigwig party in our living room. They don't look happy to see us. We aren't happy to see them. They don their hats, like fedoras are part of their uniform.

Swan notices the two suitcases on the steps. "You're going, Mrs. Hastings?"

"Is my husband going?"

"Yes."

"Then so am I."

The sun has made its way into the yard. My parents put on their hats. Browning opens the trunk. "Ready?"

In answer, Dad and Mom exchange handshakes and hugs with those of us staying behind.

Murmurs and tears.

I feel empty.

"Mr. Unser will be here Tuesday and Friday mornings to take the milk and butter to the co-op, Bobby," Dad says before giving me a sighing, watery, crusher of a hug. "The payments will go into our account."

"I'll have everything ready."

Mom hugs everyone, even the captain, once more, saving me for last. I don't want to let her go. *When will I see her again?*

But Browning has the suitcases in the trunk. He slams the lid shut, shattering the quiet and putting an exclamation mark on the reason the two G-men are here.

Swan clears his throat. Pete glares at the uncaring asshole. I try to tell myself that he's just doing his job.

They get in. Doors close. In the back seat, hands wave, faces sag, tears glisten. In the front, eyes are everywhere but on us. Swan starts the car, maneuvers back and forth and away. Mom and Dad's faces appear in the rear window. We wave.

And they're gone.

Dust and exhaust.

Loss and foreboding.

Sunlight and darkness.

The lump in my throat almost cuts off my breathing. I blink away tears. The car is a black speck, but in my mind's eye it sprouts the wings of a giant hawk, safely carrying my parents to wherever it is they're going.

I look at Cocoa. She's trying on a brave face, but her eyes, overflowing, betray her. She's finally found a family, and now this.

But she still has me. Better than nothing.

# TWENTY-SEVEN

**W**e make it through the rest of Tuesday in an apprehensive daze. At Mom's "invitation," Pete has moved into my parents' bedroom. "To give me and the captain more stretching out room," he tells me with a wink.

Obviously, even after my promise to take care of Cocoa, Mom continued to fret about leaving Future Girl and me. Alone. Together. But Pete's nighttime presence won't bother me. Cocoa and I will still have time alone. And I have *almost* no thoughts of being anything but a gentleman.

When we're not feeding and milking and churning and cleaning and otherwise staying busy, we stick close to the phone. But there's nothing new from General Groves and no word from Mom and Dad.

The house is missing its heart and soul.

Lolly still has Cocoa. And me. But he mopes.

Wednesday arrives. Leo is waiting at the shack. The papers are stacked on the bench, higher than usual. Business continues to pick up.

"Sorry about your folks, Bobby," he says. He's a silhouette, leaning against the warmth of his old car's hood. The moon is low on the western horizon, but it's full, painting the desert in glow and shadow.

Cocoa and I drop our bikes in the sand. "Thanks. They'll be back soon." Confidence I don't feel.

"I hope so," he says. "But if you need anything—"

"My uncle Pete is living with us." I don't mention Captain Nelson. Leo doesn't know about the captain or the reason for his camping in our yard, and he won't find out from me.

"And he has me," Cocoa says. Inside, I smile. Laugh. Despite the lack of light, I'm pretty sure I see Leo's eyebrows rise.

"Good," he says. "That's good."

The sentries are being extra vigilant when we get to the checkpoint, holding up all vehicles to examine credentials before allowing them to move on. The camp itself is busier than ever. The engineers are out and moving in the dim predawn, not stopping to chat, business on their minds.

The day continues routinely. Home, radio, breakfast, chores, radio, lunch. Captain Nelson gets a call, but all I hear is a bunch of *yes-sirs* and a *thank you, sir* and he doesn't volunteer anything after hanging up. Cocoa and I go outside to pin up laundry on the backyard clothesline, and we stay out for a while, taking in the sunshine and fresh air. But we remain within shouting distance. Pete promised to yell if something happens.

Cocoa looks tired, jittery, serious. I can tell she has too much on her mind, yet she's trying to take on more. *What happens next? After Boston? After New York?*

As if he's sensed the pressure on her, Doctor Kersey shows up halfway through the afternoon. She and Lolly and me are in the barn when I hear his MG gearing down. By the time he parks, we're waiting near the front steps.

He says hello, asks Cocoa how she's doing, says he saw she had an appointment tomorrow and he knew with my parents gone it might be tough for her to keep it. He tells me he's sorry about the idiots sending them away. We invite him and his medical bag into the kitchen, where Pete sits at the table and the captain is on the phone. The radio spits out a Benny Goodman tune.

"Mind if Cocoa and I borrow the living room, Pete?" the doctor says. "I want her somewhere quiet so I can get a fix on her progress."

"Take your time," Pete says.

I sit with Pete, one ear in Cocoa's direction, one in the captain's, and page through the newspaper for the third or fourth time. I picture the instruments coming out of the black bag—stethoscope, otoscope, ophthalmoscope, blood pressure cuff, thermometer, reflex hammer, all the stuff voluptuous Marla once identified for me. I wonder what they're telling Doctor Kersey.

Still on the phone, the captain says, "She's with the doctor," and "We have the radio on, but we'll expect to hear from you first," and "We'll keep our fingers crossed, sir." He hangs up and comes to the table. "Nothing yet."

The doctor and Cocoa aren't gone long. Their voices build from a murmur and they reappear at the kitchen entrance. I study their faces for a verdict. Unsuccessfully.

"How is she?" I say.

"She's fine, Bobby," the doctor says, snapping his bag shut. "Keep feeding her. Keep getting her outside. Keep taking her on that paper route."

"She throws pretty good for a skinny girl," I say.

"Not Wonder Woman yet," the doctor says, circling his forefinger and thumb most of the way around her bare bicep. "But getting there."

"Future Girl," Pete says, and Cocoa smiles.

Captain Nelson walks Doctor Kersey to his car. I have a feeling the captain wants a more candid picture of his prize goose's health. When he comes back he looks the way I feel. Anxious.

The rest of the afternoon crawls. We're all afraid to leave the house. I picture Norfolk as it crumbles and smokes and bleeds.

*Is the same thing happening in Boston right now?*

Lolly goes out and comes in, goes out and comes in. He's used to luring us into a game of fetch or an expedition to the barn or an exploration of the desert surrounding our house. He's not used to this.

Cocoa and I are in the living room when the phone rings. In an instant, we're in the kitchen. Captain Nelson has the phone to his ear. The clock reads 4:55.

A cautious grin brightens the captain's face. "They're sure?"

From out of nowhere, Cocoa takes my hand. I already can't breathe, *and now this?* Pete, of course, notices. He looks away.

"It's the one, though?" the captain says. He pumps his fist high in the air.

The captain nods and nods. He says nothing, but his expression speaks for him.

"That's wonderful news, sir," he says finally. "Thank you for calling. Yes, I'll tell her. Them. Yes, I think we can manage that."

He hangs up. Cocoa is still holding my hand. Everyone's eyes are on Captain Nelson. His grin has turned into a full-fledged smile. He turns it on Cocoa.

"In case you haven't figured it out," he says, "that was General Groves. At a little after six o'clock on the East Coast, Navy destroyers on the outer reaches of Boston Harbor detected the presence of a U-boat. It had skirted one minefield and was approaching a series of steel nets strung up to protect the inner harbor. The destroyers pursued the submarine and sent it to the bottom. Ironically, it went down near an island called The Graves. They believe its entire crew is lost."

"They're certain it's the one?" Pete says.

"Nearly," the captain says. "But they're not relaxing their guard. And as soon as possible, divers are going down to attach lines so the wreck—and its cargo—can be towed out to sea."

"Will the public be told?" I ask.

"Soon. The harbor was essentially shut down and the military was everywhere, so there was no hiding the operation. The expectation—and fear—of Boston residents was that something was going to happen. Covering it up wouldn't work. And the War Department feels that after Norfolk the country needs some good news."

The kitchen radio has been all mumble and soft music. Pete turns it up loud enough to hear actual words.

"The general says there's no way to thank you, Cocoa," the captain says, "but that you deserve a mountain of ice cream. He says to keep up the good work, which I take to mean he wants you to keep thinking. Any new revelations in that remarkable brain?"

She shakes her head. "New York in two days," she says, "but now history has changed. Will their plans change?"

"She never stops thinking," I say. *Or doing.* Against all odds, she's turned fate on its ear, shown it can be done.

"Friday, if they go ahead with it," the captain says, "and Admiral King feels they will. He believes the U-boats are running silent, no communication in or out. If that's the case, the sub heading for New York won't know of the other one's sinking. Regardless, it won't know what we know."

"Will we be ready?" I say.

"Same as Boston," the captain says, "but more of everything—mines, nets, destroyers, torpedo planes, sonar, observers."

"The general said I deserve ice cream," Cocoa says. "I'm sure he meant *we.* So, Socorro? Slim's Diner?"

"Of course," the captain says. "And we'll start off with some dinner. On Uncle Sam. We've got a big reason to celebrate."

# TWENTY-EIGHT

## Wednesday, July 25–Saturday, July 28

There's still no word from my parents. Wednesday ends. Thursday slips past.

When we get home from the route Friday morning, our soldiers are already up and, as usual, in the kitchen drinking coffee, listening to the radio, waiting. I put Dad's paper on the table. It's full of news of the cleanup in Norfolk and the near-miss for Boston.

Tens of thousands dead.

Tens of thousands who didn't die.

The men in Washington owe Cocoa more than a chocolate sundae.

"I have a bad feeling, Captain Nelson," Cocoa says. "More shit. Huge. But so far it's just a feeling."

"That's okay, Cocoa," he says. "We know you're doing your best. This is a tough day, with all the anticipation."

"The fear makes noise in my head," she says.

"All of our heads," he says.

I make a fresh pot of coffee. Thanks to the generosity of the Army, we can drink it like water while we listen to the radio and worry and prop each other up.

Cocoa sits at the table with Pete and the captain and the *Journal*. By the time I sit, she's back up, pacing. She glares at the calendar and clock, daring them to tell her something. A date. A time. If we had a map on the wall, she'd glare at that, too.

A place.

"The next bombs won't be here," she says. "Not America."

"Oh?" Pete says. Nobody says *Where?*

But she knows questions are on everyone's mind. "I still don't know where," she says. "Or when. Soon, is all I know."

"Would it help to go back to the library?" I ask. "The movie theater?"

"I don't think I saw films of the next attack. Attacks. Everything is hazy. Phantoms and mumblings."

"Don't worry about it," the captain says. "You've alerted us to a looming disaster. When we get past that, we'll concern ourselves with what might happen next."

"*Did* happen next," Cocoa says.

"It's too early in the morning for my brain to sort that out," Pete says.

"But maybe it *didn't* happen," I say. "*Won't* happen. It did, but it didn't, I mean. Ebenezer Scrooge got a chance to alter his fate. You've already done it once, Cocoa. You'll do it again."

Pete and the captain nod, but Cocoa looks at me blankly. I decide *A Christmas Carol* isn't—won't be—on a shelf of her library. While my head spins, I tell her about Ebenezer Scrooge.

"Fiction," she says.

"But you're not," I say, marveling at this amazing girl standing in my kitchen. *How did I—and the world—get so lucky?*

During breakfast Mr. Unser arrives, but other than our brief time helping him load the milk and butter into the cavernous trunk of his Packard, Cocoa and I stay near the phone for the rest of the morning. After lunch, Pete and Captain Nelson drive to the base camp to meet with General Groves, who is checking on the progress of all the renewed activity.

I picture a flash of light and a thunderous sound and a biting wind and a mushroom cloud, and I wonder about more tests. *If the bomb worked once, won't it work again? Are the scientists and the men who give them orders willing to waste one?*

While Cocoa listens for the phone, I take advantage of "the cats" being away to drive the DeSoto to the mailbox. Aside from a bill from Ma Bell, there's nothing. I try to picture Mom and Dad, where they are, what they're doing.

To get my mind off our shared predicament, I turn onto the empty road and head east. I've never shifted gears for real, but my practice has paid off, and soon I'm rolling along with the wind blasting in the open windows and the engine singing to me.

I turn around at the Unsers' place. Cocoa and Lolly are waiting for me when I drive up to our house like a big shot and forget to put in the clutch and kill the engine. I get out, trying not to look sheepish.

"You are a good driver, Robert," Cocoa says. She has her acorn in her open hand, and as usual Lolly is focused on it.

"I need more practice."

"Any mail?"

I sit next to her, show her the bill. She's wearing shorts, and her knees don't look as bony. Her thighs no longer look like calves. They're no longer pasty white. They look nice. In the kitchen, Sinatra's "I'll Never Smile Again" flows out of the radio. With Cocoa beside me, I can't imagine never smiling again.

"Maybe tomorrow," she says. "Maybe they will call."

"Maybe."

"They are thinking of you every minute."

"And you," I say. "Before they left, Mom told me you've been a gift to them."

She doesn't respond. Her eyes are watery.

It's nearly four when Pete and the captain return. The living room is farther from the phone but cooler than the kitchen, so we migrate there with a pitcher of lemonade. A late afternoon breeze stirs the gauzy white curtains and softens the mutterings of the radio newsman.

I do some calculations. It's approaching eight o'clock in New York. "You're sure it's today?" I ask Cocoa, who's sitting a proper distance away from me on the sofa because neither of us is ready for aggravation from Pete and the captain. It's a dumb question. How can she be *sure?* But it slipped out through my loose lips.

"They could have changed their plans," she says. "If the submarine is receiving communications, it will be aware of Boston."

"U-boats don't need light to do their shit," Pete says. "Until we got a better handle on how to deal with them, they hunted Allied ships like packs of wolves, camouflaged by darkness."

"We have four hours left before it's no longer Friday on the East Coast," the captain says. "Six before it ends here."

"I don't know what time zone my memories occupy," Cocoa says.

"Even Future Girls can't know everything," Pete says.

Captain Nelson and Pete volunteer to cook supper. It involves eggs, so Cocoa and I visit the hen house. We collect an even dozen, then head to the barn to say hello to the unnamed sow and her anonymous piglets and our friends the Andrews sisters.

Captain Nelson has an Italian grandmother. He recreates her homemade noodles while Pete crafts Mom's spaghetti sauce—compliments of the Army.

Cocoa and I set the table and return to the living room. We share the couch. A foot of cushion separates us, spanned by the linking of our hands. Our fingers sweat, but neither of us lets go. Strength in numbers, but more than that.

Not for the first time, I wonder what it would be like to share a kiss.

But I've gotten used to not pushing her. And I'm a coward.

Mouth-watering aromas have saturated the living room air when the phone rings. We get to the kitchen in time to see the captain answer. Pete is at the stove, mothering his sauce, but all of his attention—and all of ours—is on the captain.

He listens. A grin appears and breaks into a smile, and he gives us all a thumbs-up.

A *thumbs-up.* I think of the Sinatra song. We all have a reason to smile, and we do.

"Yes, sir," the captain says. "She *did* do it again." His eyes go to Cocoa. "We *will* do something special for her."

He hangs up. "Same story," he says. "Same terrific story." The words erupt. "With a twist. A Navy torpedo bomber—with the appropriate name *Avenger*—spotted the U-boat near the surface fifteen miles from New York. The bomber disabled it with a torpedo and sent it to the bottom with a two-thousand-pound bomb."

We cheer. We pat Cocoa on the back. For the first time, I give her a real hug, and she hugs me back.

I can count every rib.

"Will they send divers down?" I ask, imagining that unexploded atomic bomb so close to our coast and remembering the heat and fire of the test bomb rising over the desert. I see images of Norfolk, ruined, in my head. "So it can be towed away?"

"Unless it's too deep," the captain says. "If it is, it's unlikely to be a problem. Unless you're a mackerel."

"What about the news?" I say. "Will the newspapers and radio stations be told?"

"I don't know," the captain says. "They haven't decided yet. We want people to know we're protecting them from the bad guys, but we don't want them to think the bad guys are everywhere."

"The *something special*," Cocoa says. "When can we do that?"

Pete chuckles. "You don't miss a beat, do you, Future Girl?"

"Not tonight, unfortunately," the captain says, glancing around the kitchen at the supper makings. "We've got our meal going, and it's getting late."

"Tomorrow, possibly?" she says.

"Tomorrow's Saturday," the captain says. "Perfect. What's your pleasure?"

"I liked Albuquerque. I liked the library and movie theater. I liked Big Muddy."

"Big Muddy?" the captain asks. "Why does that sound familiar?"

"An Army horse," I say. "The day we met you, Pete rode her over from the base camp."

"I remember," the captain says.

"You want to see Big Muddy?" Pete asks Cocoa.

"I want to sit in her saddle."

"You want to ride her?" Suddenly I'm jealous. Cocoa's a hero and all that, and General Groves said she should get to do something special, *but what about me?* I'm her friend, or pal, or sidekick. And I'm practically an orphan.

"She's a lady," Pete tells Cocoa. "You're a featherweight. A match made in heaven."

Saturday arrives. Although the sinking of the U-boat in Boston Harbor was big news everywhere, there's been nothing on the radio about New York, and there's no mention in this morning's *Journal.*

After breakfast, we all head to Albuquerque. At the library, Cocoa goes through the world maps and atlases again, but there's no breakthrough this time. After lunch it's the Ranch Theater, where she sits on the edge of her seat watching a new newsreel documenting the advance of Allied forces through Germany.

She enjoys the feature movie, *A Tree Grows in Brooklyn,* so much that we almost stay to watch it again. But it's nearly a two-hour drive to the base camp, where she has a date with Big Muddy, and she doesn't want to miss it.

The fact that Pete and the captain are wearing civvies doesn't slow us down as we pass the base camp sentries. We continue on to the stables. As soon as Pete turns off the engine, Cocoa leaps out and hurries to the stable doors with me on her tail. Inside there's warmth and gloom and a single horse, gazing at us curiously from her stall.

Big Muddy.

While Pete saddles her, we feed her carrots from our garden. Peace offering, but she's been peaceful from the start. She could be one of Dad's pals. But the government would probably lock her up, too. Guilt by association.

I'm sure we're a curious sight as we emerge from the stable, but we're a distance away from the main hustle and bustle of the camp, and nobody has time to come snooping.

After Pete helps Cocoa get her foot in the stirrup, she swings herself into the saddle like she's been doing it her whole life. "I like this," she says. An understatement.

Pete takes the reins and leads horse and rider around the area. They circle the stables, disappearing for a moment. When they reappear, Cocoa has the reins in her hands, coaxing Big Muddy left and right with the reins and her scrawny knees. Her smile won't quit.

Eventually I get a turn, too. Not my first time on a horse, but my first time on Big Muddy. My first time with Cocoa watching.

In the lush light of the setting sun, she radiates a light of her own.

# TWENTY-NINE

The days slip past. A letter finally arrives from Mom and Dad. Along with other pacifists and COs from southwestern states, they've been interned at Gila River Japanese American War Relocation Center in Arizona.

They have an apartment next to a Japanese American couple from California. The wife's mother was living with them until recently, when the heat killed her. Since then, everyone has been warned to stay out of their living-quarters-turned-ovens during the day.

I recall reports of Allied discoveries in Poland, Ukraine, Yugoslavia, Belarus, and now Germany: concentration camps with real ovens, where humans were reduced to ashes.

Gila River must be a hellish place, but at least my parents aren't facing extermination.

Mom has already been elected a block manager. Dad is cooking in the cafeteria.

He's traded his typewriter for a stove.

I write back, keeping my words upbeat—battle victories for the Allies, Pete's bad jokes, my bad cooking, the piglets' weight gain, the Andrews sisters' milk production, our trip to Albuquerque with Pete and Captain Nelson, Cocoa's ride on Big Muddy. I tell them about Cocoa's prediction coming true for Boston, but I leave them wondering about New York. So far, silence is the government's official position on New York, and I'll respect it.

A sunken ship shouldn't lead to loose lips.

In her odd, homegrown handwriting, Cocoa adds a *P.S.: We are missing you. Take care of yourselves. I can throw a newspaper better than Robert now.*

Each day she looks healthier. More color, more weight. Her hair looks less cobwebby. It's like she's feeding off the news on the radio and in the *Journal*, news continuing what we saw in the newsreel—the Allies moving into Germany almost unopposed. A hundred thousand men have crossed the Rhine and are swarming into the Black Forest, on their way to Berlin.

But despite all the good news, despite the fact that Hitler's plans were foiled in Boston and New York and no more bombs have shown up in US waters or blown up elsewhere, she's convinced something bad is on the horizon.

Pete and Captain Nelson are away for the morning, getting the living room radio repaired and meeting with General Groves. The general has called the captain regularly, but there's been little to pass on. Cocoa feels the burden.

Today's *Journal*—Saturday, August 4, 1945—sits between us on the kitchen table. As usual, she's gone through it and through it, but that doesn't stop her from eyeing it again, looking for something to get her going down a path that will lead to something else.

"Nothing there?" I've also looked—several times. The kitchen radio was on, but the repetition grew annoying, and we turned it off.

"I don't like this, Robert." She points at a headline: *ALLIES ROLL TOWARD BERLIN.* And another: *"INVINCIBLE" GERMAN ARMY ON RETREAT.* Below that, a third: *TONS OF INCENDIARY BOMBS RAIN DOWN ON TOKYO.*

"What's not to like?"

"The feeling I have. I had it for a moment when we were watching the newsreel at the theater, and in the days since, it has haunted me." She gets out her good-luck acorn and sets it on the table. At our feet, Lolly stirs.

"A feeling," I say.

"I feel even less adequate when you mock me, Robert. All of my recollections begin that way. This one simply doesn't want to progress."

"I'm not mocking you. I'm just trying to understand what you're experiencing."

She jabs at the front page. "My feeling tells me something isn't right with all this success."

"Have you told the captain?"

"I told him what I'm telling you. He has passed it on, but what good is it? I have nothing specific. Does it make sense for good news to be bad news?"

I shake my head. Not to me it doesn't.

"If I get something else right, will Peter and the captain let me ride Big Muddy again?"

"Even if you never get another thing right."

"I have to get more things right, Robert." She taps the front page again. "Hitler has something else up his sleeve."

"You will," I say. I get brave and put my hand over hers. It doesn't feel as bony. She leans toward me, and for an exciting, frightening instant I think she's going to kiss me.

But instead she brushes a crumb of toast away from the corner of my mouth, making me feel like a little kid. But she doesn't pull her hand away from mine. "And in the meantime, I can keep your face clean."

"They're both important."

"Do you think tomorrow will work, Robert? For Big Muddy?"

"As long as it's okay with our soldiers, we should have all afternoon for her."

She gets up from the table, holding onto my hand. "Let's go outside, Robert."

# THIRTY

**P**ete and the captain return from town, but we've barely plugged in the radio and switched it on when the regular program—a soap opera called *Front Page Farrell* that Dad once listened to religiously—gets interrupted by a newscaster's familiar but static-peppered voice. The broadcast comes from London, and although there's no introduction, I'm pretty sure the man behind the voice is Edward R. Murrow.

"Treachery is the word from the Allied front tonight, ladies and gentlemen. Extreme treachery. Reports from the rear guard of an Allied force estimated at a hundred thousand men indicate that at approximately 9:15 p.m. German local time—3:15 in our nation's capital—Nazi forces carried out a battlefield attack unparalleled in military history. In death and destruction, it is rivalled only by the bomb that exploded in Norfolk, Virginia, last month.

"The Allied force—chiefly American troops—was halted for the night when the attack occurred. Distant eyewitnesses with binoculars say a single plane—a suicide bomber—dropped a single bomb. All signs point to it being an atomic weapon similar to the one used in Norfolk. The immediate result was widespread annihilation. Some of those at the periphery of the impact are attempting to flee back across the Rhine and into France, but many are wounded or sickened. Many are dying. The German army and air forces, emboldened, are in pursuit.

"Your thoughts and prayers for our brave men, and for their families and friends, will be most welcome in the coming hours and days.

"I'm signing off for now to return you to your station, but as more information is forthcoming, either I or another CBS correspondent will dispatch it to you.

"So long, and good luck."

We sit. Next to me, Cocoa melts into the sofa. Her face is pale. Her eyes are glassy. "Sorry," she says. "Sorry, Captain Nelson."

"It's Jack, Cocoa," the captain says, enlightening me, too. "Please call me Jack. And you've no reason to be sorry. Without you, we'd be oh-for-four. The Nazis would be dancing in the streets."

"They *are* dancing," she says. "Hitler. His monsters."

"The Allies' easy advance," I say to her. "You weren't fooled, but they were."

"Suckered," Pete says.

"I should have remembered," she says. "The newsreel, the news reports. Now, too late, the memories return."

"Does this trigger anything else?" Pete says.

"It should," she says. "Because there is more. Much more. And something else has already happened. Something we don't yet know about. Everything's foggy. Dark."

"The Germans have more bombs?" Captain Jack says.

"They do, and the raw materials to produce them. There is . . . a secret facility." She closes her eyes and goes through all the facial contortions of straining to think. Reaching back.

"Not to put more pressure on you, Cocoa," the captain says, "but if you could unearth only one more nugget, that facility would be everyone's first choice. A matchless target. Twenty-four karat gold."

She nods, taps at her temple. "I know it's in here. But masked."

"Would a map of Germany help?" I ask.

"There are maps at the base camp," Pete says.

"Germany is now the focus for bomber pilots training at Kirtland," Captain Jack says. "They'll have maps of Germany in every ready room."

"Will they let us have one?" Cocoa says.

"They'll let us have whatever General Groves tells them to let us have," Pete says.

On cue, the phone rings. While I turn off the radio, the captain hurries to the kitchen.

No surprise; it's the general. After Captain Jack tells him we've heard the news, he asks about Cocoa. The captain tells him what she said about more bombs and a secret bomb-making facility. He asks the general about maps.

He returns to the living room with a plan. "In an hour and a half, we're meeting the general's courier in Socorro. The courier will bring maps and anything else the general believes will help. If you have anything you need to do before we leave, you have an hour to do it."

# THIRTY-ONE

Our rendezvous spot is Slim's Diner. Pete angle-parks at the curb. We roll down the windows and wait. Serious business, but Captain Nelson—Jack—has a spark of mischief in his eye.

After a few minutes, an army-green Chevrolet sedan parks next to us. When the driver gets out and tucks her hair under her hat, I grasp the reason for Captain Jack's mood. The courier, looking snappy in her WAC uniform, is Corporal A. E. Lewis, the general's secretary. *Is the captain, or the general, trying to play cupid?*

We get out. The corporal smiles in Pete's direction. I wonder if he's talked to her since the day they met at Kirtland. If he has, he's kept it to himself. She has a large manila envelope under her arm.

"You have time for supper, Corporal?" Captain Jack says. "We have to feed this crew, anyway, and it would make your long trip worthwhile."

"Oh, it's already worthwhile, sir," she says, glancing at Pete. "But supper would be a real treat." She has a mild accent. *Midwest, maybe?*

Inside, we crowd into a booth. Corporal Lewis sits next to Pete, who tells us that the A. E. stands for Amy Elizabeth, which removes most of the formality attached to her uniform.

Despite the chilling report from the front, the meal—burgers and fries—is fun. And tasty. Pete practically floats all the way back to our place.

He comes down, though—we all come down—when we turn on the kitchen radio.

Bad news. Again.

A guy with a British accent reports that at approximately the same time as the bomb fell on Allied forces in Germany, a similar attack was initiated on a massive assembly of Russian troops bivouacked in western Poland, preparing for the push to Berlin. There are untold casualties, and the survivors are in full retreat. The report was delayed because of the extent of destruction. Nearby civilian populations, many of them recently liberated from German rule, were also victims of the bomb.

In spite of everything that Dad has ever modeled for me and told me and tried to inject into my head, part of me suddenly itches to hitchhike to Socorro and go to the Army recruiting office and lie about my age and sign up. Another part of me feels like I've already been through a battle—shell-shocked and paralyzed.

Numb. Useless. Tits on a bull.

Cocoa has her own response. She removes a collection of maps from the manila envelope. Most are of Germany, but there's one of the entire continent of Europe and at least one of all of the countries currently or formerly occupied by the Germans or on the German border—France, Austria, Belgium, Luxembourg, the Netherlands, Switzerland, Sweden, Norway, Denmark, Czechoslovakia, Yugoslavia, Poland, Ukraine, Belarus. We help her thumbtack them to the walls of the kitchen. When we get short on space we hang the least likely three, France, Sweden, and Switzerland, in the living room. We've already kicked the Nazis' asses out of France, and Sweden and Switzerland are supposedly neutral.

We tag along as Cocoa tours the maps, pausing at each. She spends extra time on Germany.

After her third time through, I risk sidetracking her concentration. "Anything?"

"I need two separate breakthroughs," she says. "One for the location of the factory where the bombs are produced. And, even more urgent, for the location of the next attack."

"Still not the US?" Pete says.

"I'm not certain. But something tells me—*reminds* me—that the Nazis' attention has switched to Europe, where delivering a bomb will be easier."

Morning arrives. By the time I get up and dressed, Cocoa is out of bed and pacing through the house. She must have raided the clean laundry basket, because she's wearing one of my T-shirts and my Navy boxers.

I tell her good morning, but she doesn't respond. Her focus is on the map of Europe tacked to the kitchen wall. Soon she'll have all the maps carved indelibly in her brain.

Finally, radiating frustration, she tears herself away and gets dressed. We ride to the shack, say hello to Leo, and hurry through the route in record time for a Sunday, despite the fat papers and a further increase in camp traffic. The news from Europe has raised the stakes again.

When we get home the Army car is gone and there's a note from Pete on the kitchen table:

> *Bobby and Future Girl—Turn on the radio. Hitler has given the rest of the world an ultimatum. Churchill has already responded. Truman will speak to the nation at eight a.m.*
>
> *General Groves called just after you left for your route. We're leaving for Kirtland now, but should be back by this afternoon.*
>
> *You're the best!*
>
> *Pete*

After we switch on the radio, the newsman goes on and on about demands and summarizes the mad man's ultimatum: Withdraw from continental Europe and its surrounding waters; cease all bombing; halt aggression against Japan.

And last but definitely not least: *Surrender*. Cede all political power to the two remaining Axis countries. If not, beginning in three days, more bombs will be detonated. More lives, civilian and military, will be lost. Hundreds of thousands. Millions. The bombing will not cease.

"No!" Cocoa says. She's back to studying her maps.

The newsman continues. Churchill responded in less than an hour. His speech was short but to the point. "Vermin do not make demands. Vermin are hunted down and trapped and exterminated. We will never fear your threats nor accede to your so-called ultimatums. Never. The Allied forces will fight on, for the good of our countries and the world."

"The fight went on," Cocoa says, "but it was futile."

"We're going to change that. Right?"

"Right," she says, forcing a smile.

"You've already changed things," I remind her. And myself.

"Only a start, Robert."

At eight o'clock President Truman comes on the air. His voice isn't as commanding as President Roosevelt's, his words aren't as eloquent as Prime Minister Churchill's, but when he sums up his address, his meaning is clear. "We will never surrender. Hitler and Hirohito and the rest of the scum of the world can go to hell."

# THIRTY-TWO

## Monday, August 6

The kitchen light is on when I get up Monday morning. Cocoa is again studying the map of Europe, but this time when I say good morning, she says good morning back, and there's a light in her eyes. We're down to two days on Hitler's ultimatum, but there's a light.

"What?" I say.

"England," she says. "I remember. England is next."

A few minutes later we're all at the table. Lolly circles us. His morning routine hasn't been routine.

"Cocoa?" Captain Nelson says. "You've got something?" His dark hair is short but, fresh out of bed, it's sticking out in several directions. Cocoa dips her fingers in her glass of water and pats it down. He doesn't object. Anything for the precious goose. I feel a twinge of something I suppose is jealousy. *Has she ever tried to fix my unruly hair?*

"England," she says. "After Hitler's ultimatum and the responses from Churchill and Truman, I recalled that Hitler has a hard-on for Churchill. England has been a thorn in Hitler's side since the start of the war. Resisting invasion. Outfighting the famed Luftwaffe. Bringing in Canada and America. Bombing Germany."

"When?" Pete says.

"He's not lying about the timing of his next strike. His forecast of three days is correct." She glances at the calendar. "Two."

"Do you recall the city?" The captain is up and moving toward the phone. "How the bomb is delivered?"

She shakes her head. "I would say London, but that's little more than a guess. Likewise, for how the bomb arrives. I don't remember. Maybe I never knew."

"Good enough," Captain Jack says, self-consciously running his hand through his hair.

After failing to reach General Groves at his office, the captain finds him at his quarters. At the end of their conversation, Cocoa gets an invitation to talk.

"Hello," she says when the captain hands her the phone. There's a timid note in her voice that's new to me. But this is General Groves. "Thank you. I wish I could remember more." She pauses. "Yes, the maps helped. They helped me recall that England was—is—a target. Now I am hoping they *vill* provide some insight on the bomb-making plant."

Another pause. "I am eating more than ever. Sleeping well, when my thoughts don't needle me too much. Fresh air and exercise, too. Robert and I ride to the base camp every morning to do his newspaper route."

More listening. "You're welcome." She hands the phone to the captain.

The rest of Captain Nelson's conversation with the general consists mostly of *yes-sirs*. He hangs up. "He told me you deserve another outing, Cocoa. Can you think of anything?"

"I think Big Muddy misses me," she says without hesitating.

"I'm sure she does," Pete says. "We'll get you there for sure. But why don't you and Robert try to come up with something bigger, too?"

We spend the rest of the morning thinking about possibilities while we have breakfast and do chores and the captain has more conversations with General Groves. After each of them he tells us what they've discussed, hoping, I suppose, to dislodge something in Cocoa's brain.

"They're figuring on London," he says after the most recent call, "while also fortifying defenses at other major ports. Because Germany's surface ships would be easy targets, and the Luftwaffe is skeletal, they believe another U-boat may be the means. But, just in case, the RAF and Army Air Force will have extra patrols in the air."

The captain's reports don't free any of Cocoa's memories. After lunch, I talk her into taking a walk. Pete and the captain have promised us a visit to Big Muddy once the day cools.

We head out of the yard and into its vast surroundings. The sounds and smells change. Heat rises from the sand. We enter a maze of sagebrush, cactus, yucca, mesquite, burrows of small critters. Whenever we near a low-growing plant or collection of plants that might provide a hiding spot for a snake, I scan for shapes, patterns, shadows, coils, rattles, movement. The desert has its own dangers.

"It makes me feel small, Robert," Cocoa says, staring into the blue above us, at its puffy white clouds. "You should look up sometimes."

"And you should look down. A rattlesnake would like to latch onto one of those skinny ankles of yours."

"I have seen worse than rattlesnakes," she says.

"I feel sorry for you. But a diamondback won't care what you've seen."

We keep going, heading west, parallel to the mountains. Getting some peace and quiet. Some room for Cocoa to breathe and shed a little of the load. She looks down occasionally but spends most of her time gazing at the sky, the hills, white-winged doves and red-tailed hawks and meadowlarks taking flight at our approach. Like she can't believe any of it.

We pause and share a drink from my canteen. I let her go first, which allows me to think about her lips touching the cool metal barely an instant before mine.

I peer back toward the house, but it's gone from view. We could be a hundred miles from here. We could be a hundred years in the past.

*But not a hundred years in the future.* Not in Cocoa's world. In Cocoa's world, there would be no plants. There would be no blue sky. The clouds would be dark and poisonous. A writhing knot of snakes.

We've been quiet. A pocket gopher slips out of its burrow ten feet away, sits up, and gives us a once-over. It lets Cocoa get within five feet before it scurries back to its front porch.

"Not as friendly as Big Muddy," I say, thinking about our late afternoon appointment with the kindly mare, and the captain telling us to come up with a bigger sort of outing also.

"Just shy," Cocoa says. She crouches, making herself smaller, but the gopher takes the movement as a threat. It scrambles into the opening, which looks exactly like a miniature cave, and disappears into the black.

The shadowy hollow sparks a memory. Something Pete once told me. "Have you ever been inside a cave, Cocoa?"

She sheds her disappointment at the exit of her little friend. "A cave?"

"Pete discovered one near Carlsbad when I was little—five or six. He says it looked like nobody else had ever been there. He kept its location a secret, but he told me he'd take me to see it when I was older. By the time I was older, though, he was off fighting the war."

"Carlsbad?"

"A town—four or five hours east of here. But Captain Jack wants you to pick out something extra special to do. And Pete said it was amazing. Stalagmites, stalactites, pools, all that stuff."

"I've seen photos of those things. I'd like to visit this cave, Robert."

"Let's go tell the fellows you've made a choice."

# THIRTY-THREE

We leave after breakfast. A four-hour drive, according to Pete. Last night he spent an hour studying a map and estimating distances between places—landmarks, hills and valleys and creeks, dirt roads—that he'd penciled in. After all the time and turmoil, I wonder about his calculations.

Next to me in the back seat, Cocoa studies the map while Lolly hogs the window on the other side. Cocoa's our official navigator, but so far we're traveling regular roads—desert and mountains and desert again—and Pete's choices are obvious.

When I'm not stealthily watching Cocoa, I gaze out the windows and think about Mom and Dad and wonder about their surroundings. Dad has shown me photos of the Japanese American camps: plywood and tarpaper barracks, barbed wire, kids playing in the dirt, sentries with rifles aimed in, not out. *But what do he and Mom see when they look beyond the fences and sentry towers?*

With a name like Gila River, it's not hard to imagine: Rough. Hostile. Venomous.

Cocoa knows monsters, *but does she know Gila monsters?*

We pass an intersection with Highway 13 on our left.

"In about five miles we cross a river," Cocoa says, studying Pete's notes. "After that, go another mile or two to a dirt road marked by an old juniper tree. Take a right there."

"Thanks, Future Girl," he says.

"Enjoying yourself so far?" the captain asks her. He's been quiet, reading notes, writing his own. A busy guy, but he has one main focus—Cocoa.

"The world is so remarkable," she says.

"Wait till you see the cave," Pete says.

A bridge takes us across a shallow river. Two minutes later a gnarled juniper appears. Pete turns onto a two-track dirt road. We buck and bounce until the car settles into the ruts.

"Two miles," Cocoa says. "Mushroom-shaped boulder on the left. Livestock path behind it. Drivable for a mile, until we reach a creek. Park and walk. Follow the creek bed uphill."

"To a canyon," Pete says. "You're gonna be impressed. Both of you." He glances at Captain Nelson. "All of you."

The mushroom-shaped boulder is unmistakable. I picture a huge cloud, rising, blooming. We turn and follow the path. The car growls uphill to the banks of a creek.

We park and drink water from our canteens. From the trunk, Pete takes out a rope, a compass, a first aid kit, four flashlights, a box of batteries, and a knapsack full of peanut butter and jelly sandwiches weighted down with oranges at the bottom. He and the captain divvy everything up, and then we're off, following the creek upstream.

Lolly lopes ahead of us, peeing on everything, then returns to trot alongside Cocoa. I remember when he was *my* dog.

I can feel the altitude. And the heat. Like Pete and the captain, I'm in shorts and a T-shirt, but after five minutes I'm sweating. Ahead of me, Cocoa, wearing shorts and a thin blue blouse, seems to have no trouble keeping up. But her breathing sounds ragged.

There's little conversation. We save our breath. Soon the

opening of a canyon looms on our left, and Pete veers in that direction.

We go up, down, around, through shadow and out, and then, for a half mile or more, down. The canyon floor is littered with rubble from the surrounding cliffs. The air cools.

"Feel that?" Pete says. He leads us around a bend and down through more rubble. The temperature continues to drop. The only sound is Lolly's panting.

Standing against the base of the cliff is a pillar-like rock, buried deep. About fifteen feet of it protrudes from the ground. From somewhere nearby comes a stream of cold air. And the stench of an extra-tangy variety of chicken shit.

Lolly sniffs along the pillar's base. When he disappears behind it, we follow. In the shadows there's a thorny bush, eight or nine feet tall, guarding an opening where cliff face meets ground. It's maybe four feet high, three wide. Beyond it is blackness. I think of the pocket gopher scrambling into its hole.

"Nothing's changed," Pete says. "Even this acacia was here. Smaller, of course. I got a few scratches from it. So be careful."

He checks his flashlight, the rest of us check ours, and we follow him in, ducking and duck-walking. As we move ahead and down, the ceiling gets taller. We can stand.

"What is the stink?" Cocoa says.

"You'll see soon," Pete says. Ahead of us, the beam of his flashlight fades into nothingness.

We keep descending. The temperature keeps falling. If it was ninety outside, it's now seventy. The passageway widens. Another opening appears on our right, and Pete chalks an X next to it on the rock.

The walls and ceiling continue to recede. We continue to move down. It's colder. Sixty.

The path winds to the right, drops steeply. "Flashlights off," Pete says. His is the lone light as we keep going. At one point, he slows and I bump into Cocoa's butt. She doesn't complain.

The smell is thick enough to slice. Lolly's toenails click. All around us is echoing blackness. Out of it comes the sound of falling water.

Finally, Pete stops. "Turn 'em back on," he says.

We do. For an instant, I'm alarmed. We're in a giant open area. In front of us are figures, stretching from the floor to wherever the ceiling might be. *Monsters?*

No. Rock formations. Stalagmites.

We raise our flashlights. High above us, hanging from the ceiling, are more formations—stalactites. Some reach down to meet the stalagmites, forming pillars, relics from an ancient Greek temple. I sense movement. Fluttering. I move my flashlight beam across the ceiling. Unfolding. Folding. Wings. Glimmer. Eyes.

"Bats," I say. "Thousands." Lolly whines. His nose must be clogged with the smells.

"At least," Pete says. Near us, near the wall, the ground is mostly unblemished rock and sand. But a few feet away, where the overhead concentration of flying mammals begins, it's covered with a thick carpet of bat shit, a zillion years' worth.

We sweep our beams around the giant space—walls, ceiling, columns, floor. I decide Pete's right. There's no sign of anyone else. Ever. The thought is overwhelming to me, and maybe to Cocoa, too. She's gone quiet. I aim my flashlight at her face for a moment, but I can't read anything. She flashes me a distracted smile.

"In San Francisco we have hills," Captain Nelson says. "Bridges and fog. Nothing like this fairy tale place. Magic, dwarves, goblins."

I know what he means. "*The Hobbit,*" I say, picturing Smaug the dragon and a cavernous room full of gold and jewels. And bones, human or near-human.

"Exactly," the captain says. Cocoa adds nothing. *Wouldn't they have* The Hobbit *in her future library? Or would Hitler have banned it? Would he have seen himself in its monsters and monstrous ambitions?*

"Ready to move on?" Pete says.

He and the captain start off. But Cocoa stays, slowly playing her flashlight beam off the walls and ceiling and rock formations and finally the ground. Lolly doesn't budge. Neither do I.

"Something wrong?" I say.

"Nothing's wrong."

"Water?" I hold out my canteen, and she takes a drink. I follow, imagining again. An almost-kiss. Ahead of us, two flashlights halt.

"We spoke of déjà vu once, Robert," she says. "In the barn. When I barely knew you."

"I remember. It happens to me sometimes."

"I'm having that feeling again."

"It's weird, isn't it?"

"More than that," she says.

"What do you mean?"

She doesn't answer. We move ahead, catch up to Pete and the captain, and continue walking. The water sounds grow louder. The air dampens. My skin erupts with goosebumps, and when Cocoa reaches back to take my hand, my goosebumps multiply.

We enter a wide tunnel that eventually opens into another room that's half as big as the one we just left. Here are more rock formations and another ceiling carpeted with bats. When Pete aims his flashlight at a wall, a waterfall appears.

Winding through stalagmites, treading on centuries-old layers of petrified bat shit, we approach a circular pool where the falls splash down. We look into its clear depths and I imagine a lost ring, and Gollum, lurking in the shadows.

"I wouldn't drink it," Pete says. "Not with bat city overhead."

"Do they ever leave?" I say. Lolly ignores Pete's warning, His lapping sounds echo off the walls.

"Dusk," Pete says. "I was just outside the entrance. It was like a signal sounded and a river of them came pouring out."

Cocoa's silent, and Captain Jack notices. "What do you think, Future Girl?"

"I don't think," she says. "I know. I know where the Nazis are making their bombs."

For a moment, nobody says anything. Then the captain reacts. *"Where?"*

"Look around, Captain Jack." Her sassiness has returned. Her voice is a pitch higher, her words come faster. "A cave, of course. A gypsum cave. Deep. Remote. In central Germany."

"You're sure?" Pete says.

"I'm sure, Peter. I felt something as soon as we got into the large cavern. Then the memories came flooding back. I've seen photos, read descriptions."

"Does the cave have a name?" I say.

"I remember connecting its name to the savagery of the Nazis—their *barbarism*—when I first learned about the bomb facility. It's called Barbarossa."

"Amazing, Cocoa," Captain Jack says. "And it shouldn't be hard for our guys to locate."

"It was a tourist attraction," she says. "Now it's a fortress, with only scientists and workers inside and an army outside."

Pete shines his flashlight on his watch. "You did it, Future Girl. Now let's get out of here and find a phone."

Two hours later we're in Alamogordo, halfway home. Cocoa and I are sitting in a café, eating cherry pie, while our soldiers stand outside at a phone booth. The captain dials, talks briefly, hangs up, dials again, talks again. His body seems to relax. Pete smiles in our direction.

"He's reached the general." I take a bite of pie. It's not Mom's, or Dad's, but it's good.

"The wheels can begin turning," Cocoa says.

We're on the same side of the booth. She takes my hand, and when the waitress comes back with two glasses of milk, she notices, and smiles. Inside, I do too.

# THIRTY-FOUR

## Wednesday, August 8

Today is the day Cocoa predicted the Nazis will try to bomb England. Aware of the eight-hour time difference, we went to bed early last night to get up extra early this morning. The general might call. News might be broadcast. But by the time we have to leave the house, we haven't heard from the general. All we've gotten from the radio are farm reports and cowboy music.

When we return, there's still nothing. Captain Nelson and the general talked, but there's been no attack. Thanks to Cocoa, though, the defenses are ready. Sea. Air. Land isn't a concern.

We move distractedly into early afternoon. Then, at seven minutes after two the phone rings. I answer it.

"General Groves, Bobby," the general says. As if I couldn't identify that gruff but friendly voice.

"Hello, sir."

"Captain Nelson there?"

"Yes, sir." He's standing by the stove, looking eager.

"I'll speak to him in a moment, but since you're on the phone, I'll tell you what we have."

"Thank you." I barely get the words out.

"Bad-news-good-news sort of thing," he says. "The krauts sent their bomb over the channel riding a rocket. A V-2, we believe. Aimed at London, we're very certain, but it overshot the target by more than fifty miles. Exploded in pastureland halfway between London and Bath."

"A rocket," I say. Sitting at the table, Cocoa doesn't take her eyes off me. "Were people . . . killed?"

"Immediate casualties were few. Mostly livestock. But the blast could be heard and felt for miles around, and the cloud was tremendous. Unfortunately, it's drifting east, so London and then France and the rest of the continent will be in the path of its fallout."

"Mostly livestock," I repeat. "They missed London."

"That's right, Bobby."

"That's mainly good news, sir."

"It is. Can you let me talk to Captain Nelson now?"

"Of course. Thank you for talking to me."

"The least I can do. And when I get done with the captain, I want to talk to your friend Cocoa. So, warn her, will you?"

"I will." I give the phone to Captain Nelson, and for the next few minutes he mostly listens and I mostly imagine. I imagine an atomic bomb landing in a pasture and creating a shock wave that rattles windows a hundred miles away and a poisonous cloud lifting into a darkening sky and drifting over farms and towns and cities and people. I imagine what America and its allies can do to stop it from happening again.

Finished with his conversation, the captain motions Cocoa over. When she gets up, she grabs my hand and drags me with her. She says hello, holding the phone far enough from her ear that I can easily make out the general's take-no-prisoners voice.

"You were right again, young lady," he says. "We couldn't stop the rocket, but the accuracy of the information you provided gives me even more confidence, if that's possible, in what you told us yesterday."

"I am glad that Robert suggested the cave," Cocoa says. "And that Peter and the captain took us there."

"It's a team effort. But without you we wouldn't be in the

game. So, I want to thank you once again."

"You're welcome."

"Our War Department and military hotshots are busy putting together a plan, gathering essential personnel and equipment, embarking on orientation and training for the members of the armed forces involved in the upcoming effort. And it's all due to you."

"Scary," Cocoa says. "Fucking scary . . . excuse me, General."

General Groves laughs. "You're a breath of fresh air, Cocoa. Are there more like you where you come from?"

"I don't know," she says. "There are other survivors. But if Hitler is stopped, will there even *be* a place where I come from?"

I try to digest her question. *But it's rhetorical, right?* And overwhelming. I block it out of my mind as the general avoids her haunting words also, and they say goodbye.

# THIRTY-FIVE

**T**he long flight from Tinian on the plodding Skymaster gave Lieutenant Colonel Oliver and his crew plenty of time for napping. And now that he's sitting on the Kirtland tarmac in the familiar cockpit of the B-29, he feels even more rejuvenated. And elated by the prospect of a fresh start.

But it's not all sunshine. He's troubled by the reason he's been ordered here so abruptly. Two days ago, the entire crew of a B-29, in England for a mission not unlike the one he's been preparing for in the Pacific, perished during a practice flight. Oliver and his crew are the replacements, the B-team.

Regardless of the reason for this assignment, though, he'll be out from under his former squadron leader's shadow. Tibbets's shadow. Being an understudy to *the chosen one* was never on Oliver's wish list, especially because there was no chance that Tibbets, with fame in his bombsights, would allow himself to falter.

The doomed crew in England must have had understudies also. Oliver wonders how they'll feel, being ousted by strangers— well-qualified or not—from the other side of the world.

But it wasn't his decision.

The plane handler goes through his series of signals, releasing Oliver and his bomber to the runway. Once there, he orientates the big craft, brings it to a brief stop, revs up its fickle Wright engines, glances at his longtime co-pilot, Captain Jimmy Terrell, and gooses it. His first takeoff at Kirtland, but he could do this in his sleep.

The engines settle down and pull together. Because this is a dry run—no payload—takeoff shouldn't be a problem. The problem might come tomorrow, when the weight of a simulated load is added. Already on his shoulders, of course, is the weight of the performance he's been brought here to rehearse.

Already a mile above sea level, they lift off, heading south toward a town called Socorro and beyond it to the bombing range. The field drops away. The wheels come up smoothly. This isn't his old B-29, which he and the crew fondly christened *Pattern Badness*—complete with the name and a cartoonish bald devil decorating the plane's nose. But it feels almost identical. Like bedding your girlfriend's twin sister. Fewer pleasant surprises, but also fewer disagreeable ones.

He checks the instruments. All percolating properly, all in harmony. In minutes the bomber's shadow will skim over the range. They'll be flying low, getting tuned in to the terrain, getting their shit together for what's on the horizon. Trying to minimize nasty surprises. And maybe even find a pleasant one.

# THIRTY-SIX

## Saturday, August 11

A letter arrives from Mom and Dad. Cocoa and I sit on the front porch and read it together. They don't have much to report. Heat. Dust. Good health. They're trying not to complain. The Japanese Americans have been prisoners for more than three years. But my parents and their new Japanese American friends often commiserate about the food, even though Dad is one of the cooks. He refuses to take the blame. You can't make a T-bone, or *yakitori*, out of the sole of a boot, he says.

He's lost weight, which he considers a good thing. Radios aren't allowed, but internees do get day-old newspapers, so they're keeping up with war events, they say, and in the next sentence they ask how Cocoa's doing. They want to know if she's still coming up with revelations and how, if she is, the revelations have affected the news. They send their love to her and Pete and the captain.

I pass along the message to the two uniforms as they leave the house. They have an appointment with General Groves at Kirtland.

When Pete hugs me goodbye, I notice he looks even more squared-away than usual—close shave, every hair in place, sharp creases, shined shoes. I wonder if he's counting on seeing Corporal Amy Elizabeth Lewis.

When I answer the letter later in the afternoon, I don't include the specifics of Cocoa's magic act. *A censor might not even believe it, but why take a chance?* I simply say that we're all staying closely tuned to the war news, and that Cocoa has been a BIG help. I trust Mom and Dad to connect the dots.

Cocoa adds a note; she's doing fine, she's gaining the weight Dad lost, she misses them, she's working hard for her uncle . . .

She's made a big bowl of butter-drenched popcorn that sits between us on the kitchen table, half gone. Between mouthfuls, she asks a question: "Is it time for me to talk to the general about bringing Chuck and Dottie home?"

"Like extortion or something? Isn't that what they call it when you put the squeeze on someone?"

"I'd make it more like a favor. I've done a lot for Uncle Sam."

"The general wouldn't be the problem. Dad wasn't interested the last time you offered help, and he wouldn't change his mind this soon. He's probably more determined than ever to stay with his buddies. By now he's most likely formed a unity pact with his new Japanese American friends."

"I don't like them there, Robert. Being away from you. Us."

"Me, neither. But maybe if—when—we win this war, the camps will get shut down, and everybody will be free to leave." Too late, I realize I've put more pressure on her: *The faster you get this war won, the faster my parents can come home.*

But if she feels the burden of my words, she doesn't show it. She smiles. "I can't wait."

# THIRTY-SEVEN

## Tuesday, August 14

Cocoa continues to poke at her memories, but Tuesday morning arrives without any new breakthroughs. While the rest of us eat breakfast, she wanders, studying maps.

Pete and Captain Jack have told us that the details of the US plan for attacking the Barbarossa Cave are strictly need-to-know, which leaves out them, and consequently us. But being in the dark isn't helping Cocoa's frame of mind. *We know there's a strategy in the works, but when will it be put into action? Will it be before or after the next German bomb flies, or sails, or drops?*

"Breakfast, Cocoa," Pete says, and to my amazement she comes to the table and sits.

"My thoughts have dried up anyway," she says, absentmindedly buttering a piece of cold toast.

"It's gonna be another scorcher today," Pete says. "You two ready for a swim?"

"A *swim*?" Suddenly Cocoa sounds and looks less discouraged. "I would sink."

"You can't swim?" Captain Jack says.

"I've never tried."

"You never tried riding a horse until you got on Big Muddy," I say.

"If you fall off a horse you don't drown, Robert."

She has a point, but a broken neck is no better than drowning—unless there are sharks involved. "Where would we go?" I ask.

"Base camp," Pete says. "Not far from it, anyway. I know where there's a pool—deep enough for swimming, too shallow for drowning."

"A pool," I say. "At the base camp."

"You'll see," Pete says.

"Do you have a bathing suit, Cocoa?" the captain says.

"In case you haven't heard, Jack, I arrived here with nothing." She winks at me. My face warms.

The captain is grinning. "We'll remedy that. We'll take you and Robert to town this morning and see if you can find something."

"Really?" she says.

"Shopping, lunch, home, swimming," Pete says. "You can be a kid again."

I think about reminding him that she's never been a kid, but from outside comes the sound of Mr. Unser's Packard rolling down our driveway. I've nearly forgotten that Tuesday is milk and butter day. I head for the door with Cocoa and Lolly on my heels.

I've never been beyond the outskirts of the base camp. I'm supposed to keep to my route. Period. But today I'm with Captain Jack and Pete, who have their own rules. My rear end is perched on the back seat of an Army car, not on a bicycle seat. Cocoa sits next to me. Pete whistles cheerfully as he maneuvers the car past the buildings and foot and vehicle traffic of the dusty outpost and onto a gravel road that quickly puts all the activity in the rearview mirror.

"Going to tell us where we're going, Pete?" I say. "Is there some kind of oasis out here?"

"Manmade," he says. "Another ranch house. Formerly the George McDonald place. Brother of Dave and Ross, who owned the ranch houses back at base camp."

"There's a pool or something?" I say.

"Something," Pete says.

"How far is it?" Cocoa says.

"From here," Pete says, "fifteen minutes or so."

From a J.C. Penney bag Cocoa pulls out her new swimsuit. It's navy blue. There's not much to it. Of course, there's not much to her, either. "Do you still like it, Robert?"

While Pete and Captain Jack ran errands, I sat on a bench outside a J.C. Penney dressing room and gave my expert opinions as Cocoa put on an endless one-girl swimsuit fashion show. Eventually she tried on this one, and I told her I liked it, and she liked it also, mostly because it fit her like the skin of a plum rather than the skin of a prune.

"Still stylish," I say. Once you've seen a girl naked, even in the dimness of early dawn, even when she's not at her best, it's easy to resent clothing of any kind, stylish or not.

We pass one car going the opposite direction. Two guys— scientists, is my guess—in the front seat. Pete moves over to share the narrow road. Dust blows in, dust blows out.

Finally, we crest a rise and a house appears. In front of it is a windmill like the one back at base camp, and between the windmill and the front porch of the house is a concrete enclosure, half the size of the house, maybe. As we get closer I see that it's full of water.

"A swimming pool?" Cocoa says.

"Now," Pete says. "Used to be a horse trough, until Lieutenant Bush decided base security needed something faster than horses to cover all this territory. But at one time Big Muddy used to come here regularly."

Cocoa's face, already full of life, brightens like a painting on a museum wall at the mention of Big Muddy. In the angled afternoon sunlight, the canvas of her skin sheds shadow and takes on color.

Pete parks in a patch of shade near the house. The pool isn't deep. Cocoa will be able to keep her head above the water, which is cool and surprisingly clear.

Inside the house, there's little furniture, a table and a couple of chairs in one room, a desk and chair in another. Each room has its own door to the outside. There are missing windows and glass on the floor in three of them. Someone has swept it into corners.

"What happened to the windows?" Cocoa says.

"The test," Pete says.

"We're close to where it took place?" I say.

"A couple of miles to ground zero," Pete says. "You wouldn't have wanted to be here."

*Ground zero.* A new one on me. I glance at Cocoa. *How close was she? During. After.*

"This old house doesn't look like much," Captain Jack says. "But this is where the scientists put it together."

"The bomb?" I say.

The captain shakes his head. "Brought the critical components here in a car and assembled them on the table."

Not what I would have pictured. *A weapon with the power to change the world is put together in a back-country ranch house?* I imagine the secret Nazi facility: fluorescent lights, glistening steel, madmen in white coats.

A chill grips my sweaty body.

We return to the room with the table. Nothing impressive but the history.

"Then what?" Cocoa says.

"On July 13, they drove their assembled piece out to ground zero, where it was placed in a larger bomb structure that contained other components," the captain says. "The next day the entire bomb—nicknamed *Fat Man*—was raised to the top of a one-hundred-foot tower. Two days later, after a lot of preparation and fretting about the weather, Fat Man was detonated."

"The Nazis were doing the same thing," Cocoa says. "Earlier."

"There were rumors," the captain says. "Fears. Many of our scientists fled Germany during Hitler's rise, either because of ideological differences or because they were Jewish. Often both." He pauses. "They saw the gleam in Hitler's eye."

Even with a breeze blowing through the broken windows, the house suddenly feels hotter, stuffier, tainted.

The pool calls. We choose rooms and change clothes and meet up outside. Then it's everyone in.

The water feels wonderful—refreshing. I'm a desert boy, not used to *wet*, but I could learn to be. Cocoa is hesitant at first, but soon she's all the way under and popping back to the surface and trying to mimic the strokes of the three of us in the pool who can actually swim—Captain Jack, smooth and fast; Pete, lots of white water; and me, YMCA dog-paddle.

I hold up Cocoa's middle, not wanting to let go even after she's got her legs efficiently working. She has my stroke down in no time. Captain Jack brought a football, and we spread out and throw it around. In spite of her small hands, Cocoa can catch, and her strong arm makes up for her lack of know-how, the result of coming from a place where football isn't even a memory.

For a while—an hour that stretches to two—she's the happiest I've ever seen her, except maybe for her time on Big Muddy.

Pete gets a cooler from the car. We sit on the edge of the pool, soaking up the setting sun and drinking Cokes. The captain has a camera—another rule, ignored. He takes pictures of the three of us together, Cocoa and me together, Cocoa by herself, me by myself. He shows me how to use it, and I take one of the three of them. He promises he'll get enough pictures developed for everyone.

He checks his watch. "We should get dressed for our next event."

*Next event?*

Cocoa looks reluctant to leave and eager to move on at the same time.

Once changed and in the car, we start back toward the base camp but immediately take a right onto a dirt road. Judging by the positions of the mountains and setting sun, we have to be moving southwest. I can't think of anything in that direction.

Except the bombing range.

Pete and Captain Jack are tight-lipped as we drive on. Cocoa slyly takes my hand. Her excitement infects me. Her hair is already drying, turning wispy in the breeze flowing through the windows.

We climb above the flatlands. The air smells like twilight. At a curve in the road, Pete slows and stops. We're on a hillside with a sharp drop-off beyond the hood of the car and then miles of desert stretching out in front of us. Far away is the mountain range and much, much farther, the sun getting ready to settle in behind it, purpling a low ribbon of clouds.

We get out. "More pictures?" I ask Captain Jack.

"Only in your mind, Robert." He's not looking at the sunset. He's looking north, and up. So is Pete. In a moment, we all are.

It doesn't take long to find out why. From the distant sky comes a faint snarl that becomes a louder growl. A slender shape appears, traveling more or less toward us. A plane, of course.

It drops lower. Its path lies in front of us, across the expanse of desert that's suddenly become a stage.

I'm spellbound. I couldn't turn away if I wanted to. I think of Dad. *Would he?*

The plane is big—wide wings, four engines—and moving fast. The sound is a roar now.

"A B-29?" I ask.

"From Kirtland," Pete says.

"It will drop bombs?" Cocoa says.

"Keep watching," the captain says.

The B-29 thunders past us right to left, practically at eye level, a mile away at most and a few hundred feet off the ground. My heart hammers in my throat. Cocoa moves closer; I grab her hand and hold on.

The bomber accelerates as it approaches the hills. It gains altitude—slowly at first, then doubling it, then more. Something drops from its belly. Still climbing, the plane banks sharply right. The engines labor. A shaft of filtered sunlight glints off its wings. Below it, the bomb or whatever it is continues to fall.

Then, at the base of a shadowy ravine that merges two hills and the desert floor, an explosion—fire and smoke and a geyser of sand and rock and a moment later a thump. In comparison to the explosion I witnessed last month, this is hardly a firecracker. But still . . .

The B-29 levels out and circles back to the north, grows smaller, nearly disappears. The light is going out of twilight. Then it comes back, on the same trajectory—low, higher, higher, bank away. The bomb explodes. The bomber retreats. Returns again. Darkness nears. The routine continues. The plane becomes a phantom, mostly sound, the faint smell of exhaust.

"Rehearsing," Cocoa says. She's right. I'm only a kid with a pacifist father, but I know something about B-29s. They're designed to drop bombs from high elevations, where ground fire and enemy fighters can't reach them. But this B-29 isn't practicing high-altitude bombing. This is for something special.

"For the German cave," I say.

"Smart kids," Pete says.

"General Groves wanted you to see this show," Captain Jack says. "Need-to-know stuff, but he knows it'll be safe with you."

When we get in the car and drive off, the bomber is still at it. I wonder if all the rehearsing will be enough.

# THIRTY-EIGHT

Gorel Groves's outer office looks the same. But even if it had been turned inside out and upside down, I wouldn't rely on Pete to notice. Corporal Amy is the only thing catching—and holding—his eye. She notices him right back.

Cocoa and I still don't know why the general invited us to Kirtland; the mystery itself made the car ride exciting, even with Pete and Captain Jack arguing about the outcome of an imaginary football game between Minnesota, where we have family, and Stanford, where the captain attended school.

The captain has business elsewhere on the base. So, Pete accompanied us here, "worried" we wouldn't be able to manage on our own, even though Cocoa has practically raised herself.

"The general will be right back, kiddos," Corporal Amy says. She shows us into his inner office, where a metal bucket containing ice and a half dozen Cokes sits on a side table. "Make yourselves comfortable. The sodas are for you. The opener's next to the bucket."

She exits, trying not to look overly eager, and closes the door. Cocoa and I open Cokes and sit. Hushed voices come from the outer office. Small talk; a laugh, deep; a laugh, musical.

"Peter has a girlfriend," Cocoa says.

"Nothing wrong with that."

"No," she says. "Nothing wrong with that."

A latch clicks. Chairs scrape. More voices, male.

Cocoa and I stand when the door opens. General Groves strides in, followed by another officer, half the general's girth. Jimmy Stewart's body.

"Colonel Oliver," the general says, "say hello to Cocoa and Bobby. Cocoa's the reason you have your mission. And Bobby has been instrumental in bringing her to our attention and jogging her memory and helping her be a regular kid in spite of it all."

We shake hands with the colonel.

"At ease, folks," the general says, pointing to the chairs. He sits behind his desk. I open Cokes for both of them and settle next to Cocoa. The colonel discretely studies her. She's no longer so skinny or sickly, but she also doesn't look capable of doing what she's done.

"I wanted you two to meet Colonel Oliver," the general says, "although I understand you met him from a distance a couple of nights ago." He must see our puzzlement. "He's a B-29 pilot."

The hint works. I know where we "met" him.

"Will you take us for a ride in your B-29 sometime, Colonel?" Cocoa says.

"I'll be happy to, Cocoa. When this is over. Promise."

"None of this can leave this room," the general says. "But the colonel has unfinished business. This evening he'll take off for far-off destinations. Soon he and his crew and a bomb called Bigger Boy are going to pay Hitler's scientists a visit. They're going to lob that bomb into the cave and up the pimply ass of Adolf's atomic bomb project and win this war for us, once and for all."

I want to cheer, but I know the general isn't guaranteeing anything. And I'm not interested in jinxing the colonel.

Cocoa digs into her pants pocket. "You're brave, Colonel, but you'll need luck, too." She uncurls her fingers. "This acorn brought me here safely. I believe it will work for you, also."

"Really?" He takes it, rolls it around the palm of his hand. "It's from—"

"Yes," she says.

"Thank you, Cocoa. I've got just the place for it. Right up front. Best view in the sky."

"Good," she says.

But I'm not sure the gesture is all good. *What if Cocoa just gave away her own luck?*

# THIRTY-NINE

## Sunday, August 19—Germany

His buddies still call him *Junior*, even though he's no longer the youngest ranger in the company. Three other seventeen-year-olds, all younger, have filled holes left by casualties. But those replacements are still green. Not ready for this mission. Not here in the German countryside, lying low by day, shadow-humping toward a mystery target by night.

When Lieutenant Wills whittled the list of volunteers down to twenty-four, only battle-tested men made the cut. For them, that was a message, and it was clear. This is big. This is crucial. No screw-ups allowed.

Daylight comes late to the thick forest, but Junior, who goes by *Ernie* back home in Minnesota, can make out the shapes of the soldiers in front of him now, moving along in a perpetual crouch, quiet like wolves.

The trees thin. Light plays through boughs in pollen-heavy beams. Somewhere beyond the porous border of the forest is a clearing. Open country, maybe. Meadows. Prairie. Patches of blue and white are visible above the evergreen treetops.

The lieutenant raises his hand. His men shuffle to a halt as he eyes his compass, turns to face them. He's got something to say, and Junior and his companions have something to hear.

"Take a load off, men," the lieutenant murmurs, gesturing for them to sit. Sweaty, blistered, worn out, they shrug off their packs, fold to the ground, swig water from their canteens.

"We're close," the lieutenant says. "Another half-night's march. We'll rest for today, get some rations in us, check our weapons and supplies and, as soon as darkness falls, push on. Staying alert. Staying invisible. The last thing we want is to bring attention to ourselves. But if we can't avoid conflict, we'll deal with it. Quickly. Quietly. It's vital that we complete our task.

"Now it's time to tell you what that task is."

# FORTY

Accccording to the plane's radar and British Intelligence, this section of North Sea airspace is free of enemy aircraft. But Colonel Oliver feels more secure knowing he has Spitfires taking the point and other B-29s on his flanks. He survived ditching once, but this time ditching isn't in the cards. This time he has to stay aloft; he has to complete the mission. Once the bomb drops they'll have a fighting chance to survive. But nobody wanted to give them the odds.

All the planning sessions had a singular goal—stop Nazi bomb production. The colonel and his crew and his plane and Bigger Boy add up to the only hope of doing that. Every other thought in his head has been pushed aside by the one that matters: *You've got precious cargo in the bomb bay; deliver it.*

To the east, the sky is brightening, but stars are still visible. Below, the earth's surface takes on a different look—darker, with a few pinpoints of light.

"Bruges," Lieutenant Bell, the navigator, says.

"Belgium," Captain Jimmy says, loud enough to show off his geography knowledge.

They're on course, on schedule. Soon the Spitfires will have to turn back. Colonel Oliver hopes that won't be a problem. Although Belgium is supposed to be in Allied hands, the recent German successes may have emboldened the assholes, changed who controls what. He looks for signs—flashes from the ground, tracers in the air, a glint of wing. The formation drones on.

By the time they reach the German border, darkness yields. Oliver has taken the big plane to thirty thousand feet, higher than the Luftwaffe can chase him. Fuel depleted, the Spitfires have gone home. His squadron mates peel off and fan out, heading for secondary targets but mainly providing distractions from the main offensive.

Colonel Oliver is mostly on his own.

At his side is a small wooden box. In the box is the gift from that strange, unforgettable girl, Cocoa. An acorn. It represents what's at stake in this mission—the future.

He reaches down and rubs it for luck.

The two safest approaches are max high and max low. It's between them where the danger peaks. It's time to speed through that kill zone, get all the way down to where German radar will be blind.

Colonel Oliver eyeballs the shadowy terrain and its familiar features rising to meet them. Since receiving the reconnaissance photos from Allied intelligence a week ago, he's studied them keenly, over and over. The images are mapped in his brain. If he lives to be an old man, they'll still be there. He'll make drawings of them for his grandchildren.

He steepens the rate of descent. No ground fire, no Luftwaffe. His instruments glow and pulse in front of him. Lieutenant Bell keeps feeding him information. They're precisely on course, closing in. He fingers the acorn again.

He levels out the plane, following contours, skimming over forests and pastures and villages. The ground races past. He pictures Walker, the bomb expert, back in the bay with his baby. Early into the flight he reported that the bomb was armed. He sounded calm. But from the first strategy meeting on, he's been jittery over the low-altitude approach. *Has he gotten over it? Gotten drunk? Shit his pants?* The colonel grins nervously at the thought.

This kind of flying, no margin for error, is nerve-wracking for everyone. *But if they're stymieing the radar, and if the rangers did their job . . .*

"Target straight ahead," Bell reports. "Twenty-nine miles. Repeat: twenty-niner miles."

Four minutes, about. Oliver peers through the murk.

*Breathe.*

The terrain unveils itself. On a lumpish hillside directly ahead, an irregular oval of faint, flickering lights appears. The rangers have set their fires, marking the cave entrance.

Pray to God they've gotten away. Far away.

*It's time.*

"Get up," the colonel urges, finessing the controls. The big plane responds. They climb. A thousand feet. Two. Three.

The flight engineer has the plane humming. The bomb is in place and armed. The bombardier, who has already made enough calculations for ten bombing runs, just needs to complete his final instrument reading and make his final sighting and push the fucking button. And when he does he has orders to yell his ass off.

On the ground, flashes of light. Antiaircraft guns. Too late. Too inaccurate. By the time the German gunners find their range, the bomb will be on top of them.

The nose of the plane lurches up, sending a jolt through the cockpit, and immediately Colonel Oliver knows what's happened. Simultaneously the bombardier shouts "Away!" at the top of his lungs. "Away! Away! Attention Krauts! Kiss your nuts goodbye!"

The bomb falls. "Detonate," the colonel says as if issuing an order.

But that's not Oliver's only worry. He has another responsibility, and there's no time for distractions. He levels out the big beast, gives it maximum throttle. The engines howl their complaints. The airframe shudders. Someone rattles off a string of curses.

*Fuck it.* He hears the doubt, but he doesn't have to listen.

Speed equals distance. He has twenty seconds. If he goes for broke, in twenty seconds he can put another two miles between his plane and the target, and maybe another two miles will be enough to make the difference.

If not, he and his crew will be dead heroes.

# FORTY-ONE

Germany

Junior's keeping up with the others, but he's struggling with the pace. Which is now holding at double-time, after an initial burst of triple, a tempo nobody but Schuler, the miler from Illinois, could maintain.

After waiting until the last minute to light the torches, the rangers hastily regrouped and fled the target. But not even the suspicion that a monster would soon be roaring at their heels gave them the endurance to sustain what was unsustainable.

The spirit was more than willing; it was almost desperate. But the flesh? The flesh was short on sleep and food and water—and news from home. Double-time will have to do.

According to Lieutenant Wills, they're retracing last night's route, but Junior has to take that on faith. There's still not enough light to tell where they are. After surrendering to the intense glare of the kerosene fires, his night vision has returned, but still he's going mostly on sound. Footfalls, labored breathing. They're in open country—fields, an occasional stream—but the ground is lumpy and gopher-holed, perfect for twisting ankles.

"You okay, Junior?" Sanborn murmurs from a stride back. At twenty-six, he's the oldest guy in this detail, and he likes to play big brother. Junior straightens himself, adjusts his pack. Unburdened from the load of kerosene and canisters, and with all the nonessentials back at yesterday's bivouac spot, it's practically weightless.

"Just like apple pie, Sarge. You?"

"À la mode."

They go silent, saving their breath.

A new sound. At first, Junior thinks it's his imagination. A pounding heart, fearful voices in his head. But the other men speed up. He goes with them, drawing on a surprising reserve.

A distant buzz slowly becomes something deeper, louder. Closer.

And then frantic. Screaming into the pre-dawn sky. Not far. Not far at all.

Together, they surge. Triple-time. All or nothing. The lieutenant has given them a finish line—the wooded spot they abandoned last evening—where they should be safe from what's coming. They need to get there. Fast. And then hope he's right.

Ahead of them, east, tall treetops show against the first hint of morning. In moments they're back in the forest, dodging rough trunks and low limbs and undergrowth. Encouraging each other. *Go! Fly! Move your pansy asses!*

Overhead, birds cease their morning chatter.

Anticipation suddenly dissolves. A sheet of radiance flashes across the sky, west to east. Instant daylight. An eerie glow penetrates the tree boughs overhead.

They don't slow to look back. But something has happened. Something *good* has happened.

*What next? Something bad?*

Abruptly a thunderous rumble drowns out every other sound—footfalls, breathing, cursing. As the sky continues to brighten, towering trees bend under a blast of heated wind, needles and cones and debris rain down. Even in the shelter of the woods, Junior has to fight to keep his balance as he and his mates are pushed forward.

But they haven't gone up in smoke. Melted. Vaporized.

They're breathing. Moving. They've taken a haymaker of a punch and survived. They've done their job. Something *good* has happened.

*Feet, keep making tracks.*

# FORTY-TWO

## Sunday, August 19 (Late Night)

There's no bedtime tonight. General Groves has promised to call as soon as he has any word.

The four of us are in the living room. I've stationed myself closest to the phone. We don't talk about why we're up. We don't talk about success or failure, life or death, the possibility that if Colonel Oliver's plane goes down, or the bomb is off target, or if it fails to explode, the Nazi bomb-making operation could be moved. And Cocoa's guess as to its next location would be just that.

We eat Spam-and-cheese sandwiches. We eat popcorn. We drink coffee, lots of it. My already shredded nerves begin to fry. Outside, the air has cooled, but inside, the heat of the day lingers. We sweat.

Cocoa fields questions about her other life. Her answers are horror stories that make me wish we'd opened the topic of Colonel Oliver's mission. Too casually, she speaks of chaos, anarchy, ignorance, crime, abuse, abandonment, homelessness, heat, pollution, starvation, decay, disease, dying, death. Aloneness.

The stories are hard to digest, but not hard to believe. *How could we* not?

It's nearly one thirty when the phone rings. By the time I say hello, everyone else is gathered around me.

"General Groves, Bobby." He sounds younger. Buoyant. *Or am I just wishing?*

"Yes, sir."

"Mission accomplished, son."

I don't have the words. What comes out of me is a shriek.

The general laughs. "Nice of you to let the others know."

"Yes, sir. Is everyone okay?"

"Barely. They cut it close. Wanted to make sure. They limped home in a battered plane, courtesy of Bigger Boy tearing the sky apart."

"Whew," I say, giving my audience a thumbs-up.

"Yes. May I talk to Cocoa?"

"Of course."

She says hello, then mostly listens. She tells the general she didn't have that much to do with it, then claims it was the lucky acorn. But everyone knows she had everything to do with it.

Captain Jack gets on the phone. Lots of listening for him, too. When he hangs up, he tells us that General Groves will call back in the morning if damage reports arrive from Germany. In any case, he'll keep us up to date.

Pete and the captain open two bottles of beer. They pour some for Cocoa and me but keep most of it for themselves. We raise our glasses and bottles and Pete makes a toast: "To Future Girl, and her loyal sidekick, Brainy Boy. The world thanks you."

We sip. Cocoa makes a face. I know how she feels. I don't mind the *loyal sidekick* part, but *Brainy Boy?* Pete couldn't have done better than *Brainy Boy?* I prefer *Present Boy*. Compared to Cocoa's world, the present is a good place to be.

# FORTY-THREE

## Monday, August 20

General Groves calls halfway through the morning. Cocoa and I are in the barn when we hear the ringing. When we get to the kitchen, Captain Jack is on the phone. Smiling. Pete sits at the table, spellbound.

"That's great, General," the captain says. Pause. "That's wonderful." Pause. "Couldn't be better, sir." Pause. "I'll do that. Thank you for calling."

He hangs up. He and Pete try to out-hug each other, then take turns with Cocoa and me. Jubilant. Comforting. When Pete wraps me up, he's trembling, and when he finally pulls away there are tears in his eyes.

Meanwhile, Captain Jack is talking fast. "Air reconnaissance and troops on the ground report a direct hit. The cave and everything in it was obliterated. For a mile around the blast, the land has been stripped bare. Boulders were tossed like marbles. Trees that weren't vaporized were uprooted, toppled, burned. They're still burning. The German army is staying far away."

A few hours later, the news is broadcast on the radio: We've struck back with our own bomb; the heart of Germany; Hitler's kitchen; a bomb-making facility and the materials for making the bombs and the people who made them. *Made.*

Not that we ever doubted the general, but now it's official. We celebrate all over again.

# FORTY-FOUR

**Wednesday, August 22, and Thursday, August 23**

We catch up on our sleep. Cocoa looks healthier, happier, more relaxed. She, like the rest of us, is worried about Nazi bombs that might have come off the assembly line before Colonel Oliver delivered his atomic enema, but most of the pressure on her seems to have lifted.

I wonder how much Mom and Dad know. I wish I could tell them about Cocoa's role in Colonel Oliver's mission. I wish I could tell them that, without her, the Nazi scientists would still be doing their shit.

From the *Journal* and the radio we get more good news. The Allies are again heading for Berlin. The German army is battling, but the last of the Luftwaffe has been destroyed, and the airspace over Germany belongs to us. The German navy has withdrawn to the few ports still in Nazi hands.

On Wednesday, Pete and Captain Jack leave shortly after Cocoa and I get home from delivering papers. They have to drive all the way to Santa Fe, where the captain is meeting with General Groves and people from Los Alamos.

So, we have hours on our own. And I have an idea. "How about we get some ice cream?"

We're returning from the barn. She squints up at the blue sky, at the sun rising above the mountains and morning clouds. She never tires of looking at the sky and sun and clouds.

"That would be a long bike ride on a hot day, Robert."

"Not a bike ride." I nod in the direction of the DeSoto.

"The car?" she says. "You can drive it that far?"

"Why not?"

A conspiratorial smile. "I've been having a craving for ice cream."

"Me, too," I say. "And cool air blasting in through the windows." What I don't say is: *and you sitting close to me.*

"I'll go change."

She hurries off. I get the pump and begin inflating the tires, which have gone half flat. Lolly supervises. I open a back door and he jumps in.

Cocoa emerges wearing her favorite blouse—medium blue with narrow horizontal white stripes that make her look more substantial—and white shorts and white Keds. Also, a wide smile. I expected she'd be reluctant to ride with a rookie driver, but she slips into the front seat without hesitation.

The DeSoto starts easily, relieving one of my fears, and before we reach the end of the driveway, Cocoa has slid over to within six inches of me, relieving another.

The windows are down. As I turn onto the road and accelerate, a breeze kicks up inside the car, clearing out the odors of disuse and mohair and dog. All I smell is her. Cocoa.

I check the gas gauge. I shift through the gears, but I don't show off, and I promise myself I won't.

Precious cargo.

Soon we're on the highway, heading north. There's little traffic. Cocoa inches closer.

I carefully angle-park the car outside the entrance to Slim's Diner. We roll down all the windows for Lolly. He's up but not trying to escape.

The place is half full. I don't recognize anyone, which is good. Questions might follow. We sit in a window booth and glance out at Lolly and the sleepy street, and when I'm not doing that I'm looking across the table at Cocoa.

"We should get some food," I say. The more we eat, the longer we'll stay; the longer we stay, the longer I'll get to look at her like this.

She takes my hand. "And then ice cream?"

We linger over lunch and sundaes. People trickle in, setting off a cheery bell. When we're almost done, the bell rings once more. I pay no attention until I notice the worried look in Cocoa's eyes and, at the edge of my vision, someone stopping at our table.

"Hello, Bobby," Sheriff Wally says. "Cocoa."

We tell him "Hi." I try to calm my nerves.

"How are the folks?" he asks me.

I'm tempted to say something sarcastic, but I want to keep this friendly. And short. Especially short. "Making the best of it."

"All any of us can do, right?"

"Right."

"And you, Cocoa?"

"Much better," she says, masking her uneasiness with a smile.

"Glad to hear it." He peers through the window. I know what he's looking at. "You two take care." He gives my shoulder a squeeze. "And you, Bobby, have a safe drive home."

He finds a corner table, where he can keep an eye on comings and goings. We finish up and pay. I leave a nice tip, grateful for the food and service and Cocoa's company and Sheriff Wally's willingness to see the room but ignore the cracks in the walls.

When we get home, we turn on the radio and learn that the US is talking with Japan over the terms of a surrender. Even halfway around the world, the bomb Colonel Oliver dropped on the cave, and on Nazi intentions, has had an intimidating effect.

Something just as exciting arrives in a story relayed from a BBC broadcast a moment later. The Allies are closing in on Berlin, "dashing headlong toward Hitler's last stronghold," the newsman reports, "impeded only by the horror at what they've discovered in Nazi death camps, discoveries that at the same time urge them on."

Cocoa and I decide to take Lolly for a walk. We fill a canteen and head into the desert. Lolly runs ahead, comes back, runs ahead, comes back. Investigating. Reporting. All clear. All clear.

He trots back, whining, tries to herd us left, right. Cocoa laughs, throws a stick, but he isn't swayed. He holds his ground, paces back and forth. She sidesteps him and backpedals on while I try to figure him out. He doesn't always think like a human.

She takes another step backward. With no warning, from a thicket of low-growing cactus inches from her bare legs, there's a blur of motion. Dark. Lightning-fast. A rattler, striking.

She makes a noise. Suddenly I've got Lolly by the collar and I'm trying to hold him back and grab Cocoa's hand at the same time. Just as suddenly, the snake recoils, invisible again.

I pull her from danger but I'm sure she's been bitten and I'll need to get her to the doctor before the venom gets to where it wants to go.

Nearby we reach a clear area. I drop to my knees while she stands frozen, wide-eyed, hand to her mouth. "I'll carry you," I say. "The poison won't move as fast."

"Okay."

Her legs are right in front of me. I know we have to hurry— even Lolly, who's whining, knows we have to hurry—but I need to look.

The snake struck from her right side, just above ground level. But when I hold her right foot and study her skin and run my fingers over her ankle and calf, there's nothing. No puncture wounds, no redness, no swelling.

I take different viewing angles. I make her rotate into direct sunlight like a slow-motion ballerina. I do the same for her left leg, although it was an unlikely target.

"No wound," I say.

"Really?" She rests her hand on the top of my head. Balancing herself.

"Not a trace." Something in my voice makes Lolly settle down. He noses at Cocoa's pocket, where she once kept the acorn.

"It must have missed me."

"It must have." But I saw the lethal wedge hit, clamp, retract. All in a blurry instant.

"That's good, right?" She looks for herself, runs her hands everywhere.

"You made a sound."

"Maybe I was just startled. Out of the corner of my eye I saw movement, then—"

"I thought we were gonna have to go see Dr. Kersey."

The panicky feeling is leaving, but side effects linger. Pounding heart, watery eyes. *What kind of spell am I under? What is it that I feel for her? Can an almost-sixteen-year-old be* in love?

"False alarm," she says, not sounding convinced. We're both still sneaking looks at her unbroken skin.

We cut our walk short.

When we get back to the house, Pete and Captain Jack are sitting on the back steps, drinking beer from dewy bottles. They've traded their uniforms for shorts and T-shirts.

"You two look like you've seen a ghost," Pete says.

Cocoa gives me a glance. *Loose lips.* "We took Lolly for a walk," she says.

"He chased after a rabbit," I say.

"Notice anything?" Pete says.

We follow his gaze. The Army truck has returned. It's backed up to the Airstream.

"You're leaving?" I ask the captain.

He looks dejected. "General Groves wants me back at Los Alamos."

"No more babysitting, Captain Jack," Cocoa says, faking cheerfulness.

"My loss," he says.

I get some lemonade for Cocoa and me. We join Pete and the captain on the steps, but I'm ready to drop the sad-parting conversation. "Did you hear the good news?" I say. "Japan, and Berlin?"

"We had a briefing this morning," Pete says.

"Word is that German forces are turning on Hitler and his hoodlums," Captain Jack says. "That he's in hiding, planning to run. But we'll have the whole city surrounded by then."

The words are comforting. They should be exciting. But the image of the rattler haunts me. Cocoa is sitting next to me, close, and I gaze at her ankles, puncture-free, then her face. She looks healthier than ever.

"I have something for you two," the captain says. "Pete already has his."

He goes to the trailer. He returns with photos from our day at the pool. There are five for each of us—one of Cocoa, Pete, and me together, one of Cocoa and me together, one of Cocoa by herself, one of me by myself, and the one I took of the three of them.

My favorite? Cocoa and me, of course. We're sitting on the wall of the pool, close, and she's leaning into me. She's smiling. So am I.

During the night, I wake up to a rectangle of dim light where my bedroom door is supposed to be. The light is coming from down the hall somewhere—the bathroom, probably. A figure is silhouetted against the glow. *Cocoa* is my only thought, but this silhouette has curves—shoulders, waist, hips. When did *that* happen?

I wonder if the silhouette is naked. The silhouette looks naked.

I'm hot. I'm tangled in my sheets. But I wait patiently. For something. Finally, unsure, I whisper her name.

"I went into the bathroom," she announces.

"Doing okay?" I manage.

"I looked in the mirror," she says dreamily.

*And?* I want to say, but I hold my tongue. I can't tell if she's sleepwalking or just taking her time. Either way, I don't want to butt in.

"I could not see myself, Robert."

"What?"

"I could not see my fucking reflection."

*Sleepwalking*, I decide, as the silhouette turns and glides into the hall and the door closes with a click, leaving me in the dark.

Sleep refuses to return. I get up with my flashlight and retrieve the ranch house photos from my dresser. In bed, I go through them one by one. Nothing has changed. Swimsuits. Happy faces. A good day. More good days have followed. Will follow. Cocoa's here. Pete's here. Mom and Dad should be coming home soon. But as I slowly drift off, something continues to needle me.

On our way to the shack in the morning, Cocoa tells me she had a strange dream last night. It was too creepy to talk about, she says. It's still haunting her, she says.

When we return home, Pete and Captain Jack are making breakfast—pancakes, eggs, bacon. A goodbye gift from the captain, maybe. When we sit down to eat, he has news for us.

"General Groves called," he says. "Word from the German front is that Hitler is either captured or dead. Apparently, he was attempting to flee to an airfield through a system of tunnels, but he and his confederates ran into a resistance group that cut them off and at last report had them pinned down with gunfire. The general will call back if he gets anything more definitive."

Smiles all around, but they're cautious. *Can it be true?*

"And there's more," the captain says. "Secretary Stimson and President Truman want to thank both of you in person. Not publicly, because how would anyone ever explain it? But as soon as the dust settles, you'll get an invitation to travel to Washington to shake hands with the president and the war secretary."

I'm glad I'm sitting down. *The president?* I've met important people lately, but President Truman is in a class of his own, even if he did come in through the back door—even if he is responsible for imprisoning my parents.

*And Cocoa and me? Together? In Washington?* I've never been outside New Mexico. I get this warmer-than-toast feeling in my lower chest, and it's not from what I'm eating.

"I can't believe it," I say.

"Maybe we can go shopping again," Cocoa says. Under the table, she takes my hand. Pete and the captain pretend not to notice. I pretend I'm unaffected, above and below the belt.

"That won't be a problem," Pete says.

I decide to press my luck. "What about Mom and Dad?" I ask him.

Pete shakes his head in a way that tells me the same question has been on his mind. Dad may not be his favorite fellow, but Pete's big sister is locked up, too. "No news," he says. "But this war is about to end. And then things will look better for them."

# FORTY-FIVE

I t's a bittersweet morning. There was the news of Hitler's likely capture or death, and the invitation to meet the president. Both sweet.

But now the bitter. From the back steps, Cocoa and I watch Pete and Captain Jack hitch up the trailer and move the captain's belongings from trailer to truck. Pete will be back, of course, but not the captain.

Cocoa sighs. She's biting her lip, trying not to cry. When Captain Jack walks over, we shake hands. He gives Cocoa a long hug. I'm not even jealous.

"I won't be far away, Cocoa." Like Pete, he's in uniform. He hands me a slip of paper. "My Los Alamos number. You can both call me whenever you want." He grins his Captain Jack grin. "Within reason. We'll figure out a time—soon—to get together and talk about all of this."

Cocoa is still fighting tears. Pete wraps her up in an embrace. "Everything's going to be okay, Future Girl," he murmurs. "Thanks to you."

Lolly follows our soldiers to the truck. His own goodbye. Doors slam. Truck and trailer rumble and roll away.

The yard looks empty.

Out on the road, familiar shapes accelerate, grow smaller, disappear.

"I haven't hugged you yet, Robert." Cocoa's voice is watery. "Today, I mean." In an instant, we're in each other's arms. I sense that there's more—and for some reason, less—to her than there was the last time we were this close. Like the rest of the morning, the embrace feels bittersweet. A hello and a goodbye. But neither of us is going anywhere for a while, and when we do, we'll be together.

"Can we visit the Andrews sisters?" she says.

We walk to the barn holding hands, passing the hens and Franklin the rooster and the sow and her unnamed piglets. Cocoa gazes intently at them, like she's committing them to memory.

Unlike the chickens and Franklin and the sow and her piglets, the Andrews sisters acknowledge our presence. Their big Jersey-brown eyes close with pleasure as we scratch their foreheads and feed them handfuls of fresh alfalfa.

Walking back, Cocoa spends most of her time staring up at the sky. A wind, undetectable at ground level, pushes a slender white cloud across the blue. A minute hand, marking time.

"It's so nice," she says. "Can we go for a car ride? Just to the Unsers' house and back?"

I get the keys. When I return, she's sitting in the middle of the front seat, with Lolly riding shotgun. When I get behind the wheel, she fills in the space. Our hips and shoulders touch. I breathe her in.

The windows are rolled down. Lolly's head is already hanging out. As we turn onto the road, fresh air pours in. A smile lights Cocoa's face. Then it fades. By the time we pass the Unser place, her smile's gone.

"Want to go farther?" I glance at the gas gauge. "We could drive into town."

"Let's go home." She sounds different. Defeated. *But how can that be, when she's just taken on the bad guys of the world, and won?*

We head back. Inside the house, Lolly sticks with her like a burr as we pour glasses of lemonade and go to the living room. While Cocoa sits on the sofa and Lolly plops down at her feet, I turn on the radio. I tune it away from the news until I find music, the beginning notes of Glenn Miller's "Moonlight Serenade." A sad song, but three minutes of sadness should be okay.

I sit next to her. She's quiet. Tears glisten on her cheeks. Her skin seems almost translucent, like waxed paper.

"Is it the music?"

She shakes her head. "He's dying. I can feel it."

"Who?"

"Hitler."

"That makes you *sad*?"

"Of course not. But what he would have done—what he did—won't happen now."

*Tears of joy*, I decide. They must be.

I get brave. I put my arms around her. She melts into me, cradles my face in her hands. Her fingers are feathers, her palms are dust.

"You can't wait any longer," she says. "You have to kiss me."

I do. I kiss her, and she kisses me back. Sweet, like desert air. Morning. Springtime.

Forget meeting President Truman. Forget Hitler dying. This, right now, is the highlight of my day. Of my life.

"I love you, Robert," she says.

*A dream?*

Our faces are close. Inches. I want to kiss her again, but first I need to tell her. "I love you, too, Cocoa." Saying it isn't that hard, at all.

"Remember me." Her voice sounds far away. "I could not ever forget you."

*What?* The words make no sense. "*What?*" But even as I think it and say it, her body—its radiance, its *essence*—seems to flare, like a shooting star, then dim. The skin of her face thins, her eyes brighten, then darken. Their spark dwindles. Her melancholy smile fades. She grows light in my arms, papery. Her clothes loosen, deflate.

Lolly is up, whining. He noses into her.

Panic strikes. *What's going on? What the hell is going on?* I can't breathe.

But I can cry. Tears blur my vision.

A nightmare.

Everywhere, her skin—face, neck, arms, hands, legs—suddenly transforms into a million transparent beads, microscopic marbles, separating, swimming, fusing, separating again. They radiate color, like stained glass. Under her, the cushion rises. She's weightless, a desert mirage.

In an instant, she's gone. I tell myself, *It can't be true, it can't.* But her blouse, still buttoned, dangles from my arm. Inside it, barely noticeable, is a beginner's brassiere. Her shorts, still buttoned and zipped, along with her underpants, are crumpled on the sofa. Her shoes, still tied, and socks are on the floor, empty.

Everything is empty.

I try to comprehend. It's incomprehensible.

In the stifling living room air, the final notes of "Moonlight Serenade" die. In less than three minutes, everything that was just beginning has ended.

Lolly circles the room, still whining. I glance around. It's possible she's still here. It's possible she hasn't vaporized, turned back into the atoms that created the essence of the girl named Cocoa.

*Future Girl.*

But in my heart, I know she's gone.

I think of Mom. I promised her I'd take care of Cocoa. I promised her I wouldn't let Cocoa break my heart. And now *this*.

I lay Cocoa's blouse on the sofa and go to my bedroom. Afraid to look, I pick up the photos from my dresser.

But the pictures are unchanged. She's there, alive, close to me, smiling. Not a dream or hallucination or mirage. For a while, she did exist.

*Where is she now?*

Leaving Lolly in the barn with the Andrews sisters for company, I get on my bike and ride. It feels good to have the hot wind in my face, blowing away the tears. It doesn't feel good to be alone.

At the spot where I found her a lifetime ago, I slow, still hopeful. A breeze whispers through the desert grass and scrub and cactus. It's not whispering my name. *Robert.*

I continue on to the base camp. I find Pete alone, coming out of the stable. The tears resume. My story unfolds in fitful scraps. Hitler's dead. Cocoa's gone. My heart's breaking. Even though I fear he won't believe my unbelievable story, he does. I see it in his eyes, in the sag of his shoulders.

"She must've been right about Hitler," he says. "His death will—*did*—change everything."

"For the better," I say. "But not."

"I'm so sorry, buddy. She was special. One of a kind. But I guess that's obvious."

"I was holding her. I can still feel her going."

He puts his arms around me and squeezes, not letting go. "I know." What he doesn't know is that I'm a contagious weeper. He's a soldier, and tough, but when I start in again, he sighs, and the sigh becomes a sob. We hold on, crying quietly, while I think about Cocoa, and where she is, and *if* she is. I gaze into the gloom of the stable and wonder if Big Muddy is in there, deliberating over the odd scene of two humans standing in the heat of the desert sun, doing nothing other than propping each other up.

I wonder if she remembers Cocoa. *How could she not?*

Pete takes me to the mess hall, where we find a corner table and nurse a couple of Cokes. He forces smiles, but his eyes don't lie. While I wait, he goes to Dr. Bainbridge's office. *How will he explain this to a scientist?*

When he returns, he has keys to the Army car and condolences from Dr. Bainbridge and an okay to leave. We jam my bike into the back seat and take off. For the first time, I ride up front, which is okay.

The windows are rolled down. Fresh air blasts in. Once more I'm on the edge of tears. I can't help but think of sharing the back seat with Cocoa, holding her hand, watching her stare out at our surroundings and try to absorb this world that is—*was?*—

so different from hers.

I assume we're on our way home, but Pete gets us going west and then north, toward Socorro. Before long, I give him a look, like *what's going on?*

"Lolly okay by himself for a while?" His voice is full of conflict—false cheer versus sympathy and grief. A mismatch.

"He's in the barn. He has water."

"Good."

"So where are we going?"

"I need to chase down Captain Jack," he says. "I called, but he hadn't arrived yet. I'd rather talk to him in person, anyway. I also need to make a phone call."

"They have phones pretty much everywhere now, Pete."

"I'm predicting a long conversation." He says this mysteriously, which ordinarily would prompt me to ask more questions. But this isn't an ordinary day. Every thought and feeling I might have had on an ordinary day gets overwhelmed by thoughts and feelings about something, *someone*, extraordinary.

*She can't be gone. Like the photos, shouldn't she still be here? Shouldn't there be a device—a new, top-secret invention— that could detect her? Some modification of radar or sonar or photography or X-rays or one of the instruments—stethoscope, otoscope, ophthalmoscope—in Dr. Kersey's office?*

*Couldn't the smart guys at the base camp or Los Alamos come up with something? She saved the world, for Christ's sake.*

"You know some German words, right, Pete? From your interrogation days?"

"A few. The ones for making excuses. Shifting the blame."

"How about goodbye? How do you say goodbye?"

His hand rests on my shoulder. He squeezes. Tears flow. Mine and, through the blur, his.

"Their way is better than ours. *Auf Wiedersehen.* It means 'Until we meet again.'"

"*Auf Wiedersehen.*" I say it out loud, then to myself, over and over. *Auf Wiedersehen. Until we meet again.* I look up. The sky is cloudless, but the blue has paled.

◆➤

Three hours later we're approaching the gate at Los Alamos. I was expecting another base camp, but this is a small city, plopped down in the remote New Mexico hills. The gate guard gives us directions to a building that looks a lot like most of the other buildings. There are dozens of people walking the grounds, hurrying from place to place. I wonder how many of them know about Hitler—that the head has been cut off the snake.

The snake. I picture Cocoa miraculously dodging the rattlesnake's strike yesterday. *Or did she? Was the rattler attacking something that was already fading away? Filmy? Elusive?*

I remember her in my doorway in the night. Her creepy dream that wasn't a dream.

*"I could not see my fucking reflection."*

Captain Jack's office is down a corridor that feels a mile long. Our footfalls reverberate off the near walls, the ceiling, the far wall. Echoes. Displacements of time.

*Was Cocoa the echo? Or am I?*

The captain is surprised and happy to see us, but not happy when Pete tells him why we've come. Unlike Pete and me, he doesn't cry, but invisible tears curdle his words.

"We need to tell the general," he says. He dials his phone, gets a busy signal. We walk back down the corridor to another office. General Groves's name is on the open door in stenciled letters, and inside, behind a desk, on the phone, sits Corporal Amy. I study Pete's face, wondering if he had more than one reason to pay a visit to Captain Jack.

She smiles. Pete manages one of his own. The captain glances at me with a half-hearted wink.

Amy hangs up and opens the inner door to announce the captain's arrival. He leaves us in the outer office and closes the door behind him. We sit, listening to the rumble of voices, and then what sounds like the general only, on the phone with someone. I read a *Stars and Stripes* and imagine a full-page headline—*HITLER DEAD*—fronting the next edition. Pete and Corporal Amy make eyes at each other, but his half of the exchange looks sad and distracted, and I wonder if she notices.

Maybe he's also wondering. And worrying. He pulls his chair

close to her, and they murmur back and forth. A couple of times she glances at me. I see sympathy, and pity.

I don't want either. I want Cocoa.

The captain comes out. "The general would like to talk to Bobby privately, Sergeant," he says. "These walls won't allow that. So why don't you and the corporal go have a soda, or something stronger if you'd like." He glances at the wall clock. "Give us until sixteen thirty."

Sixteen thirty. Four thirty, civilian time. More than a half hour away. *What conversation that I'm part of could take more than a half hour?*

Pete and the corporal don't need to be told twice. Pete leaves me with a smile as they exit. A smile for me, and, for Corporal Amy?—his hand, gently placed at the small of her back as they head down the hallway.

"He's got it bad, Robert," the captain says.

Robert. I've grown accustomed to it. "I know how that feels."

"Right," the captain says. "I'm so sorry."

"Will I get over it, Captain Jack?"

He hesitates. "I've never experienced what you have. Nobody has. But I was one of the saps who got a *Dear John* letter when we were battling across France. I lost good buddies there and before and after. The memories survive, the pain too. But with time, it gets duller. And if you're lucky—and I believe you will be, because you have a generous spirit—you'll have heartwarming experiences that will stand in front of the heartbreakers, cast shadows on them. Make them less visible. And intrusive. You can't pretend them away, but there's no need to wrestle with them every day."

He gestures toward General Groves's door. I walk in, apprehensive. But the general is on his feet with his hand outstretched. I shake it. "Robert," he says, and I wonder if the *Robert* thing is contagious. "Tragic about Cocoa," he says. "I know you two were close. I can hardly believe the story. Hardly comprehend it. But it was incomprehensible from the start, wasn't it?"

"I didn't believe her at the start," I say, remorseful. Embarrassed.

He points to a pair of chairs. The captain and I sit. "None of us did. Not until she proved us wrong." He lights a pipe. "Helluva thing," he says between puffs. "Helluva thing."

"It is," I say.

"Have you moved her clothes, son?" he says. "The ones she was wearing when—"

"I might leave them there forever."

He clears his throat. "I've just talked to Secretary Stimson, who has been avidly following this story from the start. He passes along his condolences to you and your family."

My *family*. I haven't even *told* my family.

"And he has a request," the general says.

"Sure."

"We're going to send him the photos of Cocoa—and the rest of you—from the day you went swimming. But additionally, the secretary would like the captain, with your permission, to take photos at your house tomorrow morning. Your sofa, her clothes and shoes, you sitting nearby. We don't want to aggravate your pain, but the secretary would like something for the record. Which, given the circumstances, will likely never see the light of day."

I decide I don't mind the idea of the captain taking a few pictures. It will involve wrestling with memories, no doubt, but that's already a given. "That would be okay."

The general looks relieved. "Would ten hundred hours work for you, Captain Nelson?"

"Yes, sir."

"Expect the captain then, Robert. No preparation necessary or desired."

"It won't be hard for me to stay away from the living room. And I'll keep Lolly, our dog, out of there, too."

The general stands, opens his wallet, removes a twenty-dollar bill. "Take this young man to supper, Captain, or have the sergeant do it when he returns. Make sure it happens before the town of Santa Fe shuts down for the night. He may have no appetite, but he needs to eat."

I take a deep breath, working up my courage. "I have a request, too, sir."

"Of course."

"My mom and dad have been sent to Gila River. They don't know about Cocoa. Can I—or someone—call them to let them know?"

"As soon as Corporal Lewis returns, I'll have her place the call."

We go to the outer office to wait. At exactly 1630 Pete and the corporal return. I tell her that the general has authorized a call to my parents.

Pete jumps in. "I'd planned on calling them. I was going to ask to use your phone, Captain Nelson."

"It might help to have the general pave the way," I say to Pete. "They wouldn't give him any shit."

"I can be pretty convincing," Pete says. "If we need the general, we can still call on him."

"Fine plan," Captain Jack says. "Okay with you, Robert?"

"Whatever works."

Corporal Amy locates Gila River's number. We go back to the captain's office. Pete reaches the long-distance operator, supplies the number, and waits. Someone answers on the other end and gives him the runaround: Phone conversations aren't allowed, it's too difficult to locate a "resident" at the spur of the moment, *blah, blah, blah.*

Pete doesn't accept any of it. He tells the person who he is—a brother, an Army sergeant, a wounded veteran—and why he's calling—*a death in the family*—and forecasts what's coming if he doesn't get cooperation. Next, they'll be talking to an Army captain and, if that doesn't work, an Army general will get on the line and give their boss a tongue lashing he'll never forget.

Whoever Pete is talking to has a change of heart. He or she sends out a "runner" to track down Mom and Dad.

Ten minutes later, with the phone still to his ear, Pete's face brightens. "Yeah, Dottie, it's me. I've got Bobby here. He needs to talk to you."

I take the phone, half wishing Pete had given her the news, but knowing it's my job. So, after saying hello and hearing how good I sound and how much she misses me, I tell her about Cocoa. I have a hard time saying the words, and at first she has a hard time grasping them. But she trusts me, she trusts Pete, and eventually she seems to accept the weird and troubling tale. She tries to sound calm as she relays my part of the conversation to Dad, but I hear the struggle—and the tears—in her voice.

Pete and Captain Jack step into the hall and wander away, heads together. Dad gets on the line. He sounds mystified, and upset. He tells me how sorry he is. He says he and Mom are doing okay, and the direction of the war means the outlook for them is improving.

Pete and the captain return. Pete takes the phone, says hello to Dad, asks to speak to Mom.

The captain squeezes my shoulder. "There's a place here called Fuller Lodge, Robert. Famous for its ice cream. Let's go pay a visit."

He steers me away and outside while I puzzle over what Pete has to say to my parents that he doesn't want me to hear. On foot, I get a better feel for the size of the settlement. More than six thousand people, the captain says. The lodge is impressive. And although I thought I'd never be hungry again, the ice cream is irresistible. When we get back to the captain's office, Pete is done talking. I try to read his face, but it's unreadable.

Less than an hour later, my uncle and I are in Santa Fe, sitting in a nice restaurant called Mountain View, ready to spend General Groves's twenty dollars. The ice cream is history. I'm hungry again, and I order like it. Pete seems distracted. "What he's having," he tells the waitress.

"I need to get something out of the way, Bobby," he says when she leaves. "Otherwise I'll not be able to eat, and I'll be too preoccupied to drive home. And I owe it to you. I've owed it to you for a long time. But I've . . . put it off."

My heavy heart stalls. This feels like another punch to the gut, on its way. "Is this about your talk with Mom?"

"And your dad."

*My dad? What's going on?*

"I've always been proud to be your uncle, Bobby." He takes a breath, gazes across the table at me. "But the thing that's made me even prouder is being your father."

I hear the words, but they don't register. It's been an emotional day. An emptying day. "*What?*"

"I'm your dad," he says. "Your original dad, I mean. You have another one now, of course, and he's been great. He *is* great. You're so lucky to have him."

I can barely speak. My heart is lodged in my throat, quaking. But I manage one word. "How?"

He takes another breath. My imagination soars. I know I'm adopted. I've known it forever. I've gotten used to the idea that I'll never meet my first parents. *But now? My mother's brother is my father?*

"I don't know what Dottie, your mom, has told you about my younger self," Pete says. "Let's just say it took me a while—too long—to grow up. In high school, though, I thought I was a finished product. A man. I had a job, a Model T Ford, a girlfriend."

He hesitates and I leap ahead. I know what kind of consequences having a girlfriend can have. And I know it's worse for the girl. Guys don't get pregnant and get gossiped about and deliver babies that they have to raise. Or give up for someone else to raise.

*Who was this* girlfriend?

Slowly the story comes out, interrupted only by the arrival of our food, which is mostly ignored until it's gone cold.

Her name was Martha. They loved each other. Or thought they did. By the time she told him she was pregnant, she'd already told her mother, who told her father.

With the exception of chance encounters at school, she was forbidden to see Pete again. Her parents monitored her every minute, screened her friends, took over her life, and she wouldn't defy them. By the end of the summer between their junior and senior years of high school, she was gone. But not before she and her parents agreed to let the boyfriend's more-than-responsible older sister and her husband adopt the infant boy. Robert.

"What happened to her?"

"They didn't tell anyone where they were going. Even her best friend claimed ignorance. She might've been lying, but it didn't feel like it. Martha's family had roots in the Midwest—Minnesota or Iowa—so that was most people's guess. My mom—your grandma—was still alive at the time, and after I ran out of ideas, she poked around for me with Midwest relatives and friends and friends of friends. But Martha and her parents didn't want to be found."

"You never heard from her? Mom never heard from her?"

"I hoped. For a long time, I hoped. But hope has its limits."

I look out the window at the fading light. I pick at my food. For my whole life, I've thought of my original parents as faceless kids who'd made a mistake. Now I have a face, and it's a familiar one.

It's one I love.

*What can be wrong with that?*

Only that the three most important people in my life have lied to me for fifteen years.

"Why didn't anyone tell me?"

"Mostly my idea, Bobby. Turns out I wasn't a big shot after all. I was irresponsible. Immature. Barely employed. Embarrassed. I thought I'd be a poor example. I didn't want you confused, wrenched in two directions."

It's his turn to gaze out the window. But I'm certain he's not contemplating the quiet street, the few people wandering past on the sidewalk. He's looking backward, at his own life, decisions made, aftermaths.

His eyes shift to me. "When your mom and dad agreed to adopt you, I thought the best thing I could do was stay in the background. Be a good uncle. Step in if necessary. Tell you someday. But it was easy to keep putting off the *someday*."

For a long, silent moment I return his gaze. He's the same, but he isn't. He has Uncle Pete's face, but he's my dad.

Suddenly I have two.

*What do I call him?* After years of *Uncle Pete*, I'm just getting used to *Pete*. "Why now?"

"An awful day for you. I wasn't trying to give you another load to bear. But the way you've handled everything has impressed me so much. Your courage in the face of all this, the way you treated Cocoa, the way you've handled losing her, it's all been an inspiration. I decided that if my kid can be that brave, it was time for me to step up."

"*Brave?* You're in the *Army*. You've *fought*. You've been *wounded*."

"Different. You do what you're told and hope for the best."

"Mom and Dad didn't mind you telling me?"

"They were excited."

"Do you have a picture of her? My mother?"

"The best I can do is my yearbook. Junior year. I'll dig it out when we get home."

Back in the car, with my mind settling down after a day that's emptied it and filled it and sent it gyrating wildly, I ask a question that's haunted me since Cocoa vanished.

"Do you believe in God, Pete?"

Even to me, the question feels like it came out of left field. Like in the middle of an everyday conversation, someone asking about ghosts. Or time travel.

He's silent, eyes on the road and the twilit sky above it. "You should probably ask your other dad that one, Bobby," he says finally. "You'd be more likely to get a positive response."

"I'm not fishing for a positive response. I want you to tell me what you think."

"I've prayed," he says after a while. "When the bullets were flying and the shells were dropping, lots of guys prayed."

"Did you think the prayers would be answered?"

"I hoped," he says. "I hoped I'd live through the hour, the day, the week. And if I didn't, I hoped there'd be an afterlife."

"An afterlife," I say. "I guess that's what I'm most curious about. With Cocoa and all. She was here. She was alive. Where did she go? Where is she *now*?"

No words. Road noise. Wind rushing in the open windows. Desert smells.

"Cocoa was a special case," Pete says at last. "In every way. And one of her most special qualities was making us question what we take for granted. Life. Death. Being."

"Time," I say. "I'll never think of it the same way."

"Future Girl," Pete says. "She defied—defies—time."

# FORTY-SIX

A week can be a lifetime when you're waiting for heartache to loosen its grip. I haven't noticed time making a difference, but other things have. Looking in the mirror and detecting, for the first time, the resemblance between my chin and Pete's. Seeing my original mother's face in Pete's yearbook and recognizing myself, and a glimmer of expectation, in her sixteen-year-old eyes. Having late-night talks with Pete about his life and Mom and Dad. And Cocoa.

News of world events has also improved my frame of mind. Hitler's death has been confirmed. Germany, and then Japan, surrendered. The front pages of the *Journal* are filled with uplifting stories and photos—victory parades, celebrations, smiles, embraces, kisses. Joy.

Whenever I see a photo or read a story or hear something on the radio, I think about Cocoa. Without her, none of this would be happening. Without her, the venom of the snake would have spread throughout the world.

Desert walks—Lolly and me, usually—have helped, too. Today Pete has already left when I get home from my route, so my lonesome buddy and I head right out into the cool of the morning. The rising sun casts long shadows. Lolly sticks close. He's stuck close to me since the episode of the snake and closer since Cocoa left. He's constantly on alert, as if he knows I'm searching and he wants to help.

I *am* searching. Not consciously, because unlike Lolly, who regularly sniffs through Cocoa's room for some trace of her, consciously I don't dare to hope. But without intentionally thinking about it, I notice things that are *not* there—Nazi soldiers goose-stepping across the desert floor, Nazi tanks crushing cactuses and yuccas and chicken coops, Nazi concentration camps full of American undesirables.

A skinny girl, standing naked at the side of the road.

We walk on. I notice more things that are not there.

Pocket gophers.

Rattlesnakes.

A girl riding toward me on a chestnut mare named Big Muddy.

When I get melancholy, I recall the adventures we were supposed to have: returning to the cave; searching for meteorites; soaring through the skies in a B-29; shaking the president's hand.

Like Cocoa herself, vanished.

But we got to kiss. And that makes up for all of it.

A meadowlark spooks and darts straight up, warbling and whistling. I follow its flight—flashes of brilliant yellow—into the brightening blue and its cottony clouds. Still thinking of that girl, I continue to stare as the puffs of white and pink drift east to meet the sun.

In the afternoon, the mailman brings a letter from my parents. Rumors have begun about releasing all of the internees— Japanese Americans, pacifists, and other threats to the war effort that no longer exists. The rumors say it could happen "soon."

I don't know exactly what "soon" means. But for now, the word is enough.

It's the end of August, but the summer heat hasn't backed off. I have all the windows in the house open, allowing a breeze to move the air. Allowing the sound of an approaching car to reach the kitchen, getting my attention, perking up Lolly's ears. The car turns off the road, moves down the driveway. It's not the sound of the DeSoto, not Pete. I think, *Mom and Dad—have they somehow almost beat the letter home?*

I go to the front door, step out on the porch. The car stops. It's not Mom and Dad. A man sits behind the wheel of a shiny black Pontiac. He's alone, and disguised by the glare of the glass, but when he gets out, smiling, he looks familiar.

"Bobby," he says.

And despite the fact that he's in civvies and I've only met him once before, I put the voice together with the face and the smile and the easy way he moves when he comes over to shake my hand. "Colonel Oliver," I say. "Are you here to see my uncle?"

Lolly noses at the colonel's pants pockets, his crotch. He laughs. "You," he says. "I've come to see you."

I grab the scruff of Lolly's neck. "Can you come in? We have lemonade. I could make popcorn."

"That would be great," he says. "It's a long, dry drive from Kirtland."

"I can't believe you've come here," I say as we climb the steps.

"So sorry to hear about Cocoa," he says. "To be honest, I don't understand the whole thing. All I know is it's beyond sad. And she was beyond brave. And without her, we all would've been screwed."

I nod. Other than that, I can't answer. I'm too busy swallowing my tears.

We go to the kitchen. I make popcorn, pour lemonade. I practically have to sit on Lolly to get him to quit pestering the colonel, but finally he curls up under the table.

"The night you bombed the cave," I say, "General Groves called to tell us. I thought my heart was going to explode I was so excited. Especially when he said you were okay."

"It was an adventure," he says. "An honor."

"You're a hero."

"I took orders. Fly the mission. Complete the mission. Come back alive, crew and plane intact. Heroes are people who go beyond that. Too often, they end up dead. I didn't want to be a hero, or dead."

"You changed the world."

"Cocoa changed the world."

"And me," I say. "She changed me."

"When I met her, I promised her a ride in a B-29."

"I remember."

"She won't get that ride, now. But when she asked about it, she said *us*. She was asking for *both* of you, and I made a promise. If you're interested, I want to offer you the chance to go."

"*Interested?*"

He smiles. "That's a yes?"

"Who would say no?" I couldn't. For a couple of reasons. Cocoa. Me. And a third: *us*.

"We'll arrange a flight for you, then," he says. "The wild blue yonder and all that. I'll talk to your folks. We'll figure it out, schedule it on a school day. Get you a chance to play a little hooky."

"I can't believe it."

He smiles. For a long moment, we sit in silence.

Finally, he has a question. "Dream about her at night?"

His words feel like a punch to the chest, to the heart. But I recover. "Only when I'm asleep."

"You can tell her about it. The ride, I mean."

"I will."

"One other thing," he says. He reaches into his pants pocket. Lolly sits up, points. And he's not even a pointer. "Not for you, buddy," the colonel tells him. He holds his closed fist palm-up over the table and unfurls his fingers. And for the zillionth time in the past month or two I feel my throat constrict. Lying in the palm of his hand is an acorn. A burr oak acorn. And I know where it came from.

Unlike Cocoa, it's still here.

"It was my good luck," Colonel Oliver says. "Now it's yours."

# FORTY-SEVEN

## Saturday, November 10

I feared this day would always dangle out of reach, but finally it's here. I'm outside with Lolly, doing chores, enjoying the warmth of the afternoon sun, and keeping my eyes and ears open for the approach of a car. The thermometer reads sixty; fall has definitely set in.

Pete is still *Pete*, although he feels more like *Dad* every day. He left the house early for Trinity. He's part of the skeleton crew of soldiers maintaining security, although there's not much to keep secure. The workers and most of their equipment have departed. The buildings are mostly empty. I no longer have a paper route.

The phone rings. I run to answer it.

Doctor Kersey. I invited him to the homecoming, but he's calling to say he's stuck at the hospital with a woman in labor and doesn't know if he'll make it. He apologizes, but I tell him not to worry. We'll be here for a long time.

When we hang up, I think about the newborn baby, arriving in a better world.

Because of Cocoa.

I go back to waiting. I've had one false alarm—Mr. and Mrs. Unser returning from their Saturday shopping—but otherwise the road has been empty.

Lolly senses something is up. Several times he's trotted down the driveway and returned, still fidgety.

Finally, a small dark object appears on the horizon, and then the sound of an engine rises above the shifting breeze and bird songs and my own heartbeat.

After an eternity, an army-green Plymouth turns into our driveway. Lolly gives it an escort. From the porch steps, I notice that they're all in the front seat. Mom and Dad. Captain Jack, who picked them up at the Albuquerque train station.

The car stops, and they pop out, and in an instant, we're all hugging and dancing around and saying how much we've missed each other and they're telling me how much I've grown and I'm telling them they look good but skinnier and we have this big group embrace that even includes Captain Jack, who looks only slightly uncomfortable. Lolly completely forgets his manners, leaping up on everyone.

I wish Pete were here, but duty calls.

The reunion goes on and on, turning bittersweet when Cocoa's name comes up, but still the sweet is there, overriding everything else for now. Later we can think about the person who isn't part of the celebration and the void she left.

"The place looks good, Bobby," Dad says, finally getting a chance to look around.

"Nothing died," I say, and immediately regret it.

But she didn't die. She *didn't*.

"The Andrews sisters are making lots of milk," I add, "the unnamed piglets are not really piglets anymore, the hens are still laying lots of eggs, and Franklin is still late—but no later—with his morning wakeup song."

The sun is dropping over Dad's shoulder, and looking into it, I notice movement above the distant desert sand. Mirage-like. But it's not the season for mirages.

I sense everyone, even Lolly, shifting to follow my gaze. The not-mirage takes shape, enlarges. It's heading our way. A horse. A rider. A familiar horse. A familiar rider.

"Big Muddy," I say. "Pete." Maybe Pete's name should've come first, but I see him every day, and I don't remember when I last saw Big Muddy. I thought she was gone with the rest of the camp horses.

Mom's face brightens. To my surprise, Dad's does, too. Captain Jack looks pleased, but also distracted. *Now what?*

Grinning, Pete rides into the yard and dismounts, holding the reins. Mom hurries over and locks him up in a huge hug. Dad is right behind her, pumping Pete's free hand.

"Your typewriter, Chuck," Pete says. "It's on the kitchen table. Hoping for attention."

"Thanks," Dad says. "I have some stories to tell. I'd like to tell one about a young girl who saved the world."

"Who would believe it?" I say.

"Speaking of Cocoa," Captain Jack says to me, "I've been asked to pass along a message. I'm doing so, but reluctantly."

He has my attention.

"Because she isn't able to make the trip to meet President Truman," he says, "his staff is wondering if you'd reconsider your decision to accept the invitation." He's embarrassed. I feel sorry for him, not me. "They say something could still be arranged, if you'd prefer to go ahead with the visit."

"I didn't figure it would still happen," I say. "I was nervous about it, anyway. Besides, my B-29 flight with Colonel Oliver should make up for a handshake with the president."

The nervous part is true. Until now, though, I still entertained the idea of going. But I understand why the enthusiasm has cooled. Cocoa saved the planet. She was Future Girl. I was just the sidekick. *Why would the president want to meet the sidekick?*

"I know it was promised, Bobby," the captain says, "and I apologize—"

"It's okay, Captain Jack. Really. I've already met enough bigwigs for a lifetime." I think about McCloy. *Did he have a hand in putting the lid on his fellow politicians' hospitality?*

No matter. Cocoa would've said "Fuck it."

"Tuesday, Bobby?" Mom says. "The B-29 flight?"

"I get to play hooky."

My parents smile. Barely. Pete laughs. Maybe he hasn't

read the chapter of the *Rule Book for Dads* that suggests only restrained support for activities that aren't quite aboveboard.

After Mom and Dad change into comfortable clothes, and we get Big Muddy fed and watered and hitched up in the barn, I announce that everyone has an important ceremony to witness.

Pete's in on it, but I let the mystery linger for the rest as they follow me to the back of the house. From a spot near the barn I pick up a mess-hall-size coffee can and carry it to a sun-drenched little knoll fifty feet from my bedroom window. At the top of the knoll I've dug a hole, and next to it is a mound of loose dirt and a watering can full of water.

I show everyone what's in the coffee can—a special concoction of desert soil and barnyard manure that Pete and I mixed together, and growing out of it, looking healthy and strong and raring to reach for the sky, is a seedling burr oak.

"From Cocoa's lucky acorn," I say.

Dad shakes his head. Like it wasn't so lucky for her.

"It got her here," I say. "To us. It was lucky for the world. And Colonel Oliver."

Captain Jack knows all about Colonel Oliver, of course, but the blank stares I get from Mom and Dad remind me that they don't. They know he's a famous pilot who has invited me to take a ride with him, but that's it.

So, I explain what he did and that Cocoa and I got to meet him before his mission and she gave him her acorn for luck and he took it with him when he bombed the cave and he came close to getting blown out of the sky and I'm pretty sure the acorn is what saved him and his crew. I tell them that he brought it back to me, that I planted it in the coffee can the next day.

"It's the perfect time of year to plant it," I say. "And this is the perfect place. It's sunny, and a little higher than the rest of the backyard, and now that I've relocated the clothesline, I can see it perfectly from my bedroom. I can watch it grow. Someday it'll be a tree, big and strong. We can hang a swing from it, and your grandkids can play in its shade."

"Does this mean we can never move?" Dad says. He's smiling. He loves this house.

"Why would we want to?" Mom says. She didn't even blink

at my mention of the clothesline. Or grandkids. After what she's been through, it's going to take a lot to bother her.

"Yeah," my other dad says. "Why would you want to? The Unsers are thinking of selling soon, and they said they'd give me first crack at their place."

News to me. Smiling to myself, I wonder if Pete has plans to share the Unser place with someone. A certain lady corporal, to be specific.

"You'd want to live that close to a pacifist, Pete?" Dad says.

"There's enough elbow room," my new dad says. "Besides, I learned some things from Cocoa. I learned that the pieces of life that I've always considered either right or wrong, black or white, real or unreal—lots of them aren't. They're gray. Marbled. Spotted. Striped. Sometimes they're flipped. Black is white. White is black. The past is present. The future is now. Cocoa—Future Girl—taught me that."

"She taught all of us something," Captain Jack says.

"I taught her to swim," I say, as the images of that day at the pool overwhelm my brain.

And my heart. "She taught me how to love," I add, mostly to myself because the words catch in my throat and sound kind of dopey coming out. Through blurry eyes I see the others exchange glances, like they're wondering if this kid is okay.

I am okay. Not good, not where I once pictured myself, but okay.

I turn the coffee can on its side, trowel out the cylinder of soil, and place it in the hole. Before the root ball falls apart I scoop in the loose pile of soil and manure and compact it until it's firm and level with the surrounding ground. Then I give the little tree a long drink of cool water.

Like Cocoa, it's upright, and perky and, for such a skinny little thing, sturdy.

I'll do my fucking best to keep it that way.

Mom claps. Everyone else joins in. It's a heartening way to say hello. And goodbye.

Pete and I were planning on making supper, but Mom insists on taking over. She'll be back at work Monday and won't get much opportunity—as if that's an opportunity—to cook.

While she's bustling around the kitchen and humming along with the radio, Lolly tags along at her heels, and Dad, Captain Jack, and Pete sit in the living room listening to football scores and summaries on the other radio. Number-one-ranked Army thrashed Villanova, which puts smiles on the soldiers' faces.

I go to my room and look out the window at the sapling. Even from this distance it looks happy standing in the last of the muted sunlight. I imagine it growing, spreading, reaching up toward Cocoa's blue sky.

Heading out, I pause at my dresser to study the framed photo Captain Jack took at the ranch house. Cocoa and me. Close. Touching. Smiles.

I leave the adults to their evening and go outside and get on my bike. I can't help but notice Cocoa's, leaning against the barn wall, gathering dust.

I start down the driveway. But before I get past the front door, Pete steps out, followed by everyone else. "Going somewhere, Robert?" he says.

"A ride. I'll be back for supper."

"Hold up for two minutes," he says. He heads for the barn. There's small talk, but I'm not part of it. I'm too curious.

After a long two minutes, Pete emerges from the shadows, leading Big Muddy. She's saddled again. She looks rested. Ready.

They stop a few feet away. "Hop up," Pete says, grabbing my handlebars. He's not talking about the bike.

My heart thumps. I don't hesitate. I grasp the saddle horn and slip my foot in the stirrup and in an instant, I'm high on the mare's back, looking down at the grins.

"How's she feel?" Pete says.

"Like a dream," I say.

"Good," Pete says. "Because she's yours."

"*Mine*?"

"Pete's idea," Captain Jack says. "The horses were surplus. I talked to the general. The least he could do, he said. He pulled a few strings. It was easy."

There are no surprised expressions in the gathering. At some point, maybe during the drive from Albuquerque, Mom and Dad were let in on the scheme.

"I can't believe it," I say. The truth. I lean over and wrap my arms around Big Muddy's neck, feel the warmth of her hide, her soft mane against my cheek.

Pete hands me the reins. "Take her for a spin."

"You don't have to hurry back," Mom says.

Dad gives me a thumbs-up. His eyes are glassy.

"Have fun, Robert," Captain Jack says.

"Thank you" is all I can manage past the knot in my throat, but I let my eyes wander from face to face to show that the words are meant for all of them.

The mare's coat is velvety against my bare knees. I give her a gentle squeeze. She eases ahead. I can hardly believe she's mine.

We start toward the road, but if you're riding a horse, you don't have to take the road. We veer left off the driveway and cross the yard and enter the shadowy vastness of the desert.

I don't look back.

I don't have a destination in mind. But I know what direction I'm going. The newspaper shack, and beyond that, the base camp—*Trinity*—and its empty buildings, and memories.

Already there's no need for the shack or the buildings.

But the memories. There will always be a need for the memories. Even if you have to wrestle with them.

Ahead of us, the sun, already obscured by overcast, slips behind the mountains. The Mockingbirds. We move toward them, toward the place where desert meets sky, where time has a different meaning.

Twilight sets in.

I picture us—Big Muddy and me—returning here over and over. This sky, this terrain, this direction. If we stay away, there's no telling what I might miss seeing.

And imagining.

There's no telling what I might forget.

*Auf Wiedersehen. Until we meet again.*

I flick the reins, nudge Big Muddy's ribs, and she picks up her pace. The smells of the desert fill my nose. My eyes water, but I keep them open wide, scanning my surroundings from side to side—sand, cactus, mesquite, yucca, willow, shadow.

Once upon a time, something different—not sand, not cactus,

not mesquite, not yucca, not willow, not shadow—suddenly materialized in the heart of this landscape. Something, *someone*, that tested and then expanded the limits of what I understand and accept and feel.

*Cocoa.*

It could happen again.

You never know.

You never know.

# ACKNOWLEDGMENTS

My thanks go to all the citizens and soldiers, mostly gone now, who worked for peace and fought for peace during the "Devil's War." Your real-life stories provided immeasurable inspiration. To the good folks at the World War II Museum in New Orleans, where I spent a fascinating, too-short day touring and experiencing the exhibits and gathering valuable information. To the Army hosts at the Trinity Site, New Mexico, for allowing an intimate gathering of several thousand visitors (including me) to get a close-up look at history during your October 2015 open house. To the libraries of Seattle and King County, for providing resources for research and quiet spaces for a writer-guy to spread out and work. To the members of my critique group, who saw this story in its rough-and-tumble days and spotted the wheat amidst the chaff. And to publisher John Koehler, who discovered a manuscript and envisioned a book, editor Joe Coccaro, part story tuner, part detective, and part wizard of English usage, and Hannah Woodlan, proofreader extraordinaire and no friend of the wimpy, botched, or extraneous.

CPSIA information can be obtained
at www.ICGtesting.com
Printed in the USA
LVOW10*1704170518
577553LV00007B/119/P